In the Company of Witches

In the Company of Witches

AN EVENFALL WITCHES B&B MYSTERY

AURALEE WALLACE

BERKLEY PRIME CRIME
New York

BERKLEY PRIME CRIME
Published by Berkley
An imprint of Penguin Random House LLC
penguinrandomhouse.com

Copyright © 2021 by Auralee Wallace
Excerpt from *When the Crow's Away* copyright © 2021 by Auralee Wallace
Penguin Random House supports copyright. Copyright fuels creativity, encourages
diverse voices, promotes free speech, and creates a vibrant culture. Thank you for buying
an authorized edition of this book and for complying with copyright laws by not
reproducing, scanning, or distributing any part of it in any form without permission.
You are supporting writers and allowing Penguin Random House to continue to
publish books for every reader.

BERKLEY and the BERKLEY & B colophon are registered trademarks and BERKLEY
PRIME CRIME is a trademark of Penguin Random House LLC.

ISBN: 9780593335833

First Edition: October 2021

Printed in the United States of America
1   3   5   7   9   10   8   6   4   2

Book design by George Towne

*For my mom, who made me
promise to keep writing.
Love you.*

Chapter 1

I'M GOING TO kill her."

The corner of my mouth twitched, but I kept my gaze on my book. I was very cozy curled up in the green velvet sofa by the fire. I did not want to encourage the tear my aunt was working herself up to.

"I never should have agreed to this," she went on, completely ignoring the fact that I was ignoring her. She was also ignoring the annoyed cat on the chaise lounge behind her, thumping his tail. He was trying to sleep. "You know I can't tolerate the vast majority of people for longer than a day or two—"

I would have said a couple of hours tops, but who was I to quibble?

"—but to let that woman stay for five days? Madness."

I reached for my mug of Honeybush orange tea. It was very soothing. I probably should have made a pot to share. And I don't know if I would call it madness. The woman in question was paying for her stay while her historic home was undergoing some much-needed renovations, and when you run a B&B you have to expect that on occasion you are going to have demanding guests. Although some guests really were more demanding than others.

Case in point, Constance Graves.

Constance had been staying with us at Ivywood Hollow the past week, and it hadn't taken long for us to discover it was not going to be an easy stay. Evenfall, Connecticut, was a small town, so we knew Constance could be demanding, but we really hadn't been concerned. After all, we had always been able to win over hard-to-please guests in the past—we were *very* good at what we did—but Constance turned out to be a special case.

To begin, she insisted there be no other guests staying at the B&B while she was there. It was a completely reasonable request given she was willing to pay for all the rooms, and it seemed like it would make our lives a whole lot easier. Less people, less work, right? Not so. Not. So.

Personally, I knew we were in for trouble when I showed her where she'd be staying. The Rosewater Room. It's gorgeous. Four-poster bed. Floor-to-ceiling windows. Silk upholstered divan that was perfect for reclining when life became too much. What Constance saw, however, was the white Egyptian cotton sheets peeking out from under the damask comforter on her bed. They were too white. She was afraid of the glare they might give off in the morning sun. When I changed them to a lovely taupe, she found the shade a bit too muddy. I was able to get away with a blush-colored set, but I'm pretty sure that was only because she couldn't think of an objection to throw at them quickly enough.

And it didn't end there.

The meals were always too hot. Or too cold. Too spicy. Or too bland. And all these complaints usually came before she had even lifted her fork, if she lifted it at all. Oh! And her room temperature. We could never get that right. Seventy-four degrees at Ivywood Hollow Bed-and-Breakfast did not feel like the seventy-four degrees she was used to in her house. My absolute favorite, though, was when she told me she found the antique blue inlay of the fireplace to be a little garish. I asked her if she'd like to change rooms, given she was paying for them all, but she told me with a drawn-out sigh that she'd suffer through.

I couldn't help but feel for her though. She was obviously unhappy, and someone that unhappy deserved a little leeway.

"I could push her off the balconette."

Or not.

I smiled at my aunt Nora. She couldn't help herself. She was fiery by nature. Constance had just asked for the flower arrangement in her room to be replaced because the fresh-cut hydrangeas were a little *much*, and it was a miracle Nora hadn't finished her off then and there. Most people had the good sense not to trifle with my aunt and her plants.

Nora, along with her sister Izzy and I, ran the B&B together, but she was the one who took care of the gardens and general *ambiance* of the bed-and-breakfast. It was amazing how she could take the simplest of places and transform it into something warm and welcoming, especially given the fact that *warm* and *welcoming* were probably two words that had never been used to describe her. When she walked down the street, usually dressed in black with her red hair flowing, you'd find at least two or three kids following behind. It was a game of bravery for them. Nora was a lot like a tiger in a rickety cage, beautiful to look at and dangerous. Those kids knew at any moment she might turn and lunge at them, giving them the thrill of a lifetime. Not that she ever really lunged. The turn was enough to send them off in peals of terrified laughter.

"I don't think pushing anyone off of anything will be necessary, Nora," a voice came from the top of the stairs. "I believe I finally have Constance settled for the night. She just needed a little help with the bath water."

My aunt Izzy came down the stairs, tucking some wayward strawberry blond curls back up into the loose bun on her head. Izzy did the cooking and baking at Ivywood Hollow, and she was fabulous at it. She knew it too. Izzy could get anyone to do just about anything with her culinary creations. Thankfully, she was also just about the sweetest woman to have ever lived, given it wasn't uncommon for guests to promise their firstborns for another bite of dessert. Izzy sat herself down beside me on the sofa and patted my leg companionably.

"Oh, you think you have her settled, do you? I'll believe that when I hear it," Nora drawled. "And by the way, I will never forgive you for giving that woman a bell."

My smile widened. That's right. Izzy had given Constance a bell. Our esteemed guest had found all the stairs of the house difficult to manage, and she felt she required a way to get ahold of us should she need anything. I didn't really think the stairs were that much of an issue for her, but Constance needed a lot of things, so if she had to go up and down the stairs every time she needed one of those things, well, that would be a lot. For an Olympic athlete it would be a lot.

"Did you hear it ringing last night at 3:00 a.m.?" Nora asked me. "No, of course you didn't. Tucked away in your little nest."

I lived in the loft above the old carriage house, now garage, of the B&B, unlike my aunts whose rooms were in the house. The small loft certainly wasn't as beautiful or as impressive as any of the spaces inside Ivywood Hollow, but it was cozy, and I had come to believe a little bit of privacy was good for the soul.

"She needed me to fluff her pillow. At three in the morning. Oh! I just realized I could have smothered her with it, and this would all be over."

"Evanora," Izzy chided with a laugh. As the older sister, she was the only one permitted to use Nora's full name. It wasn't a harsh reprimand though. We both knew Nora was just being Nora. "What a terrible thing to say. And, really, she's a lovely woman. She just knows what she likes."

"Don't be ridiculous," Nora replied. "She's a horrible woman, and you know it. Brynn and I were just discussing how much we'd both like to strangle her."

"What?" I asked in the high-pitched voice of the falsely accused. I straightened up on the sofa, which wasn't easy because it was ridiculously plush. "We'd *both* like to strangle her?" I was pretty sure Nora had had that particular conversation all by herself.

"She finally speaks." Nora collapsed dramatically back against the chaise lounge and draped her arm over her forehead. The cat resting above her peeked one eye open, probably trying to determine if my aunt was actually settling down or just resting momentarily before she worked herself up again. "And yes, you might not have said the words, but I could tell you were thinking them."

"I didn't realize mind reading was one of your many talents." I took another sip of my tea.

"What else can I do? You've become so quiet. You're practically a—"

Nora caught herself before she said the word out loud, but it was too late.

Ghost.

A softness came to her face as she met my eye. "Brynn, I'm sorry. That was insensitive."

"It's okay. I know." I gave her a weak smile. How could I be upset? Maybe she shouldn't have said it, but she wasn't exactly wrong. I had changed a lot. My life had fallen apart over a year ago now, and I wasn't the person I used to be.

"Let's just enjoy what's left of the evening, shall we?" Izzy said, giving my knee a squeeze. "It's the perfect fall night to be snug inside by the fire."

I smiled, grateful to let the subject drop. My aunts had been expressing more and more concern about my well-being lately, and I didn't feel up to yet another discussion about how I was doing. Besides, this was very cozy, the three of us listening to the wind whistle outside while the firelight danced over the dark honeyed walls of the parlor. It was a nice moment.

"When was the last time you tried a little mascara?"

And the moment was over.

I slid my gaze over to Nora.

"What? You have such beautiful eyes. Do you think everybody has that shade of green? And what about your hair?" She swirled a finger in the direction of the black braid that hung over my shoulder. "Is this style permanent now?"

"Evanora, leave the girl alone," Izzy said. "Now's not the time. We've all had a long day."

I shot her a thankful smile.

"Nonsense!"

My smile dropped.

"Since the subject has been raised, we should discuss it. You know as well as I do, Sister, that this situation isn't healthy. And we're all pretending it isn't happening. She doesn't want to *help*. She doesn't want to do that other job she used to go on about. All she wants to do is hide herself away here in the house doing chores. And, again, just look at her."

I frowned.

"What? You look terrible."

I didn't look that terrible. Nora's expectations for everyday fashion were child-beauty-pageant high.

"Soon enough she'll be up in the attic with Gideon. Is that what you want?"

The cat behind Nora finally gave up on getting rest anywhere near my aunt. He dropped to the floor with a thud and padded over to the foot of the stairs.

"Oh, see now," Izzy scolded. "You've upset Faustus."

Faustus, the B&B's resident Maine coon cat, was a lovely large beast. He was covered in black fur except for a faint frosting of gray across his face, which gave him quite the dignified look. We did lose some business from visitors with allergies, but that was the price of beauty I suppose.

"I'm sure his highness will survive," Nora said before shooting up to a seated position. "You have got to be kidding me!"

A half second later a bell tinkled upstairs.

"That woman is insufferable!"

A loud crack sounded from the fireplace as flames surged up the chimney.

"Calm down. Calm down," Izzy said, getting to her feet. "I forgot I said I'd bring her up some chamomile tea. I'll go get it. You get the door. It's almost nine o'clock. I wonder who it could be?"

Before the words had left Izzy's mouth, the doorbell rang.

Nora swept to her feet as Izzy headed for the kitchen.

"I've finally got it," Nora said, pointing a finger in the air while reaching with the other hand for the door. "I could shove that bell down Constance's throat. Wouldn't that be poetic? Oh, it's you."

"That's a fine way to open the door. Who are you trying to kill now?"

I stifled a laugh as a cold little wind rushed through the door along with Williams, our neighbor from across the street.

Now, I really liked Williams. I found her to be super stylish, not unlike Nora, supremely intelligent, and incredibly interesting. She had moved in ten years ago when she started teaching music history at the university—although Nora still referred to her as the *new* neighbor—and since that time she had become a valued member of Evenfall's town council. I knew Izzy felt the same way about our neighbor as I did, but the rapport between Nora and Williams was a touch more contentious. Like most neighbor relationships we did have the occasional issue to work out, and Nora, unfortunately, was willing to fight to the death over each and every one them. Once a branch from one of the B&B's many trees was blocking light to Williams's azaleas, and she requested we prune it back. Nora was horrified. They had argued about it in the street for nearly three straight hours before Izzy was able to negotiate a peace treaty. In all honesty, though, I think both women liked sparring.

That being said, Williams's latest complaint was proving a touch more difficult to resolve.

"I'm sorry," Nora said, moving to shut the door, "but we're very busy discussing how to murder one of our guests right now, so if you've come to complain about Dog, we'll have to discuss your murder at a later date."

"Nora!" Izzy said, sweeping in from the dining room with a silver tea platter. "I can't leave you alone for a second. Is that any way to greet a guest? Come in, Williams, please. The nights are getting chilly, aren't they?"

Williams raised a finely sculpted eyebrow at Nora before stepping past her.

"What brings you by?" Izzy asked. "Not that it isn't always a pleasure to see you."

"Don't lie, Izzy," Nora said before Williams could answer. "It's bad for the complexion."

Izzy ignored her. "I was just bringing up some tea for Constance Graves, but I could always pour you a cup if you'd like."

Williams cringed a little at Constance's name. Evenfall really was a small town. "That explains somebody's bad mood."

"What mood?" Nora asked, shooting up to her full height again. "I can hardly be blamed for—what in the world is going on up there?"

Just then the bell from upstairs started ringing again and then a door slammed.

Faustus let out a low meow. I eyed the cat as he adjusted

his feet on the bottom step of the staircase. He didn't often deign to speak to us, so I could only imagine Constance's behavior was getting to him too.

Nora rolled her eyes back to Williams. "If you'll excuse me, I have to go take care of something. Or rather someone."

Izzy's eyes widened. "Oh, don't you think I should be the one to check on Constance?"

"Oh no, no," Nora said, waving both hands in the air. "I'll take good care of our guest. Williams, please feel free to share your stories of doggy woe with my sister. After all, she has the more sympathetic ear."

I couldn't help but think Nora *taking care* of Constance was probably not the best plan. I snapped my book shut and pushed myself up, but the moment I got to my feet, Nora pointed at me and said, "Sit."

I plopped back down.

Izzy took a step to head off her sister's path. "Are you at least going to take the—"

Nora swept by her and up the stairs, Faustus leading the way.

"—tea?" Izzy finished, her shoulders slumping. True to form, though, my aunt recovered quickly. "So sorry about that," she said, hurrying over to Williams. "How are things at the university? I used to love the beginning of the fall semester. The smell of new books. The start of sweater season. The crisp fall air so ripe with possibility!"

Izzy tended to ramble when she got nervous.

"Well said," Williams agreed. "And it will be at least a few more weeks before all the students are beaten down and sleep-deprived. Now, could we discuss the reason for my visit?"

"I know. It's Dog. He's still—goodness!"

We all looked up. Something had hit the floor with enough force to rattle the chandelier.

I was much more successful getting myself up off the sofa on my second attempt. "Why don't you go see what's going on up there?" I suggested to Izzy. "I'd be more than happy to entertain Williams."

"Oh, well, if you don't mind," Izzy said, looking to our neighbor. Ever the hostess, my aunt could hardly imagine being so rude as to leave a guest mid-conversation.

"Not at all," Williams said, looking just the teensiest bit annoyed at having to begin her complaint a third time.

I waited until my aunt had made it all the way to the top of the stairs before I turned back to Williams. "Let me guess. Dog's been after Oscar again?"

"I don't know what to do, Brynn. That crow of your uncle's just won't leave him alone," she said, worry creasing her otherwise unlined forehead. Williams could be aloof at times, definitely professorial, but she really loved her dog.

I nodded sympathetically. Dog, the crow, just to be clear, did have a habit of plucking at our neighbor's English bulldog's tail. But in fairness, Oscar did also have a habit of losing his mind barking every time he saw Dog, and if Dog dared land anywhere near his yard, he'd go tearing after him. Well, tearing after him as fast as an older, heavier English bulldog can. "I get it, but I'm not sure you could say Uncle Gideon owns Dog. He just feeds him occasionally."

"And that's another thing. I'm finding peanut shells everywhere. In the garden. On the walk. Over the—"

"Brynn!"

I shot a quick look over to the stairs. Nora's voice sounded panicked. I looked back to Williams and took a step toward the door. "We may have to finish this later."

"Certainly, but could you at least talk to him?"

Another crash came from upstairs. This time it sounded like the tea service.

"Absolutely," I said, opening the door so that she could step out. "I'll have a word with Gideon tonight."

"Brynn! We need you!"

"Bye!" I clicked the door shut probably a little too close

to my neighbor's face and hurried up the stairs. "Coming!" I raced for Constance's room. The door was open, as was the one to the adjoining bathroom. I jumped over the teapot and tray toppled on the floor, then rushed past Faustus standing guard at the threshold of the en suite. "Sorry. I just had to see Williams out."

I stopped dead in my tracks.

Constance Graves lay motionless on the floor, her eyes open and lifeless, blood seeping from her head.

"Oh my, is she . . . ?"

"She's dead," Izzy said, twisting her fingers together. "Dead. Dead. Dead. Oh dear. She's very dead."

I looked to Nora.

"What are you looking at me for?!"

"I don't know! No reason!"

"If you're looking for confirmation, she's really dead. We checked."

The three of us stared down at poor Constance.

It seemed like ages before any of us even breathed.

It was Nora who finally broke the silence.

"You know, in hindsight, Brynn, I think *our* previous conversation may have been in poor taste."

Chapter 2

"OH MY, DOESN'T this all look tasty."

"Thank you so much for coming, Beatty."

"Anytime. Anytime." Beatty smiled at Izzy as she placed a tray of fresh brewed coffee and dulce de leche cookie sandwiches on the glass-topped coffee table.

It was a perfect fall day, and there was no better place to take it all in than from the porch of the B&B. The sky was bright blue, the only bit of white coming from the waxing crescent moon, the crickets were singing, and the deep pink roses that lined the front of the house were still blooming, filling the air with their rich scent.

Unfortunately, all the beauty made what had happened last night even worse.

Emergency services had been at the house until the early morning. We had only managed a couple hours of sleep, but rest would have to wait. Beatty, short for Bartholomew Barnes, the family lawyer, had called first thing as soon as he'd heard the news. Beatty handled all the legal business for Ivywood Hollow, although what had happened to poor

Constance obviously wasn't in the realm of his normal duties.

Once Izzy had arranged the tray on the table, I reached for the coffee, only to have my hand swatted away.

"Brynn, where are your manners? Guests first."

I rubbed my hand and smiled at Beatty. "She's right of course. Please."

He chuckled. "I think you all might need it more than me. Oh, hello, Nora."

Nora strode toward us wearing a dark green, gauze, kimono shawl with velvet embroidery over a fitted black dress. Her long red hair was piled up on her head, held in place with two gold hair pins. Even distraught, she managed to look terrific. The oversized black sunglasses may have been a bit much though. "Beatty," Nora said by way of greeting before snatching up the coffee mug he was reaching for.

"Evanora!" Izzy scolded.

"Beatty doesn't mind," Nora said matter-of-factly, sinking into one of the oversized rattan armchairs. "After all, it's not the coffee he's interested in."

Poor Izzy's eyes widened with embarrassment. Beatty Barnes was Izzy's crush. No one could fault her for it. Beatty was generous and thoughtful, the kind of person you could really count on, and to be completely honest, he was turning into a real silver fox, of the slightly chubby variety. He really seemed to like Izzy too, but things never progressed past cookies and coffee. It made Nora nuts. Like she was anyone to talk.

That being said, I couldn't exactly judge either one of them. The Warren women were not lucky in love. In fact, you might even call us cursed. I know I certainly felt that way.

"Nora's right," I said. "It's not the coffee Beatty's after. It's the baked goods." I picked up the plate and held it out to him. "Weren't these one of your favorites?"

"I have to admit, they're all my favorite," Beatty said, placing a cookie on a napkin. "Izzy always manages to outdo herself."

My aunt shot me a grateful smile.

Nora, however, let out a disgusted sigh before moving on with, "I suppose they've filled you in on all the grisly details?"

"I'm not sure I would call them grisly." Beatty reached for the notepad in his leather bag. "My understanding is Constance slipped and hit her head on the bathtub?"

"That's our best guess. It all happened so fast. I had just been up to check on her a few minutes beforehand. Nora found her," Izzy said. "That poor woman. I just can't believe it. I feel terrible."

"What is our liability in all this?" Nora asked, tapping her long crimson fingernails against her coffee mug.

Izzy straightened in her chair and fixed Nora with a look that could freeze hellfire. "Could we please take a moment to honor the woman who has passed."

"You're right. You're right," Nora said, waving a hand in the air then resting it on her forehead. "Constance was a," she struggled to find the right words, "wonderful woman."

"Don't hurt yourself there, Nora," Beatty said, bringing his own mug to his lips. "Everybody in town knew that Constance was difficult. I can attest to that personally."

Nora collapsed against her chair. "Thank you. Finally, someone other than me has said it."

"Of course, everyone does say the same thing about you."

Nora shot back up. "They do not!"

Nobody answered.

"Everybody loves me," she said, easing back uncertainly.

"Regardless, Constance was who she was. There's no denying that." Beatty let out a long breath. "She didn't have the easiest of lives though."

"She didn't?" Izzy asked, placing the cookie she had

taken, untasted, back on her napkin. "I mean, I don't know much about her other than her being the owner of Graves House. Such a lovely old home. It's a shame it has fallen into disrepair."

Nora scoffed. "Disrepair? It looks like a haunted house from a children's book. The entire family should be embarrassed."

I had heard Nora express these particular sentiments before.

Evenfall was not just a small town. It was also an old one. During the later years of the industrial revolution the mainly pastoral village had gone through a boom, doing quite well with textiles and later on with financing the railroad expansion. A renowned architect, Frank Hobson Henry, had designed a number of homes for the town's founding families. Ivywood Hollow was one of them, as was Graves House. It was said the architect had given particular care to Ivywood Hollow because he was in love with my widowed great-great-grandmother, but I got this from Nora, and she tended to believe everyone was prone to falling in love with women from the Warren family. But regardless of whether Frank Hobson Henry had loved my great-great-grandmother or not, his love for Ivywood Hollow was plain. Every detail of the Queen Anne three-story tower house showed care and affection. We had strived to keep up that standard. The same could not be said of Graves House.

"Aside from that, though, I never really knew the Graves family," Izzy said, looking to her sister. "Nora?"

For the briefest moment, I thought I saw something in my aunt's expression, but she said, "No. I know nothing of the family."

Beatty tapped his pen against his notepad. "Constance was a bit older than me, but I went to school with one of her brothers. Their father wasn't the nicest of men, not after his wife died giving birth to their youngest, Mary. After that, his kids could never do anything right. He pitted all four of them against each other right up until the day he died. Made sure they'd never get along. The boys even competed for the same girl back in high school. Ugly business that. Constance took care of her father in his final years. Bore the brunt of his behavior, from what I've heard."

"That sounds awful," Izzy said. "I wish I had known. I would have done things differently."

"Done what differently?" Nora said grumpily. "Given her a nightly foot rub? You were lovely. You know you were."

The implication was of course that *she* herself had not been. I couldn't help but feel for my aunt. Nora did not do well with guilty feelings. And I didn't think it was just because of the truly awful conversation we—*she!*— had had before Constance's death. If I were to guess, I think she felt responsible for what had happened. All three of us took pride in Ivywood Hollow and the comfort we provided our guests. We wanted everyone who stayed with us to have a memorable experience. We had never had a guest hurt, let alone *die* while staying with us. And the truth was we weren't like other B&B proprietors. We should have been able to prevent this.

"I'm sure Nora's right, Izzy. You could have showed Constance all the kindness in the world, and I doubt it would have made a difference," Beatty said kindly. "We're all products of our upbringings."

Nora adjusted her gauze shawl. "Not that that's an excuse to be miserable to everyone."

"No, it's not, but Constance certainly had her fair share of people being miserable to her. All that business with her father's will?"

"What business?" Nora asked, peering at him over the top of her sunglasses.

Beatty shook his head. "It's old news. I shouldn't have brought it up. That whole affair was one of the low points of my career. I've never felt right about any of it. But suffice it to say, if I had to guess, Constance's choices resulted in a pretty lonely life. In fact, the only person I think she was friends with was Theo," he said, looking at me.

I smiled. That made sense. Theodora Holmes was a wonderful person. She also happened to be my old boss. I used to work part-time at her bookstore, Lovely Leaves, up until, well, up until I didn't. There was no sense in reliving the past.

"Actually, I think Theo was the only person able to stay friends with everyone in that family and not take sides."

"What sides?" Nora asked.

"Again, I shouldn't say."

My aunt bristled. "Beatty, must you be so infuriating?"

"I keep wondering if it was somehow our fault," Izzy said loudly enough to derail Nora. "I've always made sure we've followed health and safety regulations, but maybe we missed something."

A soft buzz sounded from the coffee table. "Sorry," Beatty said, putting up a finger before picking up his phone. "This may be important. I have a friend over at the department." A deep furrow formed in his brow as he looked at the screen. "You know what? I hate to cut this short, but I'm going to pop over to the police station."

Izzy's eyes widened in alarm. "Why? What's going on? They don't think we were somehow negligent?"

"Let's not get ahead of ourselves," Beatty said, rising to his feet. "It could be nothing. I'll call you when I know anything for certain."

"Unacceptable," Nora snapped, also getting to her feet. "Beatty Barnes, I demand to know what that message on your phone said."

"Goodbye, Nora." Beatty placed his old fishing hat on his head. "It's always a pleasure, Izzy."

Nora dropped back down into her chair. "Infuriating."

The three of us fell into an uneasy silence.

We knew Beatty had more than just one friend down at the station. He would be the first to know if there was any speculation we were somehow responsible for Constance's death. But how could we be? It was an accident. Even though the bath had been running, the floor had been dry. We had the proper bathmats. Handrails. She had fallen. That was all.

But if I were to be completely honest, I wasn't sure that was true.

Something had been bothering me since we first found Constance.

It was a small thing, and I was certainly no expert, but I couldn't seem to put it out of my mind.

There was no blood on the edge of the tub.

If she had fallen and hit her head, wouldn't there have been blood? She could have hit her head on the floor, but she was on her side, not her back. Surely her shoulder would have blocked a direct blow.

Again, I had no experience with this kind of thing, but it seemed odd.

And then there had been all of that banging and door slamming before Nora had gone up. Looking back, it had almost sounded as though someone had been up there with her. Faustus had been acting strangely too, and he did have a canny sense of when things weren't quite right.

But no, there couldn't have been someone upstairs with Constance. We would have known.

I was being ridiculous. It had been an accident. Nothing more.

Of course, in the past there was a way I could have found out for sure. But that was all a long time ago. A different lifetime. It was no longer an option.

"Brynn," Nora said, breaking me from my reverie. When I caught her expression, I knew she had been thinking the same thing.

"We've been over this," I said, putting my coffee mug down on the table with a bit of a clatter. "There's no point in going over it again."

"So, you're not even going to try?" she asked.

"I have tried."

"I can understand why you were not willing to do anything about your problem before, but, surely, given what's happened it's time to reconsider."

"You're not listening to me. There's no point."

"That's not true. There are things we can try."

"No, there are not. *I've* already tried. It's not happening."

"But you haven't tried everything. You know you haven't tried everything."

We warred gazes, but I was not backing down. My aunt was crossing a line here, and she knew it.

"Nora," Izzy said gently.

"Don't you *Nora* me," she snapped. "I'm tired of being the bad guy. You know as well as I do her behavior isn't healthy."

Izzy cleared her throat.

I should have known this was coming given the circumstances of Constance's passing. And I knew my aunts were worried about me. They had raised me from the age of five when my parents were killed in a car accident. You could say it was their job to worry about me. But I had just passed my thirty-first birthday. There had to be boundaries. I was an adult now.

I challenged Izzy with a look. She cringed but carried on. "Brynn, your aunt Nora isn't wrong. We know you've been through a tragedy. A terrible loss. And everyone is entitled to having time to heal, but we're worried you might be stuck, darling. And that you might need a little help getting unstuck."

I wouldn't say I was stuck. I was changed. There was a difference.

Recently I had come to a decision about how I wanted to live my life going forward. I hadn't, however, told my aunts about that decision yet. They would not react well.

"We are your family, Brynn. Don't shut us out. There isn't any problem we can't solve together."

I suspected she intended to say more, but all of the sudden a strange look came over her face.

"Do you hear that?"

"Hear what? What are you talking about?" Nora slapped the armrests of her chair. "You were doing so well! Don't stop now! You were saying *Nora's right and . . .*"

"No, I'm being serious," Izzy said, holding up her hand. "Listen."

I took a breath, trying to focus on whatever it was my aunt was talking about, but all I could hear was the blood rushing in my ears.

Nora slowly sat up in her chair. "Please tell me that isn't what I think it is."

What was going on with the two of them?

I took another breath and tried to refocus my energy. This was obviously important if they were willing to drop the issue we all had been dancing around for months.

I closed my eyes.

I didn't hear anything out of the ordinary at first, but then it came to me.

It was a soft trilling.

Soft because I was hearing it from a distance, but louder than it should have been. Probably because there were so many of *them* making the steady hum.

"Come on," Nora said, sweeping to her feet.

Izzy and I followed her around the side of the house, down the porch steps, and into the back garden.

Nora's garden was a sanctuary. There was no better word to describe it. Even though she tended to it daily, it had a wild feel, lush and overgrown. It was the type of place where you wanted to dance in the moonlight, trailing your fingers over flowers, or laze away a hot summer's day listening to the wind rustle in the trees.

Today, though, that feeling had been replaced with something else. It was a small sensation, like catching the faintest whiff of smoke on the wind, but it was there, and it felt almost *sinister*.

"I don't like this," Izzy said, looking up to the window of the room where Constance had stayed.

The sound swelled as we got closer.

Nora pointed. "There, by the thyme."

I looked over to the cluster of tiny purple flowers. It was late in the year for the herb to be blooming, but the rhythm of the season couldn't compete with Nora's skills.

I stepped forward carefully.

It was hard to spot them at first, but they were there.

Toads.

Twenty, maybe thirty of them, right beneath the window of Constance's room.

Izzy, Nora, and I exchanged looks.

Toads gathering like this where someone had died? That wasn't something we could ignore.

"We need to bring one of them inside," Nora said firmly.

No one moved.

"Brynn."

"Why me?"

"Because," Izzy said, waving a hand to shoo me toward them, "toads like you."

"Toads *like* me?"

She nodded vigorously. "You were always playing with them as a child."

"I never played with toads." I put my hands on my hips. "And I'm pretty sure no toad has ever liked me."

Right then a fat little toad flopped itself onto my boot. "Really?" I asked, looking down at the big-eyed creature.

The toad blinked.

"You have been chosen," Izzy said happily.

I squatted down to get a better look at the little guy. "What do you say? Do you want to be the one to come inside?"

The toad blinked again.

"Stop chatting with the beast and pick him up," Nora snapped. "This is serious."

I looked up at my aunt. Her expression mirrored her words.

I would have had a tough time explaining to an outside observer what it was we were doing scooping up a toad on a bright autumn morning the night after a woman had died, but not being able to explain our behavior was hardly a new experience for me growing up the way I had, in the family I had.

Outsiders always had questions.

Like how did my aunts always know when someone was at the door before the bell rang? Or how did Nora keep her flowers blooming long past the time when everyone else's had died? Why was it the fire raged when one of us was upset? Or a clear sky clouded over when one of us was sad?

The explanation was simple, but no one would ever believe it.

Magic.

Enchantments and conjurations. Spells and incantations. Divinations and charms. All the hocus-pocus old wives used to speak of in hushed tones by the fire. My aunts could do all of those things.

They could do them because they were witches.

I was too.

Or at least I used to be.

Chapter 3

I GAZED AT THE silvery moon peeking over the tips of the trees visible through the open window in the tower room of the attic. The cold night wind made the apartment pretty chilly, but it was nice where I was bundled up by the antique stove.

"So?"

I leaned over to glance at the notebook sitting on the coffee table in front of my uncle Gideon, completely ignoring the bid he was throwing in my direction. "Are those new haikus? I'd love to hear them."

"Brynn, I don't think you came up here to listen to my haikus."

"You don't know that," I said, straightening in my chair. "I love your haikus. Seriously, read them to me."

He looked at me skeptically. "I'm not sure now is the appropriate time."

"I could use the distraction."

He eyed me a moment longer, then reached for the notebook, adjusting his glasses on his nose. "They're still a bit rough, and I'm not sure I've weeded out all the extra syllables."

"Just read."

"Well, if you insist." He adjusted his weight in the leather armchair. "*Long year winding down, colors blaze then turn to ashes, woodpiles awaken.*"

"That's really lovely, Gideon," I said, stealing a glance at my watch.

"Oh? Did you like that?"

"I did." The last bit of light was draining from the sky. It would be time soon. "What else do you have?"

He cleared his throat. "*When does fall's promise, slip from light into shadow, shortening the days?*"

"Beautiful. Keep going."

"This is one of my favorites. *I have tasted fall, it is a warm cup of tea, too quickly it cools.*"

"Love it."

"Which part did you like? Was it the coffee?"

"Yes," I mumbled, chewing the side of my thumbnail. My aunts would be calling me any second. "Definitely the coffee. I love coffee."

He tossed the notebook onto the table and folded his arms across his chest.

"Tea! I mean the tea! Oh no, I'm so sorry, Gideon." I slumped back in my chair. "It's not the haikus. They really are beautiful. I must be too distracted by everything to truly appreciate them."

He pulled his glasses off to get a better look at me. "Brynn, you know I have to ask."

I shook my head quickly. "You don't have to. There isn't a law or anything."

He chuckled and directed his gaze over to the open window in the large exposed brick wall, probably awaiting Dog's return.

I pulled the throw I had around my shoulders more

tightly to me. "Besides, I think you already know the answer."

He looked back at me with a gentle smile. "I suppose I do. I guess that was just my inelegant way of bringing up the topic."

Inelegant was not a word I would use to describe my uncle. He didn't spend a lot of time or attention on his appearance, given he never left the attic, but there was something about his manner that was always *very* elegant. And kind. And sweet.

"Well, in answer to your question. No, I have not tried." I took a deep breath, waiting for the question we both knew was coming next.

"Are you planning to?"

"There's no point."

All the witches in the Warren family had different affinities. It didn't mean they couldn't do magic outside of their talent, but it was a little like being a specialist in a particular area.

Izzy, of course, was a kitchen witch. While I was growing up, she always used to tell me there was very little difference between a recipe and a spell. Both were simply a set of instructions for how to put ingredients together in order to make something magical. And when directions weren't followed, well, we've all messed up a dish, or in Izzy's case, turned someone's skin a very pale shade of green. It had only happened once. To me. Right before the Spring Fling dance of my senior year. But, you know, it's fine. Now.

Usually, most everything Izzy cooked came out just right. Ivywood Hollow's breakfasts were legendary in the B&B community. Her muffins and cakes were always moist, her eggs were always fluffy, and her bacon was never too soft or too crisp. But more than any of that, Izzy's food was made with *intention*. I wasn't kidding when I said she could get anyone to do, or *feel*, just about anything if they ate at her table. If she put an intention into her food, whether it be good feelings like happiness, curiosity, and excitement, or other emotions like anger, jealousy, and regret, that intention usually found its way into reality. Izzy was judicious when it came to using her influence though. She believed in a feather touch.

Now, Nora, first and foremost, was a garden witch. She understood plants; not just how to grow them, but what they could be used for. She had a deep connection with nature and loved trees more than she loved most people. The idea of a garden witch might seem cute, but only the very foolish underestimated what Nora could do with her plants. As a child, I once stuck my tongue out at her when I thought she wasn't looking, and I swear a stinging nettle smacked me on the back of the leg. I never did that again. Nora was also pretty talented at creating what I call *atmosphere*, not just outside but inside too. Much the way her sister was able to put intention into her food, Nora could put intention into a room. Cozy rooms became even cozier when she gave them her touch, and let's just say, you'd never want to go into a room my aunt had decorated for Halloween. Unlike Izzy, Nora preferred bold magic, and she wasn't always a fan of following the rules.

Then there was me and my uncle Gideon. We didn't specialize the way my aunts did in creating and nurturing magic. Our talents just *were*. And unfortunately for me— and more so for Constance—my affinity was suddenly in great demand.

You see, I was a friend of the other side.

Or to put it more bluntly, a witch of the dead.

For as long as I could remember, I'd had the ability to see and talk with ghosts just like I would anyone else.

If Constance's death had occurred a couple of years ago, we wouldn't have had to spend the day waiting by the phone for Beatty to call to tell us what was happening with the police. He hadn't, by the way, which I had to admit was a little infuriating. No, back then, I would have spent the day talking with Constance, asking her about her life and what she *thought* had happened—ghosts almost never remembered the hours before their deaths.

But that was who I used to be.

All that changed when I lost my husband, Adam.

"I know what you're thinking," I said, catching my uncle's eye.

"How exciting. What *am* I thinking?"

"You're thinking I should try. You're thinking toads gathering where a person died could be a very bad sign. You're thinking if I talked to Constance's ghost, there's a good chance I could clear the whole matter up pretty quickly."

He plopped his chin onto his fist. "I had no idea my mind was so busy."

"But it's not that simple, and you know it."

"Please, go on," he said, waggling his eyebrows. "What else do I know?"

I frowned at him. "You know I haven't seen a ghost in a very long time."

His face creased with sadness. "But Brynn, have you really tried?"

I threw my hands up. "Why does everyone keep asking me that? Don't you see? I never had to try before. My ability, it's gone. And even if I could reach Constance, you know ghosts don't always have the answers."

"Of course not."

"Don't you *of course not* me."

His eyebrows shot up.

"That was a very judgy *of course not*."

A twinkle came back to his eye. "I apologize."

"And that's a fake apology." I sank back into the depths of my chair.

"You look just like your mother when you pout."

I smiled, but I couldn't muster much enthusiasm to go

behind it. "I wish I could explain it better. It's just—" I cut myself short with a sharp breath. "I think I'm done trying. I don't want to try anymore."

Gideon looked away. He knew exactly what I was talking about. He had long felt the same way.

Growing up, I had been raised to believe our family's magical powers came with responsibility. The Warren witches had always looked over the town of Evenfall, helping where they could. It was a legacy I had been proud of. But now Nora was right when she said I didn't want to *help* anymore. At least not in the way my family wanted me to.

"Well, my dear," Gideon finally said, "I'm certainly in no position to tell you what to do. And I suppose we'll all know soon enough if the toad has anything to say about what happened to the unfortunate Constance Graves, regardless of your actions. Ah! Dog!"

Our conversation was interrupted by the flapping of wings, and Dog's thin talons scratching against the frame of the open window. "Brynn tells me you have been a very naughty bird."

Dog looked over at me indignantly.

"What?" I asked, suddenly feeling guilty. "The neighbors are complaining."

The crow continued to stare me down.

"Stop looking at me like that. You need to leave Oscar alone. He's old. You're stressing him out."

The bird held me prisoner in his gaze a moment longer before deigning to take the peanut Gideon was holding out to him.

"I've been doing some reading on crows," my uncle said, using the side of one finger to smooth down the feathers on Dog's back. "Did you know some believe they are messengers of the dead?"

He looked over at me when I didn't answer.

"Maybe he should talk to Constance, then," I answered moodily.

Gideon chuckled. "Just like your mother."

Suddenly a distant voice came up through the floorboards. "Brynn? It's time. You'll be joining us, won't you, darling?"

My uncle gave me a look that seemed to ask, *Will you?*

I put my hands on the armrests of my chair to push myself up. "I'll join them, but I'm not—Gideon?"

My uncle had gone still, his eyes focused on something far away.

"Do you see something?"

That was Gideon's gift and his curse. He could see both into the past and the future. Yes, Nora and Izzy could catch glimpses of things that were about to happen, but they could only see seconds ahead. Gideon could see years. Maybe longer. He didn't like to talk about it. Unfortunately, my uncle didn't have much control over the content of his visions, and worse yet, he couldn't always change what he saw. He had learned that the hardest way possible.

"You'd better go down," he said with a forced smile.

I got to my feet. "That doesn't sound good."

"Oh, and take this." He reluctantly passed me a pillow from the sofa. "Put it in front of the small china buffet in the sunroom. It might help."

"Okay." I took the pillow and held it against my chest. "I don't suppose you want to tell me why?"

"And I don't suppose you want to try to reach Constance's ghost?"

"Wow," I said, raising my eyebrows at him. "It's like that, is it?"

He chuckled. "It's like that."

I smiled back at him and headed for the stairs. "Your haikus really are wonderful, Gideon."

"It's far too late for flattery now," he answered, giving me a wink. "Next time, you'll positively have to drown me in praise if you expect me to forgive you."

"I promise I'll—"

"Brynn!" a voice shouted from the floor below.

"I'm coming!" I yelled back far more testily than I should have.

I climbed down the spiral steps, leaving my uncle chuckling behind me.

I THINK IT'S DARK enough," Izzy said, bustling around the parlor without really doing anything. "Now we just need to go in there and have a look."

The *there* was the sunroom. I was initially going to put the toad in the kitchen, but Izzy was not at all fond of that idea, so I had to come up with another option. Luckily, I had been able to find an old hamster cage in the garage. Not that that was too much of a surprise. The garage had pretty much everything you might need. Most witches had a minor problem with *collecting*, but my aunts and I were pretty good at staying on top of it even if the garage did look like a secondhand store. Once I had found the cage, I lined it with dirt and grass, and I left it with the toad inside, on a shady table in the small glass-walled room. I had purposefully left the lights on.

The three of us stood in the parlor, staring at the sunroom, while Faustus sat in the threshold, seemingly waiting for us to get on with it.

"Before we go in," Nora said, "we need to discuss what we're going to do if we discover the worst."

"Oh, I hadn't thought of that." Izzy stopped pacing with a sudden jerk. "What will we do? We can't exactly go to the police. But we can't ignore it either."

"Well," I said matter-of-factly, "in the extremely, *extremely* unlikely event the toad shows us something, I was thinking I would go into town tomorrow, alone, and talk to Theo about Constance. Maybe we could find out more about her life and lead the police in a direction that might help."

Suddenly, I was blinded by a mass of curly hair. Izzy had ambush-hugged me and was now rocking us both back and forth. "Going into town? To see Theo? That's wonderful!"

"But you heard the part about me going alone, right?"

"Certainly. Whatever you want. I'm just so proud of you, darling."

I smiled. I was kind of proud of myself too. I hadn't gone into town in months, especially not to the bookstore, and while it wasn't going to be easy, I really thought it was progress.

"What are you doing?" Nora whacked her sister on the arm. "Stop it!"

Nora, apparently, had a differing opinion.

Izzy turned to look at her. "What?"

"The bookstore? Oh, *whoop-de-doo*," Nora said. "Don't you think you're ignoring the more obvious issue Brynn should be tackling?"

Izzy turned away from me and whispered as though I couldn't hear, "Baby steps, Nora. Baby steps."

"Baby steps? She's a grown woman!"

I slowly backed away to let the two of them bicker and headed for the sunroom with Gideon's pillow. I really didn't need to hear them discuss how best to parent me anymore. Their styles were never going to change. Izzy had always been overly proud of every little thing I had ever done. While Nora always seemed to think I wasn't quite living up to this magnificent potential she believed I possessed. It didn't matter that I was an adult now. Once a parent always a parent, I guess.

Regardless, I was pretty happy about my plan. I was done going back and forth with my family about what I *should* be doing. I didn't need my magic to find out who Constance had been in life. I could learn about her in other ways. I could still help people even if it wasn't the way my aunts wanted me to. And besides, the whole issue was moot because what had happened to Constance was an accident. I was sure of it. We were just upset because it had happened on our watch. The toads gathering outside the house had to be a coincidence. Nothing more.

"Brynn? Are you going in without us?" Izzy called out, hurrying after me.

Nora followed behind. "And what are you doing with that pillow?"

"Gideon gave it to me," I said, placing it in front of the small china buffet with the claw feet. Faustus gave it a sniff.

"Oh dear," Izzy said, stepping to the other side of the room, "that doesn't bode well. Faustus, you might want to get away from there." The cat gave her a look then moved along.

"This is ridiculous," Nora said drily. "What exactly are we expecting to happen? If everyone's ready, I'm just going to turn off the lights."

"Hang on," I said. "I want to check on Precious."

"Precious?" Nora asked, her hand resting on the antique light switch. "You named the toad?"

"Don't judge me," I said. "I know it's a bad name, but you're the one who made me set it all up in the cage, and it kept looking up at me with those big, black trusting eyes, and I—"

"The only thing more tedious than the name itself is the story behind the name. Let's just get on with this, shall we?"

"We shall," Izzy said firmly and in a lower tenor of voice. Another one of Izzy's quirks was that she often got quite serious whenever we were about to do something witchcraft-related and her voice took on a deep timbre, much to Nora's annoyance. It was usually kind of funny, but tonight it was particularly amusing, given what we were about to do wasn't exactly spell-work. Thankfully. No, we were just going to take a look at a toad, and maybe at what the toad left us behind in the cage.

What most humans don't know, or rather, can't see, is

that some creatures, amphibians in particular, liked to feed on strong energy. Emotional energy was a big favorite. And when they fed on strong energy, that energy had to go somewhere, and oftentimes you could see remnants of said energy in . . .

The poop.

That's right, we were going to look at the toad's poop.

In the dark.

You could only see what we were looking for in the dark.

Izzy took a loud deep breath. "Let us take a moment to cleanse our energy before we begin the sacred examination."

Nora rolled her eyes so hard she practically shuddered. I mimicked Izzy's deep breath, if for no other reason than to bug Nora.

Izzy spread her hands wide. "Now, let us take another moment to thank Precious for—"

The lights clicked off.

"Oh, so sorry, Sister," Nora said. "My finger must have slipped. Now let's see what that toad has been up to."

Izzy and I crept in the dark toward Precious's cage. We were already nervous given what we might find, and it didn't help matters that the sunroom had a peculiar feel to it in the dim light, its shadows stretched across the floor.

"I don't see anything, do you?" Izzy asked softly.

"No, nothing," I murmured.

"Why are you two whispering?" Nora asked at full voice. "And why are you creeping? Brynn, just get the creature out of there so we can examine the cage."

Leave it to Nora to ruin a mood of someone else's making.

Izzy and I both straightened before I asked, "Why do I always have to be the one to pick up the toad?"

"I *could* do it," Nora said lightly, "but I'm sure you've heard some witches have been known to eat live toads."

"That's not—" My voice faltered when I looked back at her. "—true." My aunt was smiling quite widely, her teeth gleaming in the dark.

"Well, in that case." I carefully unlatched the wire door of the cage and lifted Precious out. "There you are. I promise you can go back outside after this. I bet you're missing your friends, aren't you?"

Nora pushed past me. "Get out of the way."

"I still don't see anything," Izzy said, crouching to peer inside the cage.

Nora wheeled back around and glared at the toad. "Did you even try?"

"Don't worry," I whispered to Precious. "She says that to everyone."

Unfortunately, I guess Precious *was* worried because before I could stop him, he had escaped from my grip and launched himself into the air.

"Precious!"

Both my aunts jumped back, but it was Nora who let out a high-pitched squeal and bumped into the china buffet. All the dishes rattled, but they settled just as quickly. I almost breathed a sigh of relief, but then I saw the antique vase resting on top of the cabinet teeter side to side.

"Uh-oh."

I reached for it just as it toppled over. Luckily, it landed perfectly on the pillow below.

"Oh, well done, Gideon!" Izzy shouted loud enough to reach the attic.

A tinny "You're welcome" came back through the cast-iron register by the ceiling.

I smiled at Nora, still cowering by the buffet.

She scowled at me. "What are you smiling at?"

"You're afraid of toads."

"Nonsense."

"You don't eat toads. You run from them."

"That's quite enough out of you."

"You're scared of itty-bitty little—ow!"

Nora had snapped her fingers and a corresponding snap hit the back of my neck.

"Stop that, you two," Izzy said. "We have to find Precious. Where could he be?" She whirled around, accidently knocking the cage over onto its side. "Oh, stars!"

Faustus jumped up onto the table just as the contents spilled out. I followed his gaze down to the small toad seated among the piles of dirt scattered across the floor.

No.

It couldn't be.

I bent down to get a closer look.

"Precious," I whispered. "What have you done?"

But, of course, Precious hadn't done anything but that which was most natural. And it lay glittering all over the floor.

A few tiny blue and purple crystal flecks danced in the low light coming through the windows, but they didn't worry me. It was all the green.

My body went cold.

They were everywhere. Precious must have buried them in the dirt, but there was no mistaking them now.

I knew what the color meant.

It meant rage. Fury. Wrath.

Izzy put her hands to her mouth. "It can't be."

I rose up to standing. "But is this really proof? It doesn't necessarily mean that . . . ?"

Izzy's shoulders slumped. "I'm afraid it does."

I looked to Nora.

"It's proof," she said. "Constance Graves was murdered."

Chapter 4

WITCHES HAVE AN uneasy relationship with sleep. On the rare occasion we sleep well, it's deep and restorative, usually overdue, and can last through an entire languorous day and night. But most of the time, that isn't the case. As they say, there is no rest for the wicked. Not that any of us buy into that *wicked* nonsense. In truth, most in the witching community simply believe we're blessed to need less sleep than our nonmagical counterparts. After a night of tossing and turning, though, it certainly felt like more of a curse than a blessing to me.

Murdered. Constance Graves had been murdered. Under our care.

It was almost impossible to believe. Even though my aunts were certain, after we had cleaned up the sunroom and let Precious go, I pored over every book we had on the subject. While I read, Izzy fretted and baked. Those two things often went together for Izzy. And while Izzy baked, Nora paced and ranted, tossing out plans for spells no good witch would ever dream of casting to *handle* the situation.

Gideon occasionally interjected observations from the vents, but, unfortunately, none of us got anywhere useful.

We had far more questions than answers.

Like how did the murderer get in and up to the second floor without our noticing? The assailant certainly couldn't have gotten in through the front door or used the main staircase. We had a clear view of both from where we had been sitting in the parlor. It was possible the killer had come in earlier in the day and hidden somewhere, but that was highly unlikely. Faustus would have ferreted out an intruder. Very little got by that cat. All this meant the killer would have had to have come in either through the side or the back door of the B&B and used the hidden staircase to get up to the second floor. But the entrance to those stairs was concealed behind a door camouflaged in the panels of the wall near the kitchen. It would be almost impossible to find it without prior knowledge, and we didn't often share that information with guests, as the stairs did not meet safety regulations. So how did the killer know to use them?

The whole situation was disconcerting, to say the least, and we felt foolish for having let our guards down. But in fairness, it was easy to see how. Evenfall was such a safe town and given who we were, it was hard to imagine a scenario in which we'd feel truly threatened. That being the case, we didn't often lock the doors until we were ready to turn in for the night. We were used to the comings and goings of guests. It had all seemed so reasonable.

Still, we could have done more.

Magically, we could have done more.

Before she began baking, Izzy had set to doing just that. She had warded the house and the property behind the iron fence that surrounded the backyard. That way someone could come up to the door without suffering any ill effects, but no one without our stated permission was getting beyond it or to the B&B's private grounds without experiencing an excruciating headache. It was a little like closing the barn door after the horse had run off, but it still felt necessary given the circumstances.

I was grateful when the sun's first rays found their way into my loft above the garage, so that I could give up on the idea of rest entirely.

I got up, wrapped a throw around my shoulders, and padded across the wood floor to peek out the window above my kitchen sink. A jogger loped by, panting out clouds of frosty air. Definitely scarf weather.

Any other morning, I would have made a cup of tea and started a fire in the old stone hearth to warm up the place, taking my time to get the day started. Years ago, the loft had been my great-grandmother's workroom, her cauldron still rested on the mantel, and I loved everything about it, from the exposed beams of the ceiling to the old wood floors covered in plush throw rugs. But there was no time for coziness today.

Now was the time for action.

I splashed some water on my face, brushed my teeth, then quickly dressed in jeans, a sweater, and a thick red scarf. My grandmother had knitted it years ago, but a preservation spell kept it fresh and soft. I then pulled on my boots and dropped my messenger bag onto my shoulder.

Time to get going.

I thought I had made my preference of doing this alone clear, but clarity was sometimes lacking in our household. My aunts' desire to protect and support me was wonderful. It really was. But they sometimes went overboard. I scooped up my keys. Besides, I felt pretty good about going into town today. I could go to the bookstore and see Theo. I had done it many times before. It would be fine. I didn't need my aunts hovering over me, constantly asking how I was doing. I pulled the door open.

"Good morning, darling. How are you doing today?"

I should have known.

Izzy stood waiting for me on the wood platform on the

other side of my front door. She had always known when I was trying to sneak out. I'd never got to go to any of the really good high school parties.

I sighed, but I also couldn't help but smile. She looked pretty adorable with her plaid poncho and wicker basket. Even the tip of her nose had reddened with the cold to a shade that perfectly matched her coat.

"I'm fine," I said dryly. "You're up awfully early."

"Oh, I never got to sleep. And I remembered you said something about maybe going into town, and, as it happens, I have to pay a visit of my own, so I thought why not walk together?"

I frowned.

Izzy flipped open one side of her basket. "I brought you coffee," she said, pulling out a travel mug.

I tried to resist, but Izzy made good coffee. Really good coffee. Actually, it was probably the best coffee in the world. At least that's what I was inclined to believe on this frosty morning when I'd had so little sleep. I took the mug from her, clicked it open, and took a sip.

"First pumpkin spice of the season."

I narrowed my eyes at her. "You know, you act like you're a good witch, but sometimes I wonder."

"Don't be silly," Izzy said cheerily. "Shall we?"

"Do I have a choice?"

She didn't answer, just gave me a laugh that somehow managed to sound like birds twittering.

I followed my aunt down the stairs, comforting myself with the thought that at least it wasn't Nora tagging along today. Not that I didn't love my other aunt with all my heart, but it would have been hard to lay low on this first trip into town with her threatening to turn people into frogs if they didn't confess to murder. Not that she'd do that. At least, I didn't think she would.

Izzy and I walked together to the end of the driveway, then just as she turned, headed for the shorter route into town, I touched her elbow. "I was thinking, could we maybe go the other way?"

Confusion came to my aunt's face. "But it's so much longer." Her gaze landed on the stone gates of the graveyard. It was one of the oldest in the country, dating back nearly two hundred and fifty years. It was also where my husband was buried. "Oh, of course, darling. Of course." She patted my hand, and we changed direction.

"Now, I know I don't have to tell you this," she said a moment later, "but we should really do our best to blend into the community today. No one can know we believe Constance's death was anything but an accident."

"Right."

"People are understandably upset in these types of situations, and that can lead them to fear things they don't understand."

I smiled inwardly. It wasn't the first time Izzy had lectured me on this particular topic. She had practically drilled it into me before letting me go to school. Some things never changed. "Don't worry. I know exactly what you mean. Today we are just your average, ordinary B&B proprietors. It makes perfect sense we'd want to reach out and connect with our community, given our genuine upset over the accidental death of one of our guests."

"Exactly. Today we are more ordinary than ordinary. We are mundane. Boring even." She hooked her arm through mine as we crunched over the leaves. "Everything having anything to do with us today is completely *normal*."

Suddenly a voice rang out. "Ladies! There you are!"

Oh no.

Out of the corner of my eye, I caught sight of a man holding a rake, hurrying across his lawn to catch up with us.

Izzy and I exchanged looks.

"I guess making a run for it wouldn't look all that normal."

Izzy sighed. "Probably not."

Chapter 5

OUR STREET WAS a lovely old one. Tall maples lined both sides. Houses sat far back from the road, which provided plenty of room for kids to ride their bikes in loping figure eights. Birds and squirrels flew and scurried about in abundance, and the unique scents of the changing seasons always seemed to fill the air. The overall effect was friendly and relaxing. In short, it was the perfect street to amble along, taking your time to chat with your neighbors.

"We don't have to run, but if we hurry, we can cross the street before he catches us."

"Ladies!"

"I don't know," Izzy whispered between huffed breaths. "He's gaining on us."

"We can make it."

"Yoo-hoo!"

"It's fine. Just, whatever you do, don't look over, and don't say—"

"Oh hello, Mr. Henderson," my aunt said in a voice she almost managed to make sound cheerful.

"—anything." I shot Izzy a look.

She shrugged helplessly. "He's right there."

Our neighbor leaned on his rake, his white hair standing on end, his glasses askew on his nose. "I thought I was going to miss you ladies," he said, struggling to catch his breath.

"Sorry," I said weakly. "We must not have heard you calling us."

"It's a good thing I caught up. I've been worried sick about you. Where's Nora?" he said, looking us over as though we might be hiding her behind our backs. "The ambulance the other night, it wasn't for her, was it?"

"No, no," I said quickly. "I'm sorry to say one of our guests passed away."

"Just as I thought. Anyone I would know?"

That was a hard question for me to answer. Mr. Henderson had only moved in a year ago, and he didn't overly involve himself in the community. He had his own hobbies to preoccupy him. "Um, Constance Graves? She had been staying with us the last few days."

"I can't say as I recognize the name, but"—he motioned for us to lean in, then looked side to side—"it's entirely possible I've seen her." He leaned back again, giving us room to let that information sink in.

"I'm sure you have," Izzy said. "As Brynn mentioned, she's been staying with us and—"

He waved a hand in the air, effectively shushing Izzy. Judging by her pursed lips, she did not appreciate the gesture. "I don't mean I've seen her in her earthly form."

I closed my eyes. *Oh dear.*

"I mean, I've *seen* her, seen her."

"Seen her, seen her?" I asked, forcing lightness into my voice. I really hoped this wasn't going where I thought it might be going.

He leaned in again. "I mean, I saw her *afterward.*"

Nope, it was going exactly where I'd thought.

"I saw her ghost."

Izzy and I froze as Mr. Henderson studied our faces intently, waiting for us to react to his big news.

Finally, Izzy said, "Well, that's ridiculous." She then let out a slightly hysterical-sounding laugh. "You couldn't have seen her ghost. Ghosts don't exist. Can you imagine? What a thought. Ghosts in this day and age? Preposterous!"

I put my hand on my aunt's shoulder. Did I mention Izzy rambled when she got nervous?

She snapped her mouth shut and patted my hand by way of saying thank you.

"Oh, Isabel, Isabel, Isabel," Mr. Henderson said in a patronizing tone that had unfortunately become all too familiar. It was a *really* good thing Nora wasn't with us this morning. "You need to open your eyes to what's going on all around you. There are forces at work in this town. Strange powers here in Evenfall that you couldn't possibly understand." He stopped to look up at the trees. I almost looked up too, but resisted the urge, feeling fairly certain there was nothing up there. "Really, when you think about it, ghosts are the least of our worries."

You'd think, given I'd spent the majority of my life seeing and talking to ghosts, I wouldn't easily dismiss someone telling me they had seen one of their own. But as I mentioned, our neighbor was a special case. With special interests.

And it was all our fault.

Mr. Henderson was naturally the type of neighbor who liked to peek around curtains, but we had, unfortunately, provided him with the opportunity to see some things he really shouldn't have, and in short, we had created a monster.

It had all started when another one of our neighbors, Minnie Abernathy, had accidentally left her gate open, setting her overprotective rottweiler free just as our lovely mail carrier, Bertha, was heading back to her truck. The dog had gotten it into his head to make a run at her, but, as luck would have it, Izzy was outside at the time watching the scene unfold. With the snap of her fingers, she turned a puddle to ice just as the dog was about to lunge, sending him harmlessly skidding out of the way. As a result, Bertha was able to get back in her truck, and Minnie was able to secure her dog. Crisis averted, right?

Not quite.

Regrettably, that particular incident had taken place in the middle of July, and Mr. Henderson, seeing the entire event unfold—save the snap of Izzy's fingers—made it over to examine the ice before it had fully melted.

For the record, Nora had had a word with Minnie's dog shortly after that particular event. She was quite good at reasoning with animals—aside from Dog, of course, who was a bird unto his own—and the canine had been beautifully behaved ever since.

Unfortunately, the same could not be said for Mr. Henderson.

That incident had fostered a curiosity in our neighbor, and he had been on the lookout for strange goings-on on our street ever since. We had tried our best to be careful, but there may have been a few other incidents our neighbor had witnessed that hadn't helped the situation. Like when a cloud of purple sparks had exploded from the kitchen's chimney after an experiment of Izzy's had gone wrong. Or when a pumpkin of ours grew three hundred pounds in a single day after Nora had come to the conclusion our Halloween decorations needed a *little* extra something. No, those incidents had not helped.

All of this had led Mr. Henderson to believe things weren't quite right on our street, and he had taken it upon himself to become a one-man neighborhood watch for supernatural activity.

Even worse still? He felt we, the Warren women, were in particular danger, as most of the activity seemed centered around our house. Apparently, it was his duty to protect us single ladies from the dangers lurking right under our silly little noses.

In short, the whole situation was awkward.

It also brought up a number of ethical issues regarding the use of magic.

The easiest solution to our Mr. Henderson problem would be to use a spell that implanted a suggestion in his mind that he hadn't really witnessed any of the things he had witnessed. But that sort of spell bordered on black magic, which meant there could be consequences. It was a little like the human concept of karma or the Wiccan Rule of Three that dictates whatever you put out into the universe comes back to you threefold.

But the line wasn't always clear. Intention was very important when it came to magic and often affected the severity of the price to be paid for the darker arts. Debates over right and wrong were essential to a healthy coven. A dark spell could be performed as long as it had been determined to be for the greater good, and in those cases, any consequences could be spread out among all the coven members. Dark magic was not something you wanted to try alone.

To make matters even more complicated, sometimes the consequences for dark spells never materialized at all. Not even when they were expected. *Capricious* was probably the best word to describe the forces that governed our magical choices. So, it was quite possible we could spell Mr. Henderson and get away with it. But it was also possible we could spell Mr. Henderson and all of our hair would fall out.

In the end, we had decided to leave our neighbor to his hobbies. There wasn't any real danger as far as we could see. Mr. Henderson tended to be his own worst enemy when it came to getting others to buy into his stories. Even when he was telling the truth, he had a penchant for embellishing the details to a point they were difficult for anyone to believe.

All that being said, I couldn't discount the possibility entirely that our neighbor had seen something when it came to Constance's passing. "If you don't mind me asking, Mr. Henderson," I began.

"Yes?" he replied, nodding at me enthusiastically.

"What exactly did you see? I mean, what makes you think it was a ghost? Especially Constance Graves's ghost?"

"Well, it was a woman, for starters."

"Right."

"A beautiful young woman."

"Oh, well, Constance wasn't a beautiful young woman," Izzy said, shaking her head. "I mean, she was lovely in her own way, but not young. I think she must have been in her sixties. Which some may consider young, but—"

All I had to do was look at Izzy this time for her to quiet down.

"Ah!" Mr. Henderson said, pointing a finger in the air. "That just shows what *you* don't know. Ghosts often revert back to their younger selves when they pass on."

I struggled to stay quiet this time. That wasn't true. While ghosts did take on a certain ethereal beauty, they looked mainly as they did when they died.

"Now, where was I? Oh yes, I knew it was a ghost because even though she only visited me for a moment," he said, adjusting his thick glasses on his nose, "it was long enough to see her float across my yard in a glowing white gown."

"I see." It might have seemed like I was replying to Mr. Henderson, but the words were just as much, if not more so, for myself, because as he was relaying his tale, I spotted something in the lawn of one of our other neighbors. A clothesline with shirts, pants, and towels swaying in the light breeze. Then I noticed something else. If I wasn't mistaken, it was a sheet crumpled up under the hedge that covered the fence separating our two houses. A sheet that could have easily floated from the clothesline across Mr. Henderson's backyard to ours. If I had to guess, that, with a little imagination, was Mr. Henderson's ghost. "It must have been quite the thing to witness."

"It was. It was."

"How remarkable," Izzy said, taking a step back. "Well, thank you for sharing, but we should probably be on our way."

"I wouldn't want to keep you, but you ladies be careful, and don't hesitate to pop on over should anything go bump in the night. As I always say, it sometimes takes a keen eye to see what's going on right underneath your nose." He tapped the side of his nose to really drive the point home.

"Yes, thank you," Izzy said. "We'll keep that in mind."

"No need for thanks," he called after us. "But you know I'd never turn away a slice of the B&B's pie."

"Of course! Of course," Izzy said. A moment later she started muttering under her breath. "Ah! That just shows what *you* don't know," she said, mimicking his voice. She even put a finger in the air the way he had. "And the B&B's pie? Does he think it drops out of thin air? He wants a pie? I'll make him pie. I'll make him a pie that screams when he cuts into it. Or is filled with centipedes that come spilling out." Izzy frowned. "Brynn Warren, are you laughing at me?"

"I'm just laughing because you would never do either of those things."

She made a noise that sounded a little like a *harrumph*. "Maybe you're right, but it's nice to think about."

I laughed some more.

"Do you think it's wrong for me to think about it?"

"Not at all," I said, linking my arm more tightly with hers. "Not at all."

THE SUN HAD risen far enough into the sky that the frostiness of the morning had passed by the time we reached town.

"So, who is it you're visiting?"

"Sorry?" Izzy said, meeting my eye. I suddenly noticed how tired she looked and worried.

Mr. Henderson and his ghost had distracted us for a little while, but we had fallen into silence on our way into town, allowing the seriousness of the situation to creep back in.

"You said you were going to pay someone a visit?"

"Oh," she said with a forced smile, "I thought I'd go see Roxie."

I stopped walking. Izzy turned and looked at me.

"That's a really good idea."

Her smile brightened. "I thought so."

Roxie, originally named Dorothy, was Beatty's older sister and occasional legal secretary. She also happened to be the local dance instructor, a onetime Vegas showgirl, and an infamous town gossip. If anyone knew what was going on with Constance's case, it would be her.

"Do you mind if I come along?"

She shook her head slightly. "I don't know. I thought I might like to go *alone*."

My face dropped.

"I'm teasing," Izzy said with a laugh. "Of course you can come, but would you do me a favor?"

"Sure." As soon as the word had left my mouth, a bad feeling came over me. Like somehow I had made a mistake without even realizing it.

"It's just one little spell."

Oh yes, I had definitely made a mistake.

Chapter 6

"THE LIGHTER THAN a feather charm?" Izzy raised the basket she had resting on her forearms. "This hamper is a little heavy, and I'm afraid my fingers have gone numb."

Over the past few months, I had gotten quite good at avoiding these scenarios. I always had a sense of when to leave a room, or to gather an excuse, or to steer solutions to problems in nonmagical directions, but today I hadn't even seen it coming.

Izzy asking me to perform the spell wouldn't have been a big deal in her mind. While I had lost the ability to see or talk to ghosts, the rest of my magic had remained intact, and the lighter than a feather charm was a simple spell, just a little dance of the fingers, followed by a snap. It made any load instantly lighter. Again, it was a very easy spell. I could do it without thinking.

But I wasn't going to.

"Let me take that for you." I grabbed the basket before Izzy had a chance to protest. "I should have offered from the start. Even without the weight, it's unwieldy."

I could feel my aunt looking at me, but I refused to meet her eye. If I did, I might tell her everything, and I was so not ready for that.

"All right, darling. If you don't mind."

"I don't mind at all," I said brightly. "Besides, we're almost there."

Izzy and I fell into silence once again, but this time it was much more uncomfortable. I was grateful when I heard the recorded piano music coming from the open windows of the dance hall just ahead.

"That's it! One, two, three, four. Feel the music! Let it fill your souls!"

Izzy and I stepped inside to see Roxie pounding the floor with her staff as girls in tutus and boys in shorts and white T-shirts, no older than the age of four, struggled to stay on beat.

The red wood dance hall had once been the stables for the historic inn next door. The floors had been leveled and refinished, and large windows had been put in to run the length of the building. To top it all off, literally, the peaked roof had a weather vane, but instead of a rooster or horse, a ballerina twirled prettily in the wind.

Despite the wide-open space of the hall, Roxie's larger-than-life presence managed to fill every square inch. The walls were lined with glamorous black-and-white photos of her from her professional dancing days, but it was hard to focus on any of them when Roxie was in the room, given she was usually dressed in brightly colored flowing skirts and sparkling Nehru-style jackets. And it wasn't just the loudness of her style that demanded attention, it was her personality. Her booming laugh could bring any space to life.

"Shoot," Izzy whispered, lifting one side of the basket I was holding. "I just realized I forgot to bring the squares."

"What squares?"

"The black currant walnut squares."

I frowned. "The black currant walnut squares that make people—" I made a small gesture with my hand that was supposed to mimic a yapping mouth.

She nodded.

And here I had thought Izzy had been baking frantically into the wee hours of the morning because she was upset. It turned out my aunt had been far more calculating.

Izzy's black currant walnut squares were sticky and delicious, and when she baked them just right, they also had the remarkable ability to encourage even the most laconic of samplers into prattling on. It was exactly the type of spell Izzy excelled at. While it did certainly have an effect on people's moods, when used with the right intentions, it stayed firmly in the realm of white magic, even if the taste was wickedly good.

"Somehow I don't think we'll need them with Roxie," I said with a smile. "Here, let's get out of the way. They're finishing up."

"Wonderful work, children! Simply marvelous! I will see you all next week. And remember, if no one's told you lately"—Roxie paused, letting the silence fill the room—"you're all stars!"

Izzy and I exchanged smiles. That had been Roxie's tagline for as long as anyone could remember.

As parents and children milled about trying to find one another, Izzy and I made our way over to Roxie, who was speaking to a tiny girl with big round glasses. "We're all done, Millie. You were a goddess in a tutu today."

"Thank you, Miss Roxie."

"You run along and be sure to tell your mother you're my favorite."

"I thought I was your favorite, Miss Roxie," a little boy shouted as he raced circles around the hall.

"You are, Grayson," Roxie answered with a big laugh. "You're all my favorites. Now off you go. Get some sunshine. Jump in the leaves. Bite into a ripe apple. Enjoy life!"

She then added in a quieter voice, "As long as you don't do it here. Miss Roxie needs a little break before the next class."

"Morning, Roxie," Izzy said. "Sorry to drop in on you like this."

"Nonsense! I was going to pop by the B&B myself to check in on you all after the other night. And Brynn, it's so good to see you here. It feels like just yesterday you were in a tutu prancing gracefully around these floors."

"Hmm, I can confirm the tutu, but I'm pretty sure you have confused me with someone else if you remember my dancing as graceful."

Yes, that's right, my aunts had enrolled me in ballet way back in my youth. It didn't last long though. Sally Myerson, a snotty sixth grader, said I danced like a water buffalo, and while I did not know what a water buffalo was or whether or not it could dance, I took it as an insult and chanted a two left feet spell every time she took center stage. It didn't take long for Izzy to catch on, and that was the end of that.

"So how are you two really?" Roxie asked, drawing us close. "I haven't seen Beatty this worried in a long time."

"Beatty's worried?" Izzy and I said at the same time.

Roxie grimaced. "I've done it again. And so fast. This has to be a record for me. He asked me not to say anything to anyone." She pounded the floor with her staff. "Forget I said anything."

"Oh no you don't," Izzy said, sounding quite stern. "It's one thing for that brother of yours to leave us hanging, but you're not going to get away that easily."

"Izzy," Roxie said, a smile spreading across her face. "I'm not used to seeing you like this. So forceful. I like it. Okay, well, now that you've dragged it out of me, Beatty is not at all happy with the direction things seem to be taking over at the station. He didn't say it outright, but my guess is the police believe Constance's death wasn't an accident."

Izzy and I exchanged glances.

"I thought you two would be more shocked." She raised an eyebrow. "Not that I'm surprised. You Warren women always seem to be ahead of the game."

"No, no," I said a touch too abruptly. "We're not. It's just that Beatty was acting strangely when he left our place the other day, and—"

"—he's been avoiding our calls ever since," Izzy finished.

Roxie didn't look any less suspicious, but she seemed willing to let it drop. "He probably didn't want to upset you, but the way rumors swirl in this town, everybody will be worried soon enough."

"Did he say who the police think might have *done it*?" I stumbled in my phrasing. I couldn't bring myself to use any words like *murdered* or *killed* just yet.

"He didn't have to. If the police have any sense, they won't look any farther than Constance's siblings."

I was hoping the conversation might turn in this direction. "Beatty mentioned they had a falling out. Something to do with their father's will?"

"I'll say it had something to do with their father's will," Roxie said, planting a fist on her hip. "The old goat left everything to Constance. Cut the other three right out. Didn't give it a second thought. Granted, Constance did pay her dues, but still."

I nodded. So that was the issue Beatty had been dancing around.

"We heard she took care of her father in the end," Izzy said.

"She did. And gave up quite a bit to do it. Did you know we used to do community theatre together back in the day? Constance had the voice of an angel. She always got the lead in all the musicals. We talked about going to Vegas together, but I knew she'd never do it. All the family obligations," Roxie said, waving a ringed hand in the air. "And she had a boyfriend at the time she didn't want to leave. Not everyone has what it takes to really make it, you know?"

I couldn't say if I knew or not. I was too busy trying to reconcile the Constance Graves who had stayed at Ivywood Hollow with the girl Roxie was describing. There was always more to people than met the eye.

"I had no idea," Izzy said. "But then again, every time I wanted to go see one of the town's productions, Nora would poo-poo the idea. She believes there's an entire circle of hell devoted to those involved in the production of musical theatre."

"Hmm, that does sound like Nora," Roxie said dryly. "But Constance really was quite good. She knew how to put emotion into a song. I guess that's a natural consequence of having led such a hard life."

"You mean with the death of her mother?"

"She practically raised her siblings. Can you imagine trying to raise three young children when you're still a child yourself? That father of theirs was useless. And what thanks did she get for it?" she asked as though the answer were plain. A second later her face dropped. "Well, I suppose she did get the entire estate. But still, her father should have known it would tear those four apart."

"So why did he do it? Was it just because Constance took care of him?"

"Oh, people have been speculating for years, but no one knows for sure."

Izzy shook her head. "That's a terrible thing for a family to go through, but it was all so long ago. Surely her siblings have made some sort of peace with it all by now."

"Oh, I wouldn't be so sure," Roxie said with a cat-that-caught-the-canary smile. "From what I've heard the siblings, Rip Jr. especially, have been at Constance all these years to share the estate. Rip always felt it was his birthright to live in the family home. Not that it's much to look at these days. He lives over at McGivern's apple orchard now. His in-laws' place. Lovely spot, but he's always coveted Graves House. He claims he wants to keep it in the family, but rumor has it, his kids don't speak to him anymore. Now, the younger brother, John, he always wanted the hobby farm."

"There's a hobby farm?" I asked.

"There is. You would have seen it if you've ever gone along the Blackstone River behind the house. Beautiful bit of land, but the animals are all gone now. John would have loved to have kept it going, he always liked animals more than people, but Constance kept that from him too. Then there's the youngest, Mary. I don't think she wanted anything. She was the peacemaker in the family, much good it did."

I frowned. "I'm surprised they didn't sue when it all first happened."

"I'm sure Rip thought about it, but Beatty did all the paperwork, so you can be sure he didn't cut any corners. Either way, it's really not Rippert Sr.'s will that we should be focusing on," Roxie said with a wink.

I shot her a sideways look. "What do you mean?"

She tapped the floor a couple of times with her staff. She was clearly building up to something and was enjoying taking her time getting there. "It looks as though the estate might be up for grabs again, doesn't it?"

"Are you implying one of the siblings waited all these years to do away with Constance, so he or she could finally get ahold of the estate?"

Roxie's face fell.

Clearly, I had taken the fun out of the story.

"The real question, though, is which one of the siblings?" Roxie said, recovering quickly. "That family has been torn apart for decades. If I had to guess, Constance never had any intention of leaving any one of them anything, and yet . . ."

"And yet?"

Roxie leaned back and smiled.

"Roxie," Izzy warned.

"You're such a tiger today." The dance instructor made a claw with her fingers and gave my aunt a slight growl. "I love it. But where was I going? Oh right. Beatty did tell you about Constance's father changing his will before his death, right?"

"He did," I said, "without intending to."

Roxie smiled. "Right, well, let's just say Rippert Sr. wasn't the only one."

Chapter 7

THE SHOCK ON our faces must have had the effect Roxie had been going for because she looked pretty satisfied. The look dropped a moment later, though, when she felt compelled to add, "To be clear, I'm not sure if Constance even had a will before recently. But regardless, she had Beatty draw one up for her, and you will not believe what she said to me when she did it."

The dance instructor eyed us but said nothing. She really did love putting on a show.

"Roxie," Izzy prodded, rubbing her forehead.

"So, the day she came to see Beatty, I'd asked her what brought her by, and she said she was getting her affairs in order. I then prattled on about it being a good idea for everyone to do that, and she said, *Well, it's about time I made somebody happy.*"

Izzy and I let that sink before I asked the obvious, "Who did she mean?"

Roxie shrugged. "Who knows? She drove away after that."

"So, again, you think one of the siblings stood to gain something from Constance's will?"

"Could be. Could be," she said with a slow nod. "Beatty would never tell. But, of course, none of this means you ladies are completely out of the woods."

"What are you talking about?" Izzy asked. "What woods?"

"There may be a few other rumors circulating about town." Roxie straightened, hands folded on top of her staff. "Something about Nora threatening to kill poor Constance just moments before she passed?"

I laughed. I couldn't help it. "That's ridiculous. Nora was just being Nora. Where are people getting this?" The only person aside from Izzy and me who heard Nora threaten Constance was Williams, and Williams did not strike me as a gossip. Then again, Evenfall was a small town. If Williams had told even one person, then . . .

This was not good.

"Would you look at you two," Roxie said, swatting a hand at us. "You look like you've seen a ghost."

If only.

"I was just playing. Nobody is going to believe you ladies had anything to do with Constance's death. You're pillars of the community. Really, what would Evenfall do without the Warrens looking over us?"

Just then I noticed a new batch of students filing into the dance hall. "It looks like your next class is coming in."

"We should probably let you go," Izzy added, taking a step toward the door.

"All right. But don't be such strangers. Come back anytime."

Izzy and I both waved, but Roxie was already distracted by another little girl in a tutu standing in front of her.

"Well, if it isn't Miss Molly," she said, tapping the girl's nose. "My favorite student all ready to go."

We were almost at the door, when Roxie called out to us again, "Oh! But Izzy?"

We turned around.

"You know my brother's not getting any younger, right?"

My aunt's eyes widened.

"Someone should really make an honest man out of him."

Izzy whirled around so quickly that she crashed into a coatrack.

"Not nice, Roxie!" I called back.

But all I got was more throaty laughter in return.

S HOULD WE HEAD over to Theo's now?" Izzy asked, adjusting her poncho to avoid meeting my gaze.

"I think *I* should head over to Theo's, and *you* should head home." I may have spent the early morning hours tossing and turning, but at least I got some sleep; poor Izzy, on the other hand, was looking more exhausted by the second. Not to mention the fact that I really did want to tackle this next part alone. I'd have to play dirty, though, if I had any hope of getting her to go back to the B&B. "Besides, I'm not the one you should be concerned about."

"What do you mean?" Izzy asked, frowning against the sunshine.

"Nora could be up any minute, and if I had to guess, she won't be waking in the best of moods."

My aunt's eyes darted side to side. "You're right. I never even thought of that. There's no telling what she might get up to." She looked back at me. "But darling, this is your first time going back to the bookstore. I'm worried about you."

"I will be fine." I patted her hand.

Izzy's face crumpled with sympathy. I knew she meant well, but I hated that look. "I know you'll be fine, but I just don't understand why it is you insist on doing all the most difficult things on your own."

"It really won't be that difficult," I said. "I'm just going to the bookstore. That's all." We both knew it wasn't quite that simple though.

"No. I don't like it. Nora is the one who will be fine. I really think you're underestimating how difficult this will be."

"Izzy. Stop," I said with a laugh. "You're making far too big a deal out of this. And you heard Nora last night. Remember that one idea she came up with? The one where the killer would lose a body part for every hour that passed without a confession?"

"She would never do that," Izzy said quickly, but the corners of her eyes creased with worry. "Besides, I'm fairly certain that spell doesn't exist."

"Right. Sure. As long as you're *fairly* certain."

My aunt swatted my hand. "You're terrible, you know that?"

"I know," I said quite seriously, but I couldn't stop myself from smiling.

Izzy reached forward to adjust the scarf around my neck. "Your grandmother was so talented with her needlework magic. This scarf is always the perfect shade."

My smile deepened. It was true. The color and texture of the scarf changed subtly with my moods, my outfit, my complexion. It was delicate magic, and one that could only be performed with love.

Izzy dropped her hands and sighed. "If you're sure you'll be all right."

"For the last time, I will be fine."

"Then I'd better head back home. So help me, if your aunt so much as has her cauldron out." She pressed her lips together and shook her head, making her blond curls shudder.

"You'd better get going."

Izzy cast one more concerned look in my direction, then left. I watched her bustle away before I turned to go on alone.

It was such a cheerful fall morning to be in town. The lampposts were decorated with wreaths and cornstalks, and the variety store had its cart set up outside, laden with harvest pies and tarts. The air even held a whiff of woodsmoke coming from someone's chimney.

It was a perfect day. Or at least as close to perfect as it could be.

As I turned onto Main Street, I found myself over-whelmed with the familiar sites. So much of my life had changed in the past year and a half, but everything here looked exactly the same. Like no time had passed at all.

Furry Tales Pet Shop was looking as cute as ever with all its colorfully packaged treats in the window. They spe-cialized in re-homing rescue animals. The store's name was a play on words to highlight the fact that every pet had a story. Adam and I had been planning on getting a dog.

The thought hit before I had a chance to stop it. Familiar pain gripped my heart.

I knew there would be memories coming into town today. How could there not? The cupcake store just ahead was the perfect example. I inhaled the scent of sugary baked goods as I walked by. Annie's Place. Adam and I used to stop in all the time before closing to pick up a red velvet cupcake to share on our late-night walks. But even though the pain that came with the memory was very real, it was nothing I couldn't handle. I lived with that pain every day. I just needed to keep on putting one foot in front of the other. I was fine.

I passed an older couple window-shopping at the jewelry store and smiled at the man holding what I assumed was his wife's purse. She was busy pointing at one of the display cases. He gave me a warm smile and rolled his eyes.

That was one thing I noticed a lot since becoming a widow. Couples. I couldn't help but wonder about them.

Were they happy? Were they in love? Did they appreciate what they had? I knew it wasn't a healthy pastime for me, but stopping was easier said than done.

I let the thought go and hurried my step.

Hmm, Charmed Treasures had gone through a bit of a makeover. The gift shop was certainly ready for Halloween with its purple-and-black garland of jack-o'-lanterns draped across the front window. The store had never been that festive before. There was also a young woman standing behind the door who appeared new. At least I thought she was new. I was fairly certain I would have remembered her neon pink hair. I smiled at her, but she just stared back at me. Not in an unfriendly way. More surprised. Like she had just spotted a unicorn strolling down the street.

That was odd.

And it was exactly the type of thing I would have told Adam about when I got home. I could almost hear myself saying, *The strangest little thing happened today.*

I grunted softly with frustration. I was never going to make it to the bookstore if I didn't get ahold of myself.

Suddenly a sharp bark startled me.

I brought my hand to my chest before looking down at a small dog tied to a bicycle rack.

Wait a minute, I knew that Yorkshire terrier. It belonged to Dr. Fournier, the town dentist. He was normally so friendly. The dog, not Dr. Fournier, that is. Although Dr. Fournier was friendly too.

"Hello, Buster," I said, reaching out my fingers.

The little dog scooted behind a post.

"It's all right," I said, reaching toward him a little more.

He whined and inched away.

I pulled my hand back in and straightened up.

Dogs often had funny reactions to witches. If I had to guess, our magic smelled a little different to their canine noses. We had to work extra hard to gain their trust. But Buster had never reacted this way before. Was it something else? Dogs did pick up on all sorts of things the rest of us couldn't. Scents. Pheromones. *Emotions.*

I felt my heart rate quicken. "Is it me?" I asked in a quiet voice.

The dog stared at me with worried eyes.

I backed away, bunching my scarf at my throat. Suddenly I felt the urge to get away, to just turn around and go back home. But I couldn't. I needed to do something. What was it again?

I stood on the sidewalk, looking around without really seeing anything.

Why *was* I here? Where was I going?

Theo's!

Of course, I was going to the bookshop to ask Theo about Constance.

I resumed my walk, my heart thudding.

I only made it a few steps, when a loud *snap!* sent me stumbling. A chain had broken from a flower basket suspended from one of the lampposts lining the streets.

Stars above, what was going on?

I watched the plant sway in the air, still hanging by its other chains.

I was not having the best of luck today. But suddenly I wasn't so sure if luck had anything to do with it.

I closed my eyes and willed steel into my frazzled nerves. No, one thing I knew for certain was that magic required intention and focus. It didn't just pop up out of nowhere. *That* had not been me. The thought was ridiculous. Buster may have been picking up on my feelings, but the chain breaking had been a coincidence. Nothing more. It was all the attention on my feelings and how I would handle going into town. It was putting me on edge. I couldn't let it get to me. Besides, I was almost at the bookstore, just a few more steps.

The gold letters above the storefront windows glinted in the sunlight.

Lovely Leaves.

I hurried to close the distance, reaching out for the old-fashioned handle on the dark blue door. I pressed down hard on the brass latch. It didn't budge.

My breath caught. No, this couldn't be happening. Not now. The shop should be open at this time of day, shouldn't it? Except, all of the sudden, I didn't know what time it was, or what day.

I almost turned around but stopped myself.

The entrance to the park stood behind me.

On some level I had felt it the entire time I had been walking. Almost like it was watching me. Waiting to see if I would look over. But I hadn't. I couldn't look over. That was where I was supposed to meet Adam that day. That was where he had . . .

I pressed down on the thumb latch again. Maybe it was jammed. I rattled the handle.

My throat tightened. I needed to get inside.

I shook the handle again.

Please open.

Please.

Suddenly a face appeared on the other side of the glass. I looked into the warm eyes behind the large round lens staring back at me. Theo.

She clicked open the door, and a rush of warmth washed over me.

"Brynn! It's so lovely to see you. Come in. Come in."

Chapter 8

"YOU'RE AS WHITE as a sheet," Theo said, pulling me inside. "Oh, it's gotten chilly, and—what in the earth?"

I followed Theo's gaze back outside as I tried to steady my breath. The concrete in front of the door, right where I had been standing, had a large crack in it. Several large cracks actually. Like something heavy had fallen on it.

"How strange. I'm sure that wasn't there yesterday." She shrugged. "Oh well, never mind that now. I'm just so thrilled to see you."

My former boss ushered me all the way into the shop and sat me down on a stool by a tall wood table. The intermingled smells of orange peel, cloves, tea, and old books instantly filled me with a happiness I hadn't realized I'd been missing.

"I was just making a batch of Earl Grey, and you look like you could use one."

"That would be wonderful." I smiled as Theo's thin figure rushed over to the boiling kettle by the old wood counter. Lovely Leaves wasn't just a bookstore; Theo also sold and served loose leaf tea. She was a master at making the perfect cup. I always felt she had just a touch of magic to her. Many people did. Their abilities usually manifested in a talent of some sort.

"Why didn't you let yourself in?" Theo called back to me. "Where's your key?"

I smiled. That was such a Theo thing to say. "Seeing as I haven't worked here in over a year, I thought it might be a little rude to just let myself in."

"Nonsense. That key's good for life," she said, bringing my tea over and placing it in front of me. Theo never forgot I liked just a dash of milk. She always remembered how everyone liked their tea.

I took a look around the shop. It was such a special place. I loved everything about it. Its creaking wood floors. The prized rare books underneath the glass by the counter. The two-hundred-year-old fireplace Theo spent a fortune to keep up to code. The beautiful antique grandfather clock. Keeping it wound had been one of my jobs, along with watering the plants, and picking up the mail. Theo didn't like to focus on mundane details. Not when there were books to discuss. Speaking of books, I eyed the towering stacks that had popped up around the shop. I used to be the one to reshelve them. I had to hand it to Theo, though; even with the seemingly random piles, I knew she would never forget where she had placed a single text.

I took a steadying sip of the hot liquid before me.

"That's better, now, isn't it?" Theo said with a smile.

"It is."

"It's so good to see you here, Brynn."

"It's so good to be here," I answered, meaning every word, "but I have to be honest, I've come for more than a visit."

"Oh?"

"I wanted to talk to you about Constance Graves."

Theo's face dropped in understanding. "I was so sad

when I heard what happened. Must have been awful for you all to find her like that. What a terrible accident."

I must have twitched at the word *accident* because Theo reached out and patted my hand. "What is it?"

"I'm sure you'll hear it from somebody soon enough," I said. "The police think Constance's death may not have been an accident."

Theo straightened up on her stool. "I'm sure that's not true."

"I know. It must be a shock. Beatty Barnes mentioned you were friends with her."

"I suppose you could say that," Theo said, her eyes far away. "I was friendly as anyone could be with Constance. That woman had a wall up a mile high, but she did like her books, so we had that in common. I managed to keep her well stocked in mysteries. Agatha Christie was her favorite, but she had gone through all of those a long time ago. She didn't like to come into the store. I always had to drive them out to her place."

"Really? How come?"

Theo turned her teacup in its saucer. "I think she was afraid she might run into her sister. I've been friends with Mary since we were kids. You've met her. We play cards every week."

"I have?" I sorted through the memories of my time at the bookshop. Wait, I did remember someone coming in after hours. She had been a nice woman from what I could recall. Shy though. "I didn't realize that was Constance's sister."

"The very one. And I assume someone has told you about the bad blood in that family?"

"I've heard a little."

"It's such a shame. I blame their father. Even when they were little, he'd play those kids off of one another. The only time I ever saw him amused was when the kids were fighting for his affection."

"That sounds terrible."

"It was. He was probably hardest on Mary though. He blamed her on some level for his wife's death. She just wanted his love, and that was the one thing she never got from him." She shook her head, then snapped her gaze up to mine. "I know how that must sound given the circumstances, but I can assure you it's not the case."

"What's not the case?"

"That all this hurt from Mary's past might be a motive for what happened to Constance."

I shook my head quickly. "I wasn't, I mean, it's far too soon to be thinking anything like that."

Theo's shoulders relaxed. "Not that it matters. Mary has an alibi. Me."

"Mary was with you the night Constance died?"

"Yes. It was our card night. We started late. She wasn't going to come at first, but I was able to change her mind. We didn't finish up until almost ten." Theo let out a heavy breath. "To think we were playing cards when poor Constance passed." She turned her teacup again. "I suppose it's best not to dwell on it."

Theo was probably right, but I had come to realize controlling my thoughts was not one of my strengths these days.

"I can't imagine what this news is going to do to Mary," Theo said with a sigh. "She's already been through so much."

"Sorry?"

She looked up from her cup to meet my gaze. "Mary lost her husband a few months back. He'd been sick for a while, but, still, he was her world." Theo's face softened. She left the words unspoken, but we both knew how well I could relate to Mary's loss.

I could only hold her gaze for a moment before I had to look away. It was then I noticed the newspaper on the table. It had been folded in on itself so that half of the memorial page was showing.

"Constance's obituary," Theo said. "It's already there.

Mary must have done it. She was always trying to make things right with her sister. She chose a nice photo, didn't she?"

I had to agree. It was a handsome shot. "I would have thought it had been the other way around," I said suddenly.

"What's that?"

"Why would Mary be trying to make things right with Constance? Wouldn't she have been upset with her for keeping the family estate all to herself?"

Theo looked confused. "That's true, isn't it? Mary didn't like to talk about the situation much, but every time she did, it was like she felt guilty. She was always asking me how Constance was doing, and I knew she invited her to all the family functions. Not that Constance would have any of it."

"It says here Mary has a daughter?"

"Liz. Mary's daughter from her first marriage," Theo said. "Her father was not a nice man. We were all glad when he left town. Liz was all that kept Mary going there for a while, but then she met Grant, and things were so much better. Liz played cards with us too that night for a little while."

"What time she did leave?"

Theo gave me a funny look.

"I'm sorry. I know how it sounds. I'm just trying to piece the night together."

"She left about an hour before her mother. I didn't check the time, but it must have been around nine."

Theo and I chatted a little longer, but I could tell I had upset her with the new information about Constance's death. She most likely needed some time on her own to process everything. But before I left, there was one more thing I needed to say. "Theo, I'm sorry if it seems like I just came here to ask you about Constance. I've wanted to visit so many times."

She reached across the table again and squeezed my hand. "And there were so many times I wanted to visit you. I guess I didn't want to be a reminder of that day."

"I can understand that, but please know that was never the case." I pushed myself off the stool. "And now that I've finally made it here in one piece, I think it will be easier for me to come back again."

Theo came around the table. "That would be wonderful."

As we walked toward the door, I couldn't help but hesitate briefly as we passed a towering stack of books on the floor.

Theo leaned in and whispered, "It's killing you not to shelve them, isn't it?"

"Maybe just a little."

M Y WALK HOME was uneventful, which was good, because what I found waiting for me at the B&B was far from a welcoming sight.

Four police cars and one van stood parked on the street outside of Ivywood Hollow.

I hurried my step. There were several officers on the B&B's front lawn, but I rushed past them and headed straight for the man in the fishing hat by the porch. Once Beatty caught sight of me approaching, he stepped forward to close the distance. "Brynn, I'm so sorry you had to come home to this."

"What's going on?"

"They have a warrant. I managed to limit them to the room Constance was found in and the greenhouse, but I couldn't do anything beyond that."

"The greenhouse? What could they possibly be looking for in the greenhouse?" Maybe it was the look on his face, or maybe I was just finally catching up to what was going on, but I already knew the answer. The murder weapon.

They were looking for the murder weapon. "They're not going to find anything. You know that, right?"

"Of course I do," Beatty said, sounding almost as frustrated as I felt. "But listen, you'd better go inside. They've finished up in there, but Nora's locked herself in her room. Izzy could probably use a hand calming her down."

I cast a quick glance over to the house. "Nora's locked herself in her room?"

"That's what Izzy said."

Oh dear. I resisted every impulse I had not to sprint inside.

Nora was not the type of witch to lock herself in her room.

I hurried up the front steps, swung the door open, and stepped inside. "Izzy?"

"Thank the stars!"

The shout had come from up the stairs.

"Brynn? Come quickly, darling. I could use a hand."

I raced up to the third floor. I found Izzy with her back pressed against the elaborately carved door of Nora's bedroom, purple sparks spitting from underneath.

"She's lost her mind," Izzy said, eyes wide, head shaking.

"They're going through my greenhouse, Brynn! *My* greenhouse!"

The greenhouse was Nora's private space. Her sanctuary. The room of her own. It was where, well, it was where she kept all of her stuff! And now the police were going through it. Her herbs. Her fledgling plants. Her horticulture books. Her spell books. Not that they would understand them. They were all coded as recipes. At least I hoped they were. This was just awful. I could only imagine how Nora was feeling.

"I will kill every last one of them! Boil them in a pot! Hang their parts from trees!"

Right. I guess I didn't have to imagine how Nora was feeling after all.

"Brynn, I need your help," Izzy gasped. "Join me."

I raced over. It might have looked funny that we both had our backs pressed against the door, given it swung inward, but it helped solidify the magical barrier Izzy had thrown up. I went silent to hear what it was she was whispering under her breath.

"Lock the door. Shut it tight. Protect Evanora from her own might."

I closed my eyes. All I had to do was repeat the charm and fuel the words with my own will. Nothing easier. But I couldn't.

Nora let out a shout of frustration, right before something smashed against the door. A heavy bookend, by the sound of it.

"This isn't right! We don't have to stand for this."

Neither Izzy nor I budged, even though the sparks at our ankles had a really nasty sting.

"Brynn, I need more help," Izzy panted, her eyes darting over my face.

"I'm sorry. I know." I did know what Izzy wanted from me. I also knew I couldn't give it to her. I couldn't explain why though. Now was definitely not the time. "How did you get her in her room?"

"Pull and muzzle."

Wow. That was some powerful magic. The pull would have dragged Nora backward by the waist into her room, while the muzzle would have kept her mouth shut.

"It drained me. As you can see, I've already lost half the spell. I'm not sure how much longer I can hold on."

"Let me out! I can handle them all myself. You don't have to do anything!"

"We can't let you do that, Sister," Izzy called back. "Did you see how many of them there are? Think of the consequences!"

"Consequences! You and your consequences! You take every last bit of fun out of being a witch!" Something else exploded against the door, shattering on impact. Vase, maybe? "We aren't just any witches. We are Warren witches. The very best witches! And you would have us behave like frightened mice!"

Izzy squeezed her eyes shut. "*Lock the door. Shut it tight. Protect Evanora from her own might.*" She repeated it a few more times before opening her eyes again to look at me. "I'm losing my hold. Are you giving me everything?"

I tried to answer, but I couldn't find the words.

Izzy's eyes locked on mine as she waited for me to explain, but, thankfully, Nora saved me from having to say anything at all.

She had gone completely silent.

Izzy's gaze drifted back to the door. "Sister? Is everything all right?"

"It is now," an unnaturally calm voice said from the other side.

My aunt and I exchanged glances. Somehow Nora's calm voice was even more unnerving than the objects being thrown against the door.

"Are you sure?"

"Yes. It was just a shock to have all of those police show up so unexpectedly. And, of course, being attacked by my sister's magic was *upsetting*. But I'm fine now."

Izzy and I exchanged looks again. I shook my head side to side, mouthing the words *She's not fine*.

"That's good to hear, Norrie," Izzy said in a careful voice.

"You can let the spell go now," Nora added with what I was guessing was supposed to sound like a good dose of reassuring charm but was really just terrifying. "I mean, it would be crazy for me to attack the entire police department." Nora laughed, but it didn't sound right either. "Besides, it's not like they're going to find anything. We don't have anything incriminating to hide."

"That's true," Izzy said. "I'm glad we agree."

"And now that I am calm, I would simply like to speak with the officers."

"Okay."

"See for myself what it is they are doing."

"Right. Of course."

"Maybe ask a few questions."

"I completely understand."

"So, you'll let me out of my room?"

"Absolutely not."

"I will string you all up by your fingernails!"

And there it was.

Nora let out a shout that sounded more animal than human. "What good is magic if we can't use it when we need it?"

Neither one of us answered.

"Fine. Fine! If you two won't listen to reason."

We waited for her to finish, but she had gone silent again.

"Nora?" Izzy called out weakly.

Nothing.

Suddenly I could feel energy roiling behind the door. Big, big energy. All the hairs on the back of my neck stood up.

"Sister? What are you doing?"

At first, I thought she wouldn't answer, but then I heard, "Do you think you're the only one who can cast big spells?"

"Nora?"

"Ram the door. Blast, tear, and toss. Show my family once and for all who's boss!"

"Nora! Think this through." Izzy's eyes slid side to side, searching desperately for something to stop what was about to happen. "You love this door! It's an antique."

"It's like they say, nothing lasts forever."

My aunt tightened her grip on my hand. "Hold the line, Brynn!"

"I would move if I were you two," Nora called out sweetly.

"You can't beat the both of us," Izzy shouted back, but the look on her face said otherwise. We both knew there wasn't any magic coming from my end.

"Don't say I didn't warn you!"

"Uh-oh." Izzy shoved me hard on the shoulder.

I tumbled to the floor on one side of the door, my aunt to the other. We both threw our arms over our heads, waiting for the explosion.

We stayed like that a good long time.

Nothing happened.

I watched the look of confusion come together on Izzy's face, as the doorknob above us finally turned.

Nora stepped into the hallway, smoothing down her dress.

"You two are ridiculous, you know that? I would never hurt this door." She gave it a pat. "Now, if you'll excuse me, I think I'll go have a word with Evenfall's finest."

Chapter 9

"NORA. NORA? NORA!"
Izzy and I quickly recovered ourselves off the
floor, but Nora had a pretty good head start down the stairs.

"We need to talk about this," Izzy called after her sister.

"You locked me in a room against my will. I think the
time for talking has passed."

"That's only because I knew you would react like this!"

"You knew no such thing," Nora said, sweeping down
the steps. "You don't give me enough credit. I can be very
reasonable."

"Then what are you going to say to the police?"

Nora stopped dead. Izzy and I bumped into each other
trying to stop too. She laid her fingertips lightly on the
handrail, then looked back at us. "I will ask them to kindly
remove themselves from my greenhouse, or I will destroy
each and every one of their bloodlines."

"That is not reasonable!"

We all resumed our chase.

"You two need to relax. I'm not going to do anything. If

you had come to me in a civilized manner in the first place, I would have told you I just want to supervise the search. There are rare plants in that greenhouse, not to mention dangerous ones. Don't you think it would be best if I were there to guide them?"

This time Izzy stopped her descent. "Really? That's all you want to do?"

"Yes, really."

"If that's the case, then I'm sorry," Izzy said, speeding up again. "It's just that your temper sometimes gets the better of you, and as your big sister, I'll always want to protect you."

Nora made it to the front hall landing and swirled around to face us. "I accept your apology." She spun back around and reached for the door handle. I came to her side just in time to hear her whisper, "But if any one of those filthy officers has rummaged through my herbs, I'll remove their toes and fry them up like shrimp."

"What was that?" Izzy asked, rushing in behind us.

"Nothing, Sister dear," Nora said, swinging the door open.

Izzy looked at me, but all I could manage was a weak smile.

"Bartholomew Barnes!" Nora commanded, striding down the front steps. "What is the meaning of all of this?"

Beatty's shoulders slumped. "Now, Nora, I can promise you this is all legal. They had the judge's signature."

"Who is this judge? I would like to have a word with him."

"Over my dead body," Beatty whispered, "and I think we've all had enough of those. Look. We're almost through this, and from what I've seen, they haven't found a single piece of evidence that would point to any of you as suspects in what's rapidly becoming an official murder investigation. So, if you know what's good for you, you'll stay calm."

Beatty's lecture was cut short by a couple of shouts from the backyard. Then a small group of officers came around the side, the man in front holding out a clear plastic bag. It took me a moment to discern what was inside, but once I had, it was unmistakable.

A mallet.

All the color drained from Nora's face, turning her skin a ghostly white against her dark red hair.

Beatty didn't say anything as he watched the officer take the bag to the van.

"You have to believe me," Nora said, grabbing Beatty's arm. "I was looking for my mallet yesterday. It was missing. I left it outside the day before Constance died. I haven't seen it since."

The lawyer patted her hand and gave it a squeeze. "Let's not panic. I'm going to go to the station, but Nora, I have to be honest with you. It's time you looked for another attorney. This is out of my depth." He headed toward his car as the rest of the officers packed up.

"I don't understand," Nora said, standing alone in the center of the yard. "How could this have happened?"

"I don't understand it either." Izzy took a step toward her sister. "First Constance, and now this."

"No," Nora said, whirling around to face us. "I mean, *how* could this have happened? Someone planted that mallet in my greenhouse. I checked it thoroughly the day after Constance died. And you said you warded the property."

"I did." Izzy put a hand to her chest. "No one should have been able to set foot inside that greenhouse without being overcome with pain. I did take it down when the police arrived. I was worried I wouldn't be able to give everyone permission before they came in. But the ward was up. It may not have been my best work. I was upset that night, but I did the spell."

Nora stomped past Izzy toward the house.

"Nora, wait. I'm sure I did it properly. Don't go. We'll figure this out."

"We will, will we?" Nora said, spinning around on the

porch. Thick vines crawled up and around the pillars on either side of the steps.

Izzy rushed forward. "Sister, please," she scolded in a tight whisper. "Get control. We're outside."

"I don't care where we are. As far as I can tell, someone is trying to frame me for murder, and on the one hand, I have my lovely niece refusing to use the gift she was born with to help me out, and on the other, I have my sister, who has no trouble trapping me in a room, but can't perform the most basic of spells to protect me."

"Nora," Izzy pleaded. "That's not fair."

"No, if you'll excuse me, I think I need to be alone to figure out what it is that *I'm* going to do next to clear my name. Apparently, I am all alone in this."

Izzy and I watched helplessly as Nora disappeared into the house.

I put my hand on my aunt's shoulder.

"I'm sure I did the spell correctly."

"I'm sure you did too. There has to be some other explanation." I sighed. "She's just upset. We need to give her time."

"You're right," Izzy said, but she sounded miserable.

"You did the right thing. You know she was lying to you when she said she just wanted to talk to the officers, right?"

"She would have cut off their toes and fried them up like shrimp if I'd let her. Well, maybe not really." Izzy frowned at me. "Why are you smiling?"

"I'm sorry. It's nothing." As soon as the words left my mouth, I realized how true they were. No, there was nothing much funny about this situation at all. "Let's go inside."

THE REST OF the day was quiet. Beatty called to say the mallet had gone to forensics and he was looking into lawyers for us. On top of the fact that he did not specialize in—stars help us—criminal law, he was worried about potential conflicts of interest given that he was Constance's lawyer too. Nora spent the day in her room, Izzy in the kitchen, and I just hung out on the main floor, not quite sure what to do with myself. Things were obviously not going in the direction we had hoped. I needed to do something, but the question was, what? I had to talk to Constance's siblings, but that might be easier said than done, given the rumors that had to be flying through town. It was unlikely anyone in Constance's family would want to talk to anyone from ours now.

So, until I figured out how best to approach that situation, I was left with only one other option.

The one I had been trying so hard to avoid.

After Nora had stormed off, the guilt had set in, and I couldn't help but think she was right about my role in this. Just because I hadn't been able to see a ghost since Adam had passed, that wasn't an excuse not to try. Nora was in trouble. We were all in trouble. And I needed to do everything in my power to try to get us out of it.

I could hear pots clanging and cupboards slamming open and shut in the kitchen. Izzy was cooking up a storm, by the sound of it, so it was the perfect time to slip upstairs without her noticing. And given Nora wasn't exactly speaking to us, I had little concern she would check up on me.

I clenched my hands into fists and I headed up the stairs.

It was strange to feel so nervous about doing something that had been a part of my life for as long as I could remember. Even when I was little, I had been able to see people who had passed. My tea parties had been quite well attended back then, and I was never at a loss to find someone to play checkers with even if I did have to move all the pieces myself.

I had always felt blessed to have been born with the gift even knowing that it meant I would never be able to speak to my own departed loved ones.

That's right. You could say it was the one caveat to the power.

The witching community believed that particular little twist was a sort of failsafe to protect the mental well-being of the witches of the other side. How could you possibly move on with your life if you could see and talk to your loved ones like nothing had happened? And perhaps even more importantly, there would be nothing strong enough to compel the departed to step into the light. It had always made sense to me, and I had simply accepted it as fact. But facts have a way of providing cold comfort when you're the one experiencing loss.

I climbed the last few steps to the second floor, being sure to avoid all the creaky spots along the way, then headed for the Rosewater Room.

The last rays from the setting sun stretched across the floor and filled the space with a hazy pink glow. I quietly clicked the door shut, then walked over to the plush rug in the center of the room. I sat down facing the bathroom and crossed my legs. I suppose I could have gone into the bathroom itself, but it really shouldn't matter. If Constance wanted to talk, she'd find me.

I closed my eyes and took a long slow breath. The room was completely quiet except for the steady tick of the clock resting on the mantel.

"Constance?" I called out in a soft voice. "It's Brynn Warren. If you're here, I'd like to speak with you."

I peeked one eye open, hoping she'd be there, but no such luck. I shut it again.

"Constance?"

I didn't need to open my eyes that time. I knew she wasn't there. Or if she was, the veil between us was too strong for me to be able to sense her.

I felt nothing.

When I used to communicate with ghosts, there was always a feeling present. An excitement maybe? A quickening of magic? I could feel it tingling through every cell in my body.

But now there was just nothing. Not even a spark.

I sighed. I knew that would be the case. The truth was, when my husband died, my gift left with him.

It's hard to describe how terrible those early days were. At first, all I focused on was seeing ghosts. I knew I wasn't going to be able to see Adam, but I always believed he would be able to get a message to me. We had talked about it when he was still alive. He promised me if he died first, he would wait until another person passed in Evenfall, so that he could give them his final words. Of course, we had these conversations thinking such a scenario was a lifetime away. We even laughed about what his message might be. We never imagined it would turn out this way. That we'd have so little time.

So, I waited to hear from him.

But time went on, people did pass, and I couldn't see any of them.

I panicked.

And despite what Nora thought, I *had* tried.

I tried every bit of magic ever described in every book we owned to get my powers back. I tried spells, rituals, séances. Nothing worked.

My gift was just gone.

That's why I made the decision. The one my aunts still didn't know about.

Adam was gone. My gift was gone. And I was done.

Done with magic.

I didn't set out for it to be that way. Not at first. But as the days went on, I found myself practicing magic less and less until it got to the point where I didn't cast a single spell for days. Then weeks. Then months.

And somehow it hurt *less*.

Once I realized that, everything made more sense.

Losing my husband meant my life would never be the same. I would never be the same.

I knew it in my core, but my aunts would never understand. They would try, but how could they? We were Warren witches.

I didn't realize how long I had been sitting in the room, thinking all the same old thoughts, until I looked around and saw it was dark.

"Constance?" I called out again. "If you're there, I just want you to know I'm sorry. There must be a million things you'd like to tell those of us left behind, but for whatever reason, I can't be the person to hear them anymore." I planted my hands on the floor and pushed myself up to standing. "But I'm not giving up. I'm still going to do everything I can to find out what happened to you." I walked toward the door. "It just might be a little harder without your help."

Thump!

I jumped and whirled around.

A book lay toppled on the floor.

That hadn't been there a moment ago.

And I was pretty sure I hadn't imagined that sound.

I looked over to the window. But I knew it was shut. Besides, a breeze couldn't have knocked it over.

My skin prickled as I looked around the empty room.

"Constance?"

Chapter 10

I STOOD COMPLETELY STILL, heart hammering in my chest.

It could have been a coincidence. Books did fall.

Another book tipped over and hit the floor.

My eyes widened.

Okay, there was no denying that. Something or *someone* was tipping those books over.

I waited, frozen to the spot, for something more to happen. My breath was so shallow, I started to feel lightheaded. But there was nothing to see. Or hear. Except for the tick of the clock and the scratching of branches against the window from the large oak tree out front, which, you know, was only slightly terrifying.

After another moment passed, I rolled my shoulders, forcing some tension out. This was ridiculous. Me, of all people, being afraid of ghosts.

Thump!

I yelped. I wasn't proud, but I couldn't help it! Ghosts are a lot scarier when you can't see them. Or hear them. And they're just creeping around all invisible-like.

So, this was what a haunting was like when you weren't a witch.

I did not find it pleasant at all. Would not recommend. Zero stars.

Most ghosts weren't able to move objects, but given her force of will, I shouldn't have been surprised Constance Graves would be one of the ones to figure it out.

"Okay," I called out, a little embarrassed by the shakiness in my voice. "I'm going to assume you're here, Constance. And, again, I want you to know, we're really sorry, and I'm going to do everything in my power to find out what happened to you."

Three more books tumbled over.

"Hey!" I said, planting my hands on my hips. "Take it easy."

Five more books this time.

"You stop that right now!" I walked over to the growing pile of abused books on the floor and reached down to pick one up. "Some of these are really old."

Just as my fingertips brushed the cover of an early edition of *The Legend of Sleepy Hollow*, I spotted something lit up by the streetlamp outside.

I gently picked it up.

A petal.

A petal wasn't so unusual. We had fresh cut flowers in all the rooms. But it was a rose petal. I twirled it in the faint light. A yellow rose petal.

That was all wrong.

Nora hated yellow roses. Like really, really bizarrely loathed them. I asked her several times why she hated them—I knew there was a story—but she would always brush off the question with a glib answer like, *How do you not hate them?* That was Nora. But regardless of the reason,

my aunt never would have brought yellow roses into the
house. And, as far as I knew Constance hadn't left the B&
B when she had been staying with us, so she couldn't have
brought it in.

"Is this what you wanted me to see?"

I stared at the silky petal in my hand, a big question
swirling in my mind.

If none of us brought a yellow rose in the house,
who had?

I MANAGED TO GET out into town alone the next morning. I think my aunts were overwhelmed from the previous day's events and the worry of what today might bring.
I knew I needed to tell them everything, but Nora was still
locked in her room and Izzy appeared to be sleeping in.
That was a rare event, so I thought it best to leave her to it.
I wanted to talk to Gideon too, but I had fallen asleep in the
Rosewater Room waiting around to see if Constance had
any further messages she wanted to convey—she hadn't—
and by the time I woke up, it was morning. I knew Gideon
would have gone to bed. He was mostly nocturnal.

Either way, I set out feeling galvanized. Finding that
rose petal had given me the boost I needed. Constance was
still at the B&B. She hadn't gone into the light, and that
could only mean one thing. She wasn't at peace. She wanted
something, and it didn't take much to figure out what that
was. More than ever, I needed to find out what happened
that night.

Given the apple orchard was a good distance away, I
opted to take my bike. And while I did find it easier heading into town the second time, I couldn't help but notice
there were a lot more people taking notice of me. Word
must have spread that the police had searched the B&B.

And that wasn't the only thing I noticed.

Most of the citizens of Evenfall enjoyed decorating their homes for the season, and while it was still early for Halloween decorations, mini pots of chrysanthemums and other fall flowers were just about everywhere this time of year. And there were lots out today too. The only problem was they were all sitting at the ends of people's driveways. Dead.

I didn't know what to make of it. What kind of blight spread from potted plant to potted plant?

The sight was a little unnerving, so I was thankful when it came time to turn down the dirt road that led to the apple orchard.

The uneven surface forced me to slow down, but the autumn view was enough to keep my spirits up. The leaves of the tall maples on either side of the road had changed from green to gold, and every turn of my bike's wheels sent grasshoppers flying into the air, while late monarchs fluttered about.

After a minute or two of pedaling, I spotted the orchard. My eyes trailed over the rows of apple trees lining the gently sloped hills. There was a red barn cheerfully nestled in the midst, and beyond that, a stone farmhouse with neat white fencing.

I remembered what Roxie had said about Rip Jr. wanting Graves House, but I had a difficult time reconciling the desire to live in that falling-down manor over this beautifully upkept homestead.

As I got closer to the orchard, I had to navigate my way around the many cars coming and going from the front drive. Apple-picking season was apparently in full swing.

I leaned my bike against the wood fence by the front gate and lifted up the wicker hamper I had wedged into the front basket. That's right. I had stolen Izzy's idea. I was still worried that talking to Constance's siblings might prove difficult, so I'd decided to come bearing gifts.

I followed the stream of people under the wood sign that read *McGivern's Apples*. Inside, small children dressed in fall sweaters toddled among ducks waddling just out of arm's reach while parents looked on and chatted with one another, holding cups of what smelled like apple cider. I also noticed a few people sneezing and pulling out hand-kerchiefs. Allergies. Yet another joy of the season.

Still, despite the circumstances and the itchy noses, I couldn't help but feel the warmth of the festivities.

"Give that back this instant, Jeremy!"

Clearly not everyone was feeling the love.

I spotted a girl with long pigtails and a plaid jacket giving a fearsome look to an older boy waving a maple syrup lollipop in front of her.

"That's mine," she said, fists planted on her hips. "If you don't give it back, you'll be sorry."

"What are you going to do?" the boy taunted, throwing the lollipop in the air and catching it before the much shorter girl could snatch it away.

"I'm not going to do anything," she said confidently. "The witches will get you."

I stumbled.

"What are you talking about?" He threw the lollipop in the air again.

"My mom says Evenfall is full of witches, and they'll get you if you're bad."

"That is so stupid. There are no witches in Evenfall."

The boy threw the lollipop up again, but this time I caught it before it made its way back down. His eyes widened as they met mine.

"Now, I know you know it's not nice to take things that don't belong to you."

The boy continued to stare at me wide-eyed as I handed him back the piece of candy.

"So, if this isn't yours . . ." I looked over to the girl whose mouth had dropped open.

The boy nodded, swallowed hard, and passed the lollipop back to her.

I gave them both a wink and headed on my way.

Given everything going on, it probably wasn't the best time to interfere, but I hadn't been able to help myself. Besides, no one in town *really* believed we were witches, even if some mothers were telling their children that in order to get them to behave.

As far as most Evenfall citizens were concerned, the Warren women were a just little different and *helpful*. We always, for example, had good ideas of where to look for lost pets or misplaced items like keys or reading glasses. Izzy often had just the right flavor of ice cream in the B&B's kitchen to help ease the pain of a teenager's broken heart, and Nora's natural face creams were famous for giving a bounce to people feeling down. And then there was me. I, of course, had been counted on to offer comforting words to the bereaved over a cup of tea.

Still, though, now wasn't the time to be drawing attention to myself.

After taking in the sights for a minute or two, I walked over to a teen in a green vest who was unloading vats covered in warning labels from a truck.

"My, those look heavy," I said with a smile.

The boy wiped his brow with the back of his hand. "I'll say. What can I do for you?"

"Do you know where I could find Rip Graves?"

"Sure," the teen answered. He pointed at the stone farmhouse. "You can go right up. Just make sure you close the gate behind you."

"Thank you."

I walked up to the picket fence. My hand froze as I reached for the latch.

Yellow roses.

There were yellow roses planted on either side of the gate.

I ran my fingertips over the petals. Of course, I couldn't be certain, but they appeared to be of the exact shade of the petal I had found the night before.

It wasn't conclusive proof of anything, but it was something.

I let myself inside, making sure to click the gate shut behind me, then turned to face the house—

—and the two large German shepherds racing toward me.

Chapter 11

I SQUEEZED THE HANDLE of my basket and pulled it in close to my chest.

Had this been a couple of years ago, I would have rattled off a spell that would have had the dogs far more interested in rolling around in the clover than investigating the uninvited guest on their property, but if I was truly going to live my life without magic, I had to find other ways to handle these types of situations.

Unfortunately, all I could come up with was a firm, "Sit!"

The dogs slowed to a stop, but instead of sitting, they opted to go with furious barking.

I thought about leaving but turning my back on the canines didn't seem wise. Maybe I could give them one of Izzy's squares? I knew dogs weren't allowed to have chocolate, but currant squares were okay, weren't they? Maybe I could just distract them with the scent?

"Okay, boys," I said, lifting one side of the basket, really wishing I had brought doggie treats instead of baked goods.

"We can be friends." I reached inside, without taking my eyes from the dogs, cracked open one of the containers, and pulled out a square.

Except it wasn't a square.

I was holding a dog snack, in the shape of a bone. What? How? I could have sworn both of the containers had been filled with black currant walnut squares. I had checked each one just to be sure. There had to be another explanation. Again, magic didn't just happen.

Suddenly I remembered I had two very large dogs before me ready to attack.

I tossed out the treat, then reached into the basket again and tossed out another.

Thankfully, the noise stopped.

My shoulders dropped in relief.

"Well, good morning."

I had been so focused on the dogs, I hadn't even noticed the man strolling up behind them. "I see you've met the boys."

"I'm sorry. I hope you don't mind. One of the employees," I said, turning to see if I could spot the teenage boy who really should have given me a heads-up about the dogs, "said I could let myself in."

"I guess the dogs felt differently about the situation." The man laughed loudly. "They don't react well to surprise visits. Even from pretty young ladies."

"Um, yes, I can see that." It was then I realized I was looking at Constance Graves's brother. He was an imposingly large man, with lots of bulky muscle despite being on the tail end of middle age, but he had the same watery blue eyes as his sister and the same pursed mouth.

"The dogs are supposed to be in the house during business hours, but accidents happen," he said, giving his nose a rub.

"Right." The amused glint in his eye made me think the dogs charging hadn't exactly been an accident, especially given how politely they were sitting now, watching me with hopeful expressions.

"So, is that a stack of encyclopedias you've got hidden in that basket? Because if it is, I can save us both some time."

"No, I, uh, my name is Brynn Warren."

"Brynn Warren," he said, looking at me with new interest. "As in, one of the Warrens from Ivywood Hollow?"

"Um, yes?"

"I see. What can I do for you, Brynn Warren?" He smiled. "Us founding families need to stick together."

"I came by to offer our condolences for the passing of your sister."

For a second he looked confused. If I had to guess, he had already forgotten he was supposed to be grieving. "Right. And have you brought something other than dog treats in that little basket of yours to ease the pain?"

I blinked. That wasn't quite the response I had been expecting. I took a peek in the basket to make sure all of the treats hadn't somehow been swapped out with dog snacks. Much to my relief the other container was still filled with baked goods. "Black currant walnut squares?"

"Well then, in that case, I accept your condolences. Why don't we have ourselves a little sit-down on the porch and take a moment to remember dear old Connie."

Chapter 12

I WAS ACCOMPANIED BY a German shepherd on either side of me as we walked up to the stone farmhouse. They still seemed uncertain about whether or not I could be trusted.

"Have yourself a seat," Rip Jr. said, gesturing to one of the chairs on the porch.

I sat as delicately as I could on the deep Adirondack chair and opened the wooden hamper. Rip leaned over to get a look inside as the still-drooling dogs settled down in front of me. "Sorry, guys. You'll have to ask the boss if you want more treats."

Rip smiled. I think he liked being called *boss*. He looked at the dogs and said, "You've had enough."

They shot me disappointed looks, then rested their heads on their paws in an identical motion.

I offered the container of squares to Rip, and before I could blink, he had one in his mouth. "We should have something to drink with these." He turned toward the screened window behind us. "Maureen! Get some lemonade. We have a guest!"

"Get it yourself," a voice shouted back.

Rip smiled. "She never was known for her hospitality." He then bit into another square. "I don't indulge often," he said, giving his nose another rub, "but today I think I'll make an exception."

"It's a beautiful spot you have here, Mr. Graves."

"Rip," he corrected. "My father was Mr. Graves, and nobody would want to be mistaken for that old son of a—"

"Rip, then," I said with a smile. "And speaking of beauty, those yellow roses at the gate are particularly lovely."

He frowned. "Family tradition. My mother loved them."

Hmm. I couldn't help but wonder if all the siblings grew them.

I studied Rip's face as he looked over the hills without much pleasure. "It is a nice property though. Eighteen acres. Worth nearly five million."

I wasn't sure how to answer that. I hadn't asked the value, but apparently it was important to Rip I know it.

"So, Constance," he said, tearing his gaze from the hills. "I heard you three found her. I always thought she'd die alone."

And I *really* wasn't sure how to answer that. The squares, it seemed, were already having an effect.

"It's better than she deserved."

"Rip!" a sharp shout came from inside.

"Sorry. Sorry," he said, not at all looking like he meant it. I couldn't help but notice him rubbing his nose again. His allergies must be quite bad. "It's wrong to speak ill of the dead."

"I heard there was some bad blood between the two of you."

Rip nodded, rooting around for the next square to make his victim. "I know I sound like a monster, but Connie gave us all cause." He looked up at me. "And it wasn't just because of that damned will. I know that's what everyone thinks."

The squares were most certainly doing their job. Not that they would *force* him to say anything. Izzy would never bake something like that. They were simply encouragements.

"Connie never missed an opportunity to stick it to us. I'm pretty sure it's what she lived for." He brought his baby fingernail up to dig around in the side of his teeth. "It's a disgrace the way she let Graves House fall apart. She did that on purpose, you know. Just to get at me. It was supposed to be mine. My father always said the house should be bequeathed to the eldest son." Suddenly there was a hardness to Rip's eyes. One of the dogs let out a low whine. "The Graves name is respected in Evenfall. Admired. The house was a part of that. Do you think my great-grandfather chose that location on the hill by accident?"

I didn't answer. I wanted him to speak uninterrupted.

"It was to send a message. But old Connie could never appreciate any of that. She never wanted the house or the history that came with it. She just didn't want any of the rest of us to have it."

I waited to see if Rip would say more, but when he didn't, I decided to take a gamble. "I'm not sure if you've heard, but the police have opened an investigation."

"What kind of investigation?"

"It's possible Constance's death may not have been an accident."

I studied Rip's face closely. His eyes narrowed in confusion, but I couldn't be certain if it was genuine. Seconds later an unpleasant smile broke out over his face as he muttered, "Johnny boy, who would have thought you had it in you?"

"Rip!"

"Yes, dear," he said sweetly to the window, then whispered, "I'd better keep her on my good side. She's my alibi." He winked at me before leaning back in his chair.

There was something about his smile though.

There was an excitement to it. An eagerness.

If I had to guess, it was a smile born of one of human-kind's baser instincts.

Greed.

It was clear Rip still wanted to get his hands on Graves House, but given how he spoke of his sister, I couldn't imagine Constance changing her will to make him the ben-eficiary. So why was he so happy?

"I shouldn't have said anything," Rip went on. "And I shouldn't be speculating, Miss Warren. I'm just shocked by this news."

He didn't sound shocked. He sounded amused. "Had Constance mentioned anything to you about being wor-ried? Or afraid?"

"Not to me. I didn't see much of Connie." He rubbed his nose again, now red from the rough treatment. "Now, if you'll excuse me, I have some calls to make."

"Certainly." I pushed myself to my feet. The dogs got up with me.

"Thanks for stopping by, Miss Warren," he said warmly. "I'll let the boys see you out."

"I'm sorry to have come by with such upsetting news," I said, not for a moment believing Rip Jr. was upset.

"Yes, let's all hope the police do their job." He disap-peared into the house.

I looked down at the dogs on either side of me and whis-pered, "I could be wrong, but I think he was lying about almost everything."

The dogs stuck their muzzles into my hands.

I smiled. "Shall we?"

MOST PEOPLE ARE born with a gut instinct that gives them a nudge when things aren't right. It's the feeling you get when you know someone is being insincere, but you can't quite articulate how you know. Or the strange prickle that crawls over the back of your neck when you sense someone is watching you, and it turns out, you're right.

I didn't need any of those subtle hints or clues to know something was wrong when I arrived back at Ivywood Hollow. All I had to do was look up at the dark storm cloud roiling overhead.

I hurried my step up to the front door and cautiously stepped inside.

"Izzy?"

No answer.

"Nora?"

Nothing.

After a quick search of the house, I spotted Faustus seated by the door leading to the backyard.

"In the greenhouse, are they?" I asked, bending to give him a quick scratch behind the ears. He rubbed his face against my palm, then backed away, giving me a filthy look. "Yes, I met some dogs today. I'm sorry. I washed my hands though."

He licked the side of his paw, then rubbed it against his face.

Apparently, not well enough.

I stepped out into the turbulent winds swirling up leaves and hurried for the greenhouse, being careful to step over a regiment of ants making their retreat from whatever was going on in there.

"How could you be so irresponsible?"

"I had to do something. I'm not just going to sit back and wait for them to arrest me."

I twisted the carved door handle and stepped into the sticky warmth of the conservatory. It was a beautiful structure that ran nearly the length of the property. The rectangular framework was all cast iron, and the roof had a bulbous curve that tapered up to a long running peak, ornamented with filigreed cresting. Inside there were three long tables. One at each side, both overloaded with plants, and one running down the middle that served as a workspace. On the walls at the front and back, there were bookshelves and tall cabinets. Nora had purchased the cupboards from the library when its catalog had gone digital. Now the hundreds of small drawers were stuffed with herbs, powders, semiprecious stones, and a few other ingredients that I didn't really want to know about.

I approached my aunts facing off on either side of the worktable, two large pillar candles flickering between them.

Nora was vigorously grinding something with her oversized mortar and pestle, while her older sister watched disapprovingly.

"Brynn, darling, there you are," Izzy said, dragging her gaze from Nora. "Maybe you can talk some sense into her."

I chuckled weakly. "I suppose there's a first time for everything, but what exactly is it I'm supposed to provide sense about?"

"Your aunt here decided to cast a spell on the entire town today."

I blinked a few times. "Oh, wow."

Nora closed her eyes. "You make it sound like I brought a plague of locusts to Evenfall, which I would like to point out I did not do, even though I am completely capable of such a feat, and the town deserves it for turning on me."

It was good to see my aunt's ego hadn't been affected by all the stress. "So, what exactly did you do?"

Nora folded one arm across her waist and lightly scratched the back of her neck with her other hand. "A harmless spell, really. No one will give it a second thought given the time of year."

Time of year? I gasped. "That was you? You gave everyone an itchy nose?! Why? Why did you do that?"

"I did not give *everyone* an itchy nose," Nora said grumpily. "Only the ones who told lies."

I looked from Nora to Izzy and back to Nora again. "That's bad. You're a bad witch. The powers that be are going to get you."

"You see?" Izzy said. "She's half your age, and she knows what a foolish thing it was for you to do."

"She is hardly half my age," Nora said with a scoff. "And so far, I'm still standing. We are Warren witches, don't forget, and my cause was just. There will be no consequences."

"Even if you're right, a spell like that? One that effects the entire town? There are a million different ways it could have gone wrong."

"Well, it didn't," Nora said matter-of-factly. "You have underestimated me once again."

"What did you do with it though?" I asked, jumping at the sound of something small scurrying in the terra-cotta pots behind me.

"I went into town and talked to a few people."

This was just getting worse and worse. "I'm afraid to ask but how did that go?"

Nora groaned. "Let's just say people can be infuriating. A lot of them refused to answer my questions. They simply walked away. I think I showed remarkable restraint in not striking them down where they stood."

I could picture Nora walking right up to people and asking them if they had killed Constance Graves. I mean, surely she had been more subtle than that, but the effect had probably been the same.

"But I did find out some useful tidbits."

"Such as?"

"I learned that Theo of yours at the bookstore was playing cards with Constance's sister at the time of the murder."

"I could have told you that. What else did you get?"

Nora straightened up to her full height and arched an

eyebrow. "I also found out the diner does not use freshly ground coffee beans to make their brew despite what they might have you believe."

"Oh, well," Izzy said. "I guess it was worth flouting the rules of magic to find out that little nugget."

Thunder rumbled overhead.

"Calm yourself, Sister. And again, what would you have me do? Nothing? I've studied enough history to know our kind does not do well in situations like these. I believe you've heard the term *witch hunt*?"

"Nora, you're being paranoid. Evenfall is our home."

"Um, she may not be entirely wrong." I filled my aunts in about the looks I had received in town.

"There you have it," Nora said, waving a hand in my direction.

"That doesn't excuse your reckless behavior!"

"What other options did I have? You're too afraid to cast any spell beyond your sweet dream sugar cookies, and—"

"You said you liked my sweet dream sugar cookies," Izzy said, looking hurt.

"Of course I do. Everyone does. They're sugar cookies that give you sweet dreams," Nora said. "But that kind of spell is hardly going to get us out of this mess. The truth is, you've never been willing to do what needs to be done in serious situations. And then there's Brynn. My loving niece, who won't even try to use the talent she was born with to help me."

"I tried."

Nora raged on, not hearing me. "I mean, if ever a situation called for a witch of the dead, this would be it."

"I tried."

"But no, apparently that's too much to ask." Suddenly Nora jerked up and looked over at me. "What did you say?"

I took a long, deep breath. "I tried. I tried to contact Constance's ghost."

My aunts fell silent. Even the grasshopper that had been creaking ceaselessly in the corner had gone still.

Izzy took a step toward me. "When?"

"Last night," I said, meeting her eyes. "I went up to the Rosewater Room, and I tried."

"Well?" Nora asked, also moving toward me.

"Nothing. Well, not entirely nothing. Constance knocked a few books around, which led me to find a yellow rose petal on the floor."

"A yellow rose petal?" Nora gasped, putting a hand to her chest. "How horrifying."

I gave her a look but pressed on. "That was all though. I couldn't see or talk to her."

"Oh, darling," Izzy said. "It was very brave of you to try."

"Brave of her to try? What's next? Shall we start giving merit badges for getting out of bed in the morning?" Nora asked. "Let's pull this all back a little. It was good of you to try, Brynn, but just because you didn't succeed, that doesn't mean it's the end of the story."

"I think it is."

"Don't be silly. You must try again."

"No. No. I need you to listen to me."

"No, I need *you* to listen to *me*. I've been doing some reading and there are spells we can still try."

"You don't understand." I ran a hand over my face. "I need to tell you something. Both of you."

"Whatever it is, it can wait."

"No, I've waited too long already to tell you this."

"What could possibly be more important than what we're currently facing?"

"Evanora," Izzy snapped, giving her sister a pointed look before turning her gaze back to me. "I think it's time you told us everything."

"Everything?" Nora asked. "What everything? What is going on?"

My throat suddenly felt dry. I knew Izzy had suspected something was going on when I wouldn't do the lighter than a feather charm, and then again, when I wouldn't help

her with Nora. I swallowed hard. "It's time you both knew."
I searched for the words that might make this easier. "Nora,
Izzy, I have done a lot of thinking since I lost the ability to
see ghosts, and I've made a decision."

My aunts waited breathlessly for me to go on.

"I have decided to stop practicing magic. I am no longer
a witch."

Chapter 13

NORA STARED AT me a good long moment, then, much to my surprise, she burst out laughing. "That's just ridiculous. No longer a witch. What nonsense."

"I'm serious, Nora." I took a steadying breath. "I am happier without it."

"That's absurd," my aunt said. "You're not happier without magic. You're a Warren. Magic is who you are."

"I don't expect you to understand my decision, but I do expect you to respect it."

"Respect it? Never. Absolutely not."

"You don't have a choice. I've been doing some reading, and while it's rare, there are witches who have given up their powers. If I stop practicing altogether, eventually my magic will disappear."

"Ha!" Nora shouted. "You think it's that easy, do you?"

I pulled my hair from my face and twisted it behind my neck. "I know this isn't what you want to hear. It's painful for me too."

"But it's a lot less painful than facing the real issue, isn't it?"

I shot her a warning look.

Nora studied me. I knew she was weighing her options about how far she wanted to take this, but I could tell by the resolved look on her face she wasn't going to back down. And even though I knew what she was building herself up to, it still felt like a slap when she said, "You can't even say his name, can you?"

"Don't."

"We miss him too."

"Nora," Izzy pleaded.

"No, Izzy," she snapped. "I will not abide by this a moment longer. You are a talented witch, Brynn, and you have been given a rare gift. It's wrong of you to throw it away."

"I didn't throw anything away. My gift was taken from me."

"Rubbish. Your gift is blocked because you're blocked. You've blocked everything off. You're terrified to feel anything. You've completely shut down. You never talk about him. Stars above us, forget the spells we haven't tried to regain your powers, what about the most obvious ritual we've been ignoring? Adam's funeral."

Adam's funeral.

The words were wrong. They shouldn't be said.

Nora took another step toward me. I instinctively backed away. "Don't you remember the joy you used to feel when you used your gift? You brought peace to so many people in pain."

"And what about my pain?" I snapped. "What about that?"

She didn't answer.

"You want me to share my feelings? You want me to talk about it? Here it is. I'm the one who has always been with ghosts. I'm the one who has always passed on their final messages to their loved ones. And yet, I'm the one who doesn't get to know what *his* final words would have been? Tell me, how is that fair?"

My aunts stared at me, mirrored expressions of pain on their faces.

"Here's some more truth for you. I *hate* my magic. It abandoned me that day when Adam lay dying on the grass, and it abandoned me afterward when I still had a chance to hear from him one last time."

"Darling," Izzy said, reaching for me again.

"No, I'm done." I scissored my hands. "Nora, I will move mountains to help you prove your innocence, but don't ask me about my magic again. It is not your choice. Accept it."

"Brynn," Izzy said, "this isn't right."

I turned and headed for the door.

"Don't you dare walk away from us, young lady," Nora shouted after me. "We are not done talking about this."

I was done though. I grabbed the handle and tried to twist it. It didn't budge.

"Nora," I warned. "Knock it off."

I heard some muttering from behind me that sounded like, *You undo the spell if you don't like it.*

I tried the knob again.

Still frozen.

"Nora!"

"All right! But this isn't over. I know you're in pain, but this is not the way to deal with it."

I yanked the door open and stumbled through the threshold. I only made it halfway to the house when a lightning bolt cracked directly over my head. I whirled around and gave Nora, who was leaning against the doorframe of the greenhouse, a ferocious look.

"Oh, that wasn't me," she said, planting a hand delicately on her chest. "If I had to guess that was all you, Miss

I'm-Not-a-Witch-Anymore. You think you can simply stop being who you are? It's not that easy, Niece. Your magic doesn't just die. It fights to live. But I suspect at some level you already know that."

I pressed my lips shut.

"If I had to guess, you've already had some experience with your powers going rogue."

Suddenly I could see the broken concrete in front of Theo's shop. And the dog treats that had appeared in my basket.

"It's going to keep happening, you know. At first, your magic may try to win you over, by giving you a helping hand here and there, but eventually it will get *annoyed*. And its behavior will get worse. Especially when you're upset."

"It's none of your concern. I have everything under control."

Nora laughed. "Famous last words."

"This conversation is over."

I turned back around and hurried for the house, but not quickly enough to escape my aunts' bickering.

"Oh, well done, Sister."

"*Now* you have something to say?"

"No. No. I think you said enough for the both of us."

"One more word and I'll hurl a lightning bolt down on your head."

"Please. I'd like to see you try."

L ET ME GUESS," I called up to the tree branch, "Gideon sent you to check up on me?"

Dog cawed, then swooped from his perch, sending a few golden leaves cascading down, and flew to a tree farther down the street.

"Mm-hmm."

Despite the tumult of the day before, I had flown out of bed. Not literally of course. I'd need a broom to do that. But I did wake up feeling full of purpose. I finally told my aunts the truth, there were no more secrets between us, and that meant I could focus completely on the work at hand.

And there was a lot of work to do.

I meant what I had said about moving mountains to prove Nora's innocence. No matter what she believed, I didn't need my magic. I just needed to get busy.

It was time to talk to Constance's younger brother, John.

Rip had said he couldn't believe his brother had finally done *something*. Obviously, he said it in such a way to lead me to believe his brother might be responsible for Constance's death, but given the way he had scratched at his nose, there was a good chance it was all a play on his part. If that was the case, I needed to find out why he wanted me to believe his brother was guilty. Was it to deflect guilt away from himself? Or was there something more going on?

Roxie had mentioned that John cut all the town's lawns, and given that it was a Wednesday, there was a good chance I knew where to find him.

Adam and I often went on Wednesday picnics. He had taught science at the local high school, and his schedule gave us just enough time to meet up for lunch dates. They were usually short, just paper bag meals, but they were lovely. When we weren't getting kicked off the lawn by men riding on mowers, that is. That's right, on one occasion we had met up on the lawn of the town square, only to be driven off it literally by a man on a mower. We had laughed about it at the time even though it had been a pretty aggressive move. It's easy to laugh about things when you're happy and in love.

The memory warmed me a moment before it was washed away by the pain that always seemed to follow.

I didn't have time for that today.

I quickened my step, hearing the flapping of wings over-head as Dog leapfrogged ahead of me.

Of course, so many things could have changed since that time on the lawn. There was no guarantee whatsoever John Graves would be at the town square, and yet, I had a feeling he would be. There was something in the air. I somehow knew the *powers that be* were on my side for a change. Maybe it was my reward for telling the truth.

Dog let out a loud caw. "You feel it too, don't you?" I said, looking up at him on his new perch. I noticed a woman on the other side of the street, trimming some hedges, giving me a suspicious look. She probably didn't make a habit of talking to crows.

"Good morning, Mrs. Myers!" I called out cheerily.

She held up a hand in greeting but still looked suspicious.

Well, it would take more than suspicious looks to stop me today.

Just before I turned the corner that would take me to the town square, I heard a rumbling noise. A smile spread over my face.

Lawn mower.

Sure enough, there he was. The man I remembered from that day with Adam.

I trotted across the street and stepped up onto the lawn.

Now, how to get his attention? In the past I could have used any number of little spells. A flash of sunlight directed by the snap of my fingers. A gust of wind that would have carried the cap off his head and dropped it at my feet.

But those were no longer options.

The man finished the row, then swung the riding mower back around in my direction. I raised a hand in greeting. I thought he spotted me, but I must have been mistaken because he kept on driving. I walked closer and tried again. Without a doubt he saw me that time, we made eye contact, but he kept on driving. Right past me.

Clearly, not much had changed since he had run Adam and me off the lawn.

Well, I was not about to be run off again. Not today.

I waited until he reached the end of the row and swung the mower back around.

Then I stepped directly in his path.

Chapter 14

S URPRISE FLICKERED IN the eyes of the man driving the lawn mower, but he didn't stop the engine.

I planted my hands on my hips and leveled my gaze.

If he wanted to play chicken, we'd play chicken.

John Graves rumbled toward me with a mean little glint in his eye, but I was not budging.

No, I was definitely not budging.

The distance between us closed to a few feet.

Still not budging.

The lawn mower barreled, albeit slowly, toward me.

Maybe I was budging?

Just then a blur of black wings flashed between us.

I heard a shout, then the engine died.

"What the heck is the matter with you, bird?" John shouted, watching Dog swoop back up into the trees, sending more leaves tumbling down. "You trying to get us both killed?"

"By both, do you mean you and me?" I called out. "Or you and Dog? I mean, the bird?"

John Graves shot me a look. "Me and the bird. You got two feet, don't ya? You can get out of the way."

Huh, so it was like that.

"Now look at what you've done," John said to Dog, not to me, just to be clear. "This row's a mess." John had jerked the wheel when the crow startled him, putting a jagged curve in his otherwise perfectly straight line. "Don't you be asking for any of my lunch scraps today."

I peered up at Dog. How many people did he have feeding him?

"So, you know that crow?" I asked.

"Infernal bird has been pestering me like crazy the past few days. Always bringing me other people's mail. I spend half my day delivering it back to the rightful owners." Suddenly John smiled. "He's not terrible company though." The smile dropped when he looked back at me. "So, you going to move, or am I going to run you over?"

"Hopefully neither. Mr. Graves, my name is Brynn Warren."

"I know who you are. I know who everybody is in this town. And I've heard all the stories about you Warren women."

Okay, then. This was going swimmingly. "In that case I'll skip the introductions. I wanted to come by and offer my condolences over the passing of your sister."

"Save it. I don't need to hear any of your kind words, or sorry sentiments. I've got work to do."

"You know, you don't have to be so rude," I snapped before I could stop myself. "And it's not normal to threaten people with lawn mowers."

John Graves narrowed his eyes into a nasty squint.

I matched the look with my own scowl.

We glared at each other for a good long moment before he broke out in a laugh and slapped his knee. "You're a live one, aren't you? Connie must have liked you."

I straightened up, taken aback. "I'm not sure if she did or not, but I'd like to think so."

He nodded, a somewhat sad expression coming to his face. "She could be a tough one, all right."

I took a steadying breath. I really needed to get ahold of this conversation. "Mr. Graves, again, the reason I'm here is because I wanted to talk to you about your sister."

"Okay, but drop the condolences bit, girl. I'd like to believe we've started this relationship out honestly, so don't go lying to me now. I can guess why you're here."

I blinked. This was the fastest relationship I had ever managed to get myself into. Hopefully we were just friends.

"We both know your aunt is on the list of suspects for the death of my sister," he went on, not waiting for me to answer, "and you're here to find out if I'd make a nice replacement for her on that list."

"Well, that's true," I said uncertainly. This really wasn't how I planned for this conversation to go. "But I'm also open to hearing about any other suspects you might have in mind?"

He laughed and slapped his knee again before settling back into the seat of his lawn mower, making the springs squeak. "Sorry to disappoint, but I didn't kill her."

I squinted at him again.

"I know. I know. That's exactly what a murderer would say, but I didn't. Even if people think I had motive."

I tilted my head in question.

"Bah, don't go acting all innocent." He folded his arms across his chest. "I'm sure you've heard all about my father's will."

"I heard maybe you wanted the land that came with the family house."

He nodded, suddenly looking much older. "It's a pretty spot. I used to tell Connie when we were kids all about my big plans to have a few animals back there." A smile touched the corner of his mouth. "She was a different person then."

I wanted to tell him again I was sorry for his loss, even if it had been a lifetime ago, but I wasn't sure how he'd take it.

"When the time came, though, none of that made a bit of difference. Connie had made up her mind, and there was no changing it."

"That's what I don't understand, and I know I have no right to be asking you this, but—"

"You had no right to stand in front of my lawn mower, but that didn't stop you."

I fixed him with another look. "Everyone I've talked to has made it clear how you all felt about one another, but sibling rivalries don't seem to explain the level of contempt Constance must have felt to cut you all out of your father's estate."

The question had been percolating for a while. At first, I had been focused solely on why Rip Sr. had left everything to Constance, but now I couldn't help but wonder if maybe the bigger question was why Constance hadn't split up the estate.

John's face darkened. "Now you're getting into some private family business, girl."

I knew it. There *was* more to the story. It didn't make me feel any better, though, about what I was going to say. "Your brother implied you held the most resentment toward Constance."

"My brother! You've been talking to my brother? If you're looking for a suspect, I'd start with him. He's always hated Connie, and he tried to get us to hate her too. Sure, Dad was easier on her, but that was no excuse."

I shook my head. "But what would his motive be? I know he wanted Graves House, but it's in terrible shape, and the apple orchard is beautiful."

"The apple orchard! He let you believe that was his, did he?"

"It's not?"

"It all belongs to his father-in-law. And between you and me, I wouldn't be surprised if he'll be calling him his ex-father-in-law soon. I just can't believe it's taken Maureen this long to come to her senses." A tremor ran over John's face. Beatty had mentioned the brothers had fought over the same woman. I guess Rip had been the one to marry her. Time obviously hadn't healed that wound.

If Rip and Maureen were getting a divorce that certainly put a different spin on things. Rip struck me as the type of man who liked having status in the community. He wouldn't want to live just anywhere.

"Now you're starting to get it," John said, studying me.

"But I still can't imagine Constance leaving it to him in her will."

John laughed bitterly. "My brother always has a plan. He's not a smart man, but he sure is cunning." He reached to turn the key in the ignition of his lawn mower.

"What about Mary?" I knew I was pushing my luck questioning a man I had only just met like this, and I felt terrible prying into his life, but what choice did I have?

"What about her?" John asked, not turning the key, but not moving his hand from it either.

"What role did she play in all this?"

"In Connie's death? None, I would imagine. Mary's been trying for years to make things right, but some things don't deserve forgiveness." The expression on his face made me think he was describing his own feelings rather than his sister's. "Now if you don't mind, I have a lawn to cut."

"No, wait. What things? What happened?"

Instead of answering, he turned the key.

"John," I shouted over the roar of the engine, holding up my hands. "Please!"

He drove the machine around me and didn't look back.

My hands dropped to my sides.

Dog swooped away from the branch where he had been perched, flying in the direction of the B&B. Guess it was time to head home.

I followed the large bird back to the sidewalk. My mind was full of questions, but as I watched Dog soar overhead, one in particular stood out. What would cause a crow to bring a man other people's mail? I needed to talk to Gideon. Hadn't he said something about crows being messengers of the dead? Maybe Dog was trying to give John a message.

Despite what many think, witches don't have familiars in the traditional sense. Most of us do have an affinity for animals, especially cats, but they're not the demonic helpers the old witch hunters led people to believe. That being said, there were some animals who were a touch more tuned in to the human world, and they often gravitated to witches. These familiars, for lack of a better term, could often see things that the rest of us couldn't, and in Dog's case, well, he literally had a bird's-eye view.

Yes, I would definitely bring it up with Gideon. Maybe my uncle had some other inklings as to what went on in the secret life of Dog, aside from his stealing letters and his tormenting poor—

Oscar!

I was so deep in thought I didn't even realize I was looking at the bulldog sitting contentedly on his front lawn, not even a block away.

I hurried my step to stand underneath Dog perched in a tall tree. The way he was tilting his head side to side I couldn't help but think he was weighing his options for a point of attack.

"Don't you even think about it," I called up to him.

The bird looked down at me, head still cocked.

"I mean it, Dog. We've talked about this."

He considered me a moment longer, then took off in flight, headed directly for Oscar.

"No! Dog! Bad crow!" I broke out into a run. Unfortunately, I was a lot slower than the bird, given my really cute, but impractical boots.

At the sight of us both charging toward him, Oscar startled, then ran in a circle, barking like crazy.

Dog seemed to take that as an invitation because he swooped down and snipped at Oscar's tail before soaring back into the sky.

"Why? Why are you doing this?" I cried after him. "This is a nice neighborhood."

I was about to shout at Dog again when a very professorial and very displeased voice called out, "What in the world is going on out here?"

I spotted Williams, standing on the stoop outside her front door, arms crossed over her chest.

"Brynn Warren, what are you doing to my dog?"

Chapter 15

WE WERE JUST playing?" I swear Oscar arched an eyebrow at me, but at least he wasn't saying anything.

"I see." Williams came down the wide steps of her house, her marled gray cardigan sweater wrapped tight to her body. She eyed me in a way that made me think no student would ever dare plagiarize a paper in her class. "Regardless of whatever this is, I'm glad you're here. I was hoping I'd get a chance to talk to you."

I blinked. "Williams, you know you're welcome to stop by anytime."

She looked briefly over to the B&B. "I wasn't sure how Nora would feel about that given everything that's happened."

"Everything that's happened?" I was afraid to ask exactly what it was she was referring to. I had been blindsided a lot lately.

"You are aware I was questioned by the police? We all

were," she said, looking around the neighborhood. "They took Mr. Henderson's security footage."

Mr. Henderson had security footage? I looked over at his house, really seeing for the first time the camera perched on the wall by the driveway. I was going to have to look into that. "I assumed you had spoken to them." I could suddenly see where she was going with this. "But you have to know Nora wasn't being serious that night. That was just Nora being Nora."

"Yes. I am well aware, and I did try to convey that to the police, but my sense is they were not willing to adopt my interpretation of events."

I felt my shoulders drop. This, along with the mallet they had taken from Nora's greenhouse? I knew it meant they were building a case. Obviously, I already knew that to some extent, but hearing the concern in Williams's voice brought it home.

"I'm also afraid I need to apologize for something else. The morning after Constance died, I may have relayed the night's events to a few of my fellow council members. I want you to know it was never my intention to cast Nora in a poor light. If anything, I was trying to communicate what a horrible coincidence it was that she had been joking about *taking care* of Constance just moments before she passed." She ran a hand over her face. "I was tired. I wasn't thinking."

I nodded. "I believe you when you say you had no ill intent."

"Regardless, living in a small town I should have known better."

"We all make mistakes." Despite everything, I really did feel for her, given she probably didn't make mistakes very often. That along with her love-hate relationship with my aunt must have made it more difficult to bear. "I'll certainly convey your apology to Nora."

She nodded. "Listen, I don't mean to worry you any further, but there's something else you should know." A cold, damp wind swirled around us as a gray cloud moved over the sun. "Have you heard about the upcoming town hall meeting?"

I shivered with the cold. "No, I haven't."

"I was afraid of that. Well, one has been called. An emergency meeting to address recent events."

Town hall meetings had been the form of local government used in Evenfall since the seventeenth century, so it only made sense one had been called. Everyone had to know by now the police were investigating Constance's death. "I can understand that. People want reassurance everything is being done to keep us safe."

"From what I've heard, Liz Graves is the one who organized this meeting." Williams gave me a pointed look.

I fell silent trying to process this new information. Constance's niece had organized the meeting?

Williams put her hand lightly on my arm. "I'm not sure if it's a good idea or not for you and your aunts to attend, but if I were in your position, I would want to know what was going on."

I looked at her in question. It was clear she had more to tell me.

"There have been rumors going around about strange incidents of vandalism. All nonsense, I'm sure." Williams looked uncomfortable. "But some people are linking them to you and your family."

"We'll be there." Rumors were easier to spread behind people's backs. It would be much more difficult for our *neighbors* to cast accusations with us there. Not that I could blame them entirely. Someone *had* killed Constance. It only made sense we would be among the suspects. It still hurt though. "Thank you for the heads-up."

She nodded. "And please tell your aunt I am thinking only good thoughts for her. I wish I had been able to come up with a better story to tell the police. Maybe I could have led them in another direction."

"Williams," I said, genuinely shocked. "Are you saying you would have lied to the police? For Nora?" I couldn't help but smile.

She frowned at me. "Just tell her what I said. And again, I apologize for speaking to anyone about what I heard that night."

"I'll be sure to tell Nora. Speaking of which I should probably—"

I couldn't finish the thought because the most startling sight had caught my eye.

At some point Dog must have come down from the trees, because he was standing on the grass, right beside Oscar. The two of them were staring at us, apparently following every word.

Williams followed my gaze, at which point both creatures remembered themselves. Oscar barked furiously as Dog hopped around him in a circle.

"Oh no," Williams said to the pair. "It's far too late for that now. I saw everything." She headed for the house.

The bulldog bounded after her. "To think I defended you."

Oscar barked.

"And you were complicit this whole time."

Dog and I watched the two depart inside.

Once the door had shut, I looked at the crow. "I guess one of us better tell the aunts about the town meeting."

Dog made a big flap with his wings and took off.

I frowned. "Thanks a lot."

Chapter 16

IVYWOOD HOLLOW HAS a reputation for its calm, restorative atmosphere. This time of year, one could reliably expect upon entering its doors to be greeted with a fire gently crackling in the hearth, soothing classical music playing in the background, and divine scents emanating from the kitchen.

Given that's what I had come to expect, it was a little jarring to step into the B&B just in time to hear a loud crash and someone shouting, "Slam that door one more time, Constance! Just one more! You won't like what I do!"

I quickly pulled my scarf from my neck and deposited it on the coat rack. The shouting had come from Nora on the second floor, but I wanted to get a little more information about what was going on up there before I stuck my nose in it.

I followed the sweet smells coming from the kitchen. There I found my other aunt happily tinkering away, sifting flour, with noise-canceling headphones nestled in the masses of her curly blond hair.

"Izzy?"

No answer.

I walked over to the island. "Izzy?"

Still nothing. I reached out and touched her arm.

She let out a shout and dropped her sifter into the flour, sending a cloud of powder up into the air. She placed one hand on her chest and pulled off her headphones with the other. "Darling, you startled me."

"Sorry," I said with a chuckle. "Those are some good headphones you have there."

"They're like magic. Maybe even better. And thank the stars for that," she said. "It has been quite the day."

"You've been cooking up a storm I see."

She sighed and looked around at all the dishes she had going. "Truth be told, I miss having guests. Cooking is such a simple way to make people happy, and everything is so complicated right now."

Wasn't that the truth. "Speaking of which, I heard a door slam. Is everything all right up there?" I rolled my eyes to the ceiling.

"It's Constance. At least we think it's Constance."

"You think *what* is Constance?"

"Something or *someone* has been slamming the closet door at the top of the stairs open and shut all day. The headphones are enough for me to block it out, but Nora is having a little more trouble with the situation."

We both jumped as another slam came from the floor above. "That is unpleasant."

My aunt shot me a tired look. "We've been waiting for you to get home. We're both at our wits' end. I know you're not currently using your powers, but we thought maybe you could help?"

I sighed and sat myself down at the table by the stone hearth that also served as an oven. "Izzy, I love you, but I really don't want to go over this again."

"Neither do I," she said, putting her hands up in surrender. "I'm not asking you to practice any magic. But you know ghosts better than either of us. We thought you might have a suggestion of how to—"

The door slammed again. It was quickly followed by what sounded an awful lot like a battle cry from Nora.

"Well, Constance is obviously trying to get our attention," I said. "You two did look in the closet, right? Was she trying to lead you to a clue? Something maybe the killer left behind?"

Izzy gave me a withering look, which really spoke to how tired she was. "Of course we did. There's nothing in there but extra linens."

"You're sure?"

"We took everything out. There's nothing there."

I planted my chin on my hand. "I don't know, then. Moving things around usually takes a lot out of a ghost. Most aren't able to do it at all. She should be close to tiring herself out."

The door slammed again.

Not tired enough.

Izzy closed her eyes and took a breath.

I chuckled. "That really is annoying. Did you try talking to her?"

"Brynn," Izzy said, wiping her hands on her apron, "you know we can't talk to ghosts."

"Of course you can."

"What do you mean?"

"Just because you can't see or hear spirits doesn't mean you can't talk to them. Constance?" I called out. "Slam the door twice if you want us to know there's something about the closet we need to pay attention to."

The door slammed twice.

"Right. Message received. The closet is important. We'll need to think about it, okay?"

Izzy and I waited. Only silence followed.

"Oh, darling, that might have worked. You deserve a reward." Izzy hurried over to the stove. "I was thinking earlier maybe you'd like some hot chocolate when you got home. It's blustery out there."

I smiled with happy anticipation. "I knew I smelled something sweet."

"Besides, we should talk about last night."

The smile dropped from my face. "Izzy, I really can't go another round."

"No. No. I don't want to talk about your situation. I want to talk about Nora."

I took a long slow sip of the hot chocolate. Wow, it was good. Thick, but not too thick. Rich. Silky.

Suddenly I was feeling so much love. Love for my home. My aunts. The kitchen. Chocolate.

Wait a minute.

I looked up at my aunt. "Did you just spell me?"

Izzy wrinkled her nose and shrugged.

"Rude." I took another sip. "And you don't need to do that. I'm not mad at Nora. I know this whole situation is upsetting for her. It's upsetting for all of us." I then told Izzy everything Williams had told me about the town meeting.

Izzy sat down across from me. "It's even more important we talk, then."

I frowned. "So, we're having an official talk?"

"I was hoping to give you a little perspective about why Nora behaved the way she did last night," she said, sinking back into her chair. "Now, I know your aunt comes off as this supremely confident, proud woman, and she is, for the most part, but that wasn't always the case."

I took another sip of my cocoa.

"I don't know if you know this, but when we were little, Nora had a really difficult time in school."

I pulled the mug from my lips. "Really?"

"She was painfully shy. I mean, we all knew we were

different from the other children, but Nora felt it more deeply than the rest of us. And kids being kids, they picked up on that."

"I can't imagine Nora took that very well."

Izzy looked down at the mug cupped in her hands. "For a long time, she just endured it. She always sat alone at lunches. She walked the yard by herself at recess. I think for a few years she never spoke a word in school at all, and no one even noticed."

I suddenly had a mental snapshot of Nora eating her lunch at a table by herself dressed in black, a red bun perched on top of her head.

"Your mother did her best to help," Izzy said, meeting my eye. "She was the oldest, of course, and very popular. She had a quality that drew others to her. But she was in high school by that time, so she could only do so much. Gideon and I tried to help, but we were young too. Self-involved. We should have done more."

"Huh, somehow I thought Gideon would have been the loner."

Izzy laughed. "Oh no, all the girls loved Gideon. They were drawn to his tragic poetic side. His fan club followed him everywhere."

I smiled.

"Anyway, for a while there I think Nora thought about giving up her powers altogether." She peeked up from her mug at me. "She didn't talk about it much. But we all suspected."

"What happened?"

"I think when it came right down to it, she decided she had to be herself."

"Izzy, that's not fair. I'm still me."

My aunt held up a hand. "I'm really not drawing comparisons. This is about Nora. Anyway, in order to get through it, your aunt had to develop a thick skin. Armor, really. And a certain bravado. All that nonsense about the

Warren witches being the best witches?" Izzy smiled and shook her head. "That's part of it."

"Wait, you mean we're not the best witches?"

Izzy laughed. "Well, of course we are, but that doesn't mean we should be bragging about it." My aunt's laughter ended with a sigh. "But in all seriousness, it was a good thing, for the most part, because it meant Nora finally had a way of engaging with others. And most people do find her fiery nature amusing."

"But sometimes she goes too far."

Izzy nodded. "Especially when she feels vulnerable."

I put my mug down on the table. "And she feels very vulnerable right now."

"But not just about Constance," Izzy said, reaching for my hand. "You know how much Nora loves you. You know how much we both love you."

I nodded, but I couldn't meet her gaze.

"No matter how hard you to try to hide it, we know you're in pain. My way has always been to be patient, hoping one day you'll open up to us, so we can help you through it."

I bristled but kept my mouth shut. There was no getting *through* losing my husband.

"But when it comes to your aunt. It is killing her that she's not able to fix you."

"She can't *fix* me."

"I know. I know. It's the wrong word." She looked away. "You should have seen her back when Gideon first retreated to the attic. I thought they might kill each other. It was only when your uncle threatened to leave and hole himself up somewhere we couldn't find him that Nora finally backed off. To be honest, we're both a little scared you're doing something similar. Hiding away from life, so it can't hurt you. And we don't know how to stop it."

I didn't say anything.

"Now, with all that's happened, I think Nora is feeling a

lot like that little girl again with the town against her. But it's even more than that." The corners of Izzy's eyes creased with worry.

"I'm not following."

Izzy picked at the edge of the table. "It's just, I think Nora has always feared one day she might end up like Constance. Not murdered, obviously. But alone."

"What? That's ridiculous."

"I know that. And you know that. But Constance was guarded, abrasive. She drove everyone away. And I think Nora fears one day she might do the same thing."

"That could never happen. Constance was in a class all her own. Yes, Nora has her moments, but I wouldn't call her abrasive."

Suddenly the closet door banged again upstairs. It was quickly followed by Nora shouting, "Constance! Murdered or not, I swear to every power in this plane of existence, I will shatter your soul into a million tiny pieces, scatter them across the universe, then set each and every one of them on fire for a thousand years if you so much as touch that closet one more time!"

I looked at Izzy. "She can't do that, can she? That's not like a *thing*, right?"

"No. No. No," Izzy said, chuckling and shaking her head. She then stopped suddenly, as though a thought had occurred to her. A second later she chuckled again. "No." She finished with a nod as though she had finally convinced herself.

"Good," I said with my own nod. "What were we talking about again?"

"We were saying Nora really isn't that difficult. Soul-shattering threats aside."

"Of course."

"And your aunt is right about one thing," Izzy said, tapping the table lightly with her finger.

"What's that?"

She locked me in her gaze. "It won't be easy letting your powers go."

I looked away this time. "Everything's under control."

"But if that changes. If you do start experiencing magic that isn't quite of your making, you will tell me, right? Because that could be very dangerous. For all of us."

"If things get out of control, I promise I will tell you."

"Okay," Izzy said, patting my hand then getting to her feet. "I still can't believe this is all happening. If I had just done the warding spell correctly, that mallet never would have been planted in the greenhouse, and we wouldn't be in this mess."

"Are you sure it's your fault? Is it possible someone was able to get around it?"

Izzy frowned. "It was a fairly basic spell, but no. In order to get past it one would need to have bathed themselves in, let's see, skullcap, mandrake, crushed eggshells, and graveyard dirt. Oh! Or the essential oil from a black quartz flower. But given that Nora is the only one to grow them around here, it must have been my fault."

"Izzy, mistakes happen. It wasn't intentional."

"Well, perhaps, but the pull and muzzle spell was intentional. And I do need to apologize for that. I may be her big sister, but she's an adult."

I didn't say anything.

"And you need to apologize too."

"What for?"

Izzy looked at me.

I rolled my eyes like I was a teenager again. "Fine. I probably should have told you guys I wasn't practicing magic instead of hiding it." I knew there had been more to the hot chocolate. She had this planned from the start.

"Wonderful!" Izzy said, clapping her hands together. "So, I don't think Nora will be down tonight, but tomorrow I'll make a special family dinner for us, and we can both apologize."

I didn't answer, but my feelings on the subject were made clear by my expression because Izzy said, "Careful, your face might freeze that way."

My eyes widened. We both knew she had a spell for that.

I forced a smile to my lips.

"That's better."

IZZY'S HOT CHOCOLATE had some lingering effects because when I went back up to my loft in the old carriage house, I changed into my coziest flannel pajamas, then pulled out a box of old photos from underneath my bed.

Rain gently tapped at the windows as I placed the box on my quilt and settled myself in behind it. I lifted off the lid and picked up the first photo lying on top of the stack.

I smiled. It was a Halloween shot. I must have been only five or six, and I was dressed up as Snow White. I remember Nora desperately trying to convince me to choose another costume that year—something with more *power*—but I was determined to be a princess. She stood behind me in the photo dressed as the Evil Queen, and Izzy was wearing an enormous apple costume. I brought the photo up a little closer to take in the details of my dress. Izzy had bought it at a department store, but Nora had swept it away from her the moment she'd brought it home. I was furious at the time because I thought she was getting rid of it, but it turned out she had other plans. The next morning, when I woke up, the dress was on my bed, except all the cheap fabric had been replaced with real velvet and silk and the plastic beads had been swapped out with semi-precious stones. It was ridiculous given my age, but for that one night I felt like a real princess.

I placed the photo on the bed and reached for another. It was a black-and-white shot of all the Warren siblings. My mother was sitting on the hood of her VW Bug, laughing, her long dark hair trailing down her back. Gideon was behind the wheel pretending to drive, while Izzy stood balancing, arms out, perched on the front bumper. Separate from the three of them stood a very serious-looking Nora with her hair tied back in two braids, hands folded at her waist. I smiled again. The four of them looked like trouble. Of the very best sort.

The next photo was a shot of me and Nora in the garden. She was wearing a long sundress and wide-brimmed hat. She looked quite elegant despite the fact that she was pushing me in a wheelbarrow. Suddenly I could remember that day as clearly as though it had just happened. We spent the entire morning outside. Nora taught me how to make cat's cradles with string between our fingers and a witchy version of patty-cake that ended with sparks flying when we clapped. She had, of course, gone on about Warren witches being the very best witches, and—oh! She taught me a rhyme I had to promise to never *ever* use on my classmates unless they really deserved it. How did it go? *Bumps and lumps, stumbles divine, trip up anyone from the*—enter a name—*bloodline.* It was a harmless spell really. The intention behind it was meant to be more playful than hurtful, which was probably why I had dared to use it on Nora when she went to get us some lemonade.

I laughed a little at the memory, Nora looking so sophisticated in her summer dress, tripping on the flagstone path to the house. I thought I was in for it when she whirled back around. But instead of scolding me, she scooped me up in her arms and spun me around, saying, *You, Brynn Warren, are my kind of witch.*

I sighed. Oh Nora.

How could she ever think she'd end up alone like Constance?

The thought made me wonder about the Graves family. What was life like for them before their mother died? Were they happy? United? I knew what grief could do. The destruction it could leave in its wake. But even after her mother's death, Constance had stepped in to raise her siblings. She must have loved them to take on that kind of responsibility at such a young age. Everyone, including me, had been so focused on how bitter Constance had become, but she hadn't been born that way. Life had changed her. And I suspected from what John had told me, her siblings had done something to bring about that change.

I suddenly wanted to know who Constance was before she and her family had fallen out. Roxie said she had been involved in community theatre before her father became ill. Maybe I could go to the library to see if there were any pictures in the archived copies of the *Evenfall Gazette*. I needed to know more about who Constance was. Maybe it would help me figure out who would be driven to take her life.

I put the photo I was holding down on the quilt with the others and absentmindedly reached for another from the box.

The moment I touched it my body went cold.

No. This shouldn't be here.

I had separated all those pictures. Put them away in another box.

I almost tossed the photo away, but the pull to look was too strong. I knew how much it would hurt to see it again, and normally I would have had the strength to turn away, but tonight the desire to see him was stronger than my need to protect myself from the pain.

I leaned back against the headboard of my bed, bringing my knees up close to my chest. I rested the photo against my legs.

Adam.

Chapter 17

M Y EYES STUNG as I ran my fingertips over the glossy surface of the photograph.

It was from our first date at Carmichael's Bridge. It had been his idea. Adam wasn't your typical teenage boy. Long before he'd decided to become a teacher, he'd been fascinated by nature and science; the marshy swamp around the bridge was his idea of paradise. He loved everything about it. The night song of the frogs. The way the bats danced overhead. He even loved the insects, maybe not the mosquitos, although he loved to talk about how important they were to the ecosystem, but he was pretty passionate about the rest, especially the fireflies. I told him at one point I thought they looked like stars above the water and he asked me if I knew any constellations. It turned out I did. Gideon had been teaching me for years. Andromeda, the chained maiden. Canis Major and Minor, the big and small dog. Sagittarius, the archer. Orion, the hunter. I had gone on and on, pointing them out. In fact, I got so lost in the stars, I didn't notice Adam had gone silent. When I finally looked back down, I was shocked by the look on his face. No one had ever looked at me that way before. Not like I was *magical.*

And that was all before he knew who I really was.

I stared at the teenage couple in the photo. They suddenly felt like strangers.

They were so young. They had so much ahead of them.

They had no idea all their happiness would be taken away.

Pain swelled in my chest. The same pain that always hit me when I had a happy memory of Adam. It didn't matter what it was. It was always replaced with the memory of that day. The day that marked my life into *befores* and *afters.* The day that took my heart.

We had planned to meet in the park across from the bookstore. We wanted to walk home together after I was done with my shift, and he finished classes. It was a day like any other. Nothing special about it at all. No clue about what was going to happen.

I remember so clearly walking across the street to the row of trees that led to the park. They were bright green in the afternoon sun, so alive with the first blush of spring. And the air was rich with that fresh, cool scent of earth that comes after the snow melts. I had always thought that was such a hopeful smell, a promise of things to come.

It all happened so quickly after that.

I saw him on the path that wound around the gazebo at the very same moment he spotted me. His hair fell into his eyes as he raised his hand in greeting.

I smiled, and then the strangest look came over his face.

A second later, his hand dropped, and he fell to the ground.

For a moment I stood where I was. I couldn't understand what was happening, and at the same time, I must have already known. That's why I froze. I didn't want to leave the moment where he was still with me to go to the next, where nothing made sense. But it did only last a moment, and then I was running. There was no thinking about it, my body just went to him.

He was gone before I could get there.

My memory is hazy after that. I know I called for help. Then I tried to bring him back. I don't remember how I tried, what I did exactly, but I know I tried. And I'm certain none of the spells I cast fell in the realm of white magic. I would have torn a hole in the fabric of the universe to bring him back.

Someone told me afterward that the paramedics found me unconscious when they arrived on the scene. My head resting on Adam's chest.

The doctor said he'd had a congenital heart defect. A widow-maker. It had always been there. We just hadn't known.

I closed my eyes against the memories. I could feel the emotion building, swelling, crushing me from the inside.

No, I wasn't going to do this again. Feel any of it again. Those first few days, weeks, after Adam died nearly killed me. I couldn't survive that again.

Suddenly a strange noise pierced through my thoughts. It sounded like a *crack*.

I looked up. A long fissure lay snaked across the plaster of my ceiling.

No. No way. I hadn't felt anything.

I put the picture of Adam back in the box, facedown, then piled the other photos on top of it. I roughly fixed the lid back on and then jumped off the bed to shove it back underneath.

This was a problem. I knew it was a problem. I had to be more careful. I needed to keep myself in tighter check until my magic faded.

I climbed back into bed and pulled the quilt over the top of me.

I had to tell my aunts about this. Given everything going

on, now was not the time for me to be losing control of my magic. But I also knew what telling them would mean. Nora would use it as proof she was right about everything. But I had just slipped. I knew looking at the photo was a bad idea. It wouldn't happen again.

Besides, the problem would solve itself in time. I just needed to get through it. I clicked off the light.

I tried to get some rest. I really did. But instead of sleep, I spent most of the night staring at the crack in my ceiling, trying not to think about fireflies and stars.

I WOKE THE NEXT morning to the sound of the loft's windowpanes rattling. I peeked outside at the wind whipping leaves from the trees. The sky was a fast-moving mishmash of dark clouds and patches of blue sky. My grandmother would have called it a topsy-turvy sort of day. I could still hear her telling me, *Brynn, sometimes the sun lifts you up, sometimes the clouds bring you down, but if you're a smart witch, you'll ignore all that and ride the wind.*

I dressed quickly. I was going into town. Again.

I had gone to town more times this week than I had in the previous year. I had to admit my aunts were right, not about the magic, but about having a purpose. Despite how truly awful the circumstances were, I was doing something, and that felt good.

I hurried down the steps of the garage, wrapping my scarf around my neck. It was definitely a cold one. I was about to turn to take the long way into town when I heard, "Brynn! Brynn Warren!"

I circled in the direction of the voice, but for a second I couldn't see anyone. All I could see were the gates of the graveyard.

I closed my eyes. *Get ahold of yourself, Brynn.*

When I opened them again, I spotted the woman who had called out to me.

It was hard to be sure. I hadn't seen her in a long time. Not since I worked at the bookstore. But if I wasn't mistaken, that was Mary Coleman. Constance's sister.

I froze.

I had been meaning to speak with her. Even if she had no part in her sister's murder, there were few people better positioned to give insight into Constance's life. Still, there were several things holding me back.

First, I could no longer use the pretense of offering my condolences. Not that the condolences themselves were a pretense. I did want to express to Constance's family how terrible I felt about what had happened. But in the days that had passed since her death, a lot had changed. My family was being investigated, a fact Mary had to be aware of by now. And if Williams was right, her daughter was spearheading the effort behind tomorrow's town hall meeting, which seemed centered on our family.

I wasn't prepared to talk to Mary now.

She, apparently, wanted to speak to me though. In fact, she had hurried her step in my direction, and I could tell by her expression she was upset.

When she was a few feet away, she called out again, struggling to be heard in the wind. "Please. Please don't leave. I need to talk to you." Her eyes looked desperate. "Actually, I've been meaning to talk to you for months now."

Chapter 18

MARY GRAVES HAD been wanting to talk to me for months? That didn't make any sense. It hadn't even been a week since Constance passed.

"You probably don't remember me," she went on, twisting a handkerchief in her hands, "but we've met before. At the bookstore."

The woman before me had the same color of eyes as her siblings, but everything else about her seemed softer, from the shape of her features to the rounded planes of her face.

"You're Mary Coleman," I stammered. "I wanted to say I'm very sorry for the loss of your sister."

"Please. I think it best we don't talk about Constance."

"All right." I tucked my blowing hair back behind my ears.

"Given everything that's happened, I wouldn't normally come to you," she said, looking down at her hands. "My daughter would be furious if she knew." She looked up at me with tears in her eyes. "Did Theo happen to mention to you my husband passed recently?"

I was hit with a rush of sympathy and understanding.

"I've heard you come to people sometimes when their loved ones have passed. That you bring messages." A single tear spilled onto her cheek. "I know it's been a while, but I was hoping you might have a message for me?"

I didn't have time to answer before she went on.

"His name was Grant? Grant Coleman? He passed four months ago. He wore glasses. His hair was a little thin. But he was very handsome. You might have seen him at the hardware store. He loved to fix things. Or you might have seen him sitting in the town gazebo. That was one of his favorite spots. If he was going to haunt anywhere, I think it would be there."

"Mrs. Coleman. Mary." She looked up at me, so much hope in her eyes. "Would you like to sit down?" I asked, leading her gaze over to a bench. "The wind's dropping a little. I think we can have a proper chat. I'd love to hear all about Grant."

She gave me a grateful smile. Once we were settled, Mary dabbed the tears from her face and said quietly, "You don't have a message, do you?"

"I'm sorry. I don't. I'm afraid I haven't been able to receive any messages for quite some time now."

"You don't have to explain," she said, giving my hand a squeeze. "Theo told me what happened. We're in the same boat, aren't we?"

I smiled weakly.

"Not the happiest of clubs. I haven't quite figured out how to move on without Grant. I thought a message from him might help. Even though I'm not entirely sure I believe in what you do." She looked at me apologetically.

"It's okay. I understand."

"My daughter thinks I've been spending too much time at the graveyard." She looked in the direction of the gates. "I usually visit once in the morning and once at night. I like to sit with him. Keep his site clean. Let people know he was loved. *Is* loved."

"That's lovely." I took a breath. "I haven't been able to go."

Mary leaned in toward me, trying to catch my gaze. "You haven't?"

I shook my head.

She sighed and patted my hand. "If you'd like, I can check in on him? Make sure everything's tidy?"

My eyes prickled. "That is very sweet of you. Thank you."

"Think nothing of it," she said quickly. "You know, I'd always hoped I'd go before Grant, but it wasn't meant to work out that way. Nothing seems to be working out the way it should. Not for any of us." She looked over to the B&B. "We shouldn't talk about the case, but I want you to know, I'm certain your aunt isn't responsible for what happened to Constance. Nora's a good person. She's always been kind to me."

I frowned. I could have sworn Nora had said she didn't know anyone in Constance's family. I waited, hoping she'd elaborate, but Mary clearly had other things on her mind.

"Do you think Constance is at peace?"

The question shocked me a little. I wasn't sure how to answer it. I had never met a ghost who had been murdered before, and given the way Constance had been banging on our closet, I wouldn't say she was completely at peace, but I didn't want to upset Mary with speculation, so I thought it best to tell her only what I knew for sure. "In my experience, spirits are very peaceful on the other side. All the everyday concerns seem to lose importance. The only thing that matters is the love."

Mary nodded and looked down again at her handkerchief. "That's so nice to hear. I'd like to think my family could have that. My father. My siblings. It would be nice if we could find peace on the other side."

"Mary, I apologize for what I am about to ask, but Nora is in trouble, and I know your family has been fractured for a long time. Do you think one of your brothers could have had something to do with Constance's death?"

She flinched, then quickly shook her head. "I want to help you and your aunt. I really do," she said in a quiet voice.

There was something in her eye that told me she meant it, but it was also plain something was holding her back.

"What you're asking," she began, picking at the cloth in her hand, "after all we've been through, my family needs to heal. I have to think of them first."

"You do know something." I squeezed her hand to still it. "Mary, please, you have to tell me."

"Mom! What are you doing?"

Both Mary and I jumped at the voice of the dark-haired woman striding toward us. I didn't recognize her, but this was obviously Liz Coleman. She had a hard, wiry look about her, but, admittedly, that impression was colored by the anger drawn across her face. Actually, I would say it was something more than anger. The woman coming toward us was furious.

"I've been looking for you everywhere. And this is where I find you? Talking to her?" Liz shot a hand in my direction. "What were you thinking?"

Mary stammered something I couldn't hear as her daughter pulled her to her feet.

"Her aunt killed your sister."

I jumped up, leaves suddenly swirling around us on the sidewalk. "That is a lie."

"You leave my mother alone." Liz raised her finger to my face. "I'm not afraid of you or your parlor tricks." She looked down to our feet.

"I'm sorry?"

"Don't play dumb. I know you and your aunts aren't right. Come on, Mom."

Mary mouthed the words *I'm so sorry* as her daughter dragged her away.

I TRIED TO SHAKE off the lingering emotion from my encounter with Mary Coleman and her daughter on my walk to the library, but that was easier said than done. Now that I had met Liz, I was even more concerned about the upcoming town hall and what it might mean for my family.

I was also starting to worry going to the library was a waste of time. The most I could hope to find was a picture of Constance in the *Evenfall Gazette*. It was hard to imagine how that might help. And yet, despite my misgivings, I still felt like it was something I needed to do.

I hurried up the wide concrete steps of the library. It was a lovely deep red brick building. Not large by any stretch of the imagination, but it had been built around the same time as the B&B, and the architecture, which included some pretty impressive stained-glass windows, gave it a slightly gothic feel. The enormous gnarled oak tree on the front lawn didn't hurt either.

All was silent when I walked in, just the way I liked it. Not that the Evenfall Library wasn't popular. If I had come a little later in the morning, I knew the place would be packed with kids, which was wonderful in its own right, but there was something a bit magical about the silence of a room filled with books. You could almost feel the stories reaching out to you with romance and adventure. I smiled at the thought. I was getting carried away. But even if I was, I'd never reach the heights of *carried-awayedness* our town librarian, Christina, could manage when it came to the love of books.

I walked through the foyer, eyeing the walls decorated for Halloween with colored-in pictures of black cats, jack-o'-lanterns, and witches with warts on their noses. Rude. I then turned the corner and headed for Christina perched on a stool behind the front desk.

I couldn't help but notice she looked extra bookish today. She wore a white button-down shirt with a navy crewneck sweater over the top, a tweed skirt, and brown tights. Her legs were crossed both at the thighs and the ankles, turning them into a pretzel, and she was chewing on the thumbnail of her left hand while her right held a book a few inches from her face. Her eyes were wide behind her oversized glasses. They were tracking the page in front of her at a furious rate.

"Christina?"

The librarian let out a shout and tossed the book in the air. She fumbled to catch it, but she only managed to bat it a few times before it hit the floor. "Oh no!"

Then she was gone. Disappeared behind the desk.

I peered over the top. I found her on her knees, turning the fallen book over in her hands, apparently checking for injury. "Thank goodness. You're okay." She rose to her feet, pushed her glasses back up her nose, and smiled at me. "Brynn! It's so good to see you. Sorry about all that."

I chuckled. "It must be good."

"What's that?"

"The book. It must be good."

"It is. But it's about a haunted house, and ghosts terrify me."

"Really?"

"Oh yes," she said, her face falling into a very earnest expression. "Ever since I was little. My brother used to creep into my room after it was lights out with a sheet thrown over his head. I always knew it was him, but still." She shuddered. "Even *A Christmas Carol* gives me the heebie-jeebies."

I smiled. "Then why are you reading it?"

She looked confused. "I don't know. I guess it's good to

be a little scared every now and then? Lets you know you're alive." She placed the book down with exceeding care onto the counter. "So, what can I do for you? Are you looking for a recommendation?" She snapped her fingers. "You were always a romance reader." Before the words had even left her mouth, her face crumpled. "I'm so sorry. I can't believe I said that. What is wrong with me?"

"No, Christina. Don't do that," I said, reaching across the desk to give her hand a squeeze. "You didn't say anything wrong. I hate the fact that people feel like they have to watch every little thing they say around me."

She bit her lip and nodded.

"Besides, I do need your help. And if you think what happened just now was awkward, wait until you hear what I came in for."

I explained everything I could to Christina. It was hard to put into words why I wanted to see Constance back in her youth, doing what she loved, because I didn't fully understand myself, but when I finished, Christina nodded and said, "Rosebud."

"I'm sorry?"

"*Citizen Kane*. The movie. Have you ever seen it?"

"No, I don't think I have."

"You'd remember it. I won't spoil the ending, but the idea behind it is that it's hard—almost impossible really—to ever fully know someone. One person's monster is another person's angel. That kind of thing."

"That's exactly it," I said. "Constance had a reputation for being abrasive. But I know that wasn't always the case."

"Well," Christina said, coming around the desk and rubbing her hands together, "let's see what we can dig up in the archives."

I couldn't help but smile again. This was a woman who really loved her job.

It took us some time to sort through the microfilm to find what we hoped would be the right year. We figured

Constance would have been in her early twenties when she was performing, so we went with that. It then took a little longer to get the machine up and running with the film threaded. "It would be great if we could transfer all this to the computer," Christina said, "but it's a big job. One day maybe."

It took about twenty minutes of scrolling before Christina shouted, "There!" She pointed at the glowing screen. "*H.M.S. Pinafore.*"

The picture included several people in costume on the set of the boat, including one woman out front in a white dress, holding a parasol.

I leaned forward to read the caption. "Constance Graves as Josephine!"

"Wow. She was a looker."

I couldn't help but agree. Just then the phone rang.

"I'll be right back," Christina said, hurrying away.

I nodded and turned back to the photo. There was something almost mesmerizing about it. So much life captured, frozen in time.

And yet not quite.

The strangest sensation fell over me.

It was like I could almost see the skirts of the women twirling. The furious goings-on happening behind the scenes.

I could hear something too. Sounds far off in the distance. Singing. Feet stamping out time. Gasps. Laughter. Applause.

The heat of the floodlights warmed my—Constance's—face as I stepped forward to the front of the stage, holding out one arm, then dipping in a low curtsy, head bowing to the audience's praise.

"Wait a minute," a voice said.

I jolted and brought a hand to my heart.

"Sorry," Christina laughed. "Although it's good to see I'm not the only one who can be transfixed."

"Wow. I was really in the moment." Like really in the moment. I had never been a medium for ghosts before, but those sensations had felt like Constance's memories. If I had to guess, she was in the library with us. Watching, hoping maybe I would figure out what it was she wanted me to know.

I gave my head a shake. "What was it you were going to say?"

"Just that I recognize someone in that photo," she said, pointing at a man dressed smartly as a sailor off to the side of the frame.

"Who is it?"

"My dad."

Chapter 19

THAT'S YOUR DAD?"

"Yeah, and by the way he is looking at Constance, let's just say I'm glad my mother's not here."

I shot her a worried look.

She patted my shoulder. "I'm kidding. I think they're past that stage." She leaned back and a thoughtful look came over her face.

"Is everything all right?"

"I was wondering when I last spoke to him. He never mentioned knowing Constance, and it seems to be all everyone is talking about these days. He's supposed to be coming by though. My mom usually makes a big meal on Sundays, and he brings over the leftovers. They're always worried I'm not taking care of myself."

I chuckled. "I know a little what that's like."

"You should stick around and ask him about Constance. He obviously knew her," she said, waggling her eyebrows.

"I don't know. I wouldn't want to be a bother."

The sound of a book hitting the floor startled us both.

My gaze snapped back over to the front desk, and sure enough there was the ghost story Christina had been reading earlier splayed across the floor.

"That did not just happen," she said.

Oh, but it had, and I knew just the ghost who was responsible. Clearly Constance had some feelings about me speaking to Christina's dad. But I didn't want to freak my friendly neighborhood librarian out with that bit of information. "I must have left the book on the edge of the counter."

"You didn't touch the book."

"I did. I picked it up when you came around the desk. I wanted to get the title. Thought I might give it a try."

She narrowed her eyes. "You're working with the ghost, aren't you?"

We stared at each other a half second before she laughed. "Your face. I'm kidding! I don't *really* believe in ghosts. My grasp on reality is tighter than that."

I laughed weakly. "Back to your father, you don't think he'd mind if I asked him a few questions?"

"Mind? My dad loves talking about his theatre days! Don't be surprised if he breaks out into *I am the very model of a modern major general.* Wait, that's *The Pirates of Penzance*, isn't it?"

"I have no idea what you're talking about."

"Brynn, we should hang out." Christina put a hand on my shoulder. "I can catch you up on the last century."

"I'd like that."

I helped pack up the microfilm, then headed outside. I would have waited for Christina's dad at the library, but the first round of toddlers made their way in for story time, and while they were certainly adorable, they were also very loud, and I wanted some time to think. Not that I really knew what it was I was supposed to be thinking about. Constance obviously wanted me to talk with her former co-star, and I just had to wait to find out the reason why.

Initially I thought I'd stay outside on one of the park benches, but the crisp wind had picked up again, sending me looking for warmth.

I headed down the sidewalk when I heard, almost on cue, a loud creak in the wind.

The sign for Charmed Treasures.

I peeked in the front window of the town's only gift shop and florist.

Once again, I couldn't help but note it had undergone some changes since I had last been inside. Before, all of the merchandise had been of the lacy and delicate variety, but now there were some new items added to the mix. Take the window display. The shop had always sold finely woven tablecloths, but now they were showcased flowing out from what looked to be a *cauldron*.

Hmm.

I opened the door. Instead of twinkling bells greeting me, a creepy laugh track started up. "Well," I said to no one in particular, "*Muah ha ha*, yourself."

I took a quick look around before stepping farther into the store.

"Hello?"

No one answered.

I looked back at the door. The open sign was clearly up. Shouldn't be a problem if I looked around. I headed toward the refrigerators filled with flowers at the back of the shop but was waylaid by the rows of handcrafted soaps stacked against the side wall. Those were new too. As I walked over, a bouquet of scents greeted me. I picked up one of the individually wrapped bars and brought it close to my nose. It had a very unique scent. One I was sure I had smelled before, but I couldn't quite place it. I put it down and moved on to a table covered in linen nightgowns. I placed my hand gently on the front of one of them. They were beautiful quality—the scalloped trim at the bottom looked hand sewn—but a little frilly for my taste. Next, I walked over to a glass case filled with jewelry, but before I even got to look, I was startled by a short shriek.

I spun around to see a wide-eyed, pink-haired girl with oversized jack-o'-lantern earrings standing behind the counter, looking absolutely shocked to see me.

"I'm sorry. Are you not open?"

"Brynn Warren," she squealed, "I can't tell you how happy I am you're here."

Now it was my turn to look shocked. "I'm happy to be here. I'm sorry, have we met?"

"Nope."

I waited for her to say more, but when she didn't, I nodded, then slowly turned away from the big smile she was giving me.

"Some of them are pretty pungent, but they do wonders for the skin," she said, her voice still overflowing with excitement.

"Sorry?" I asked, looking back at the girl.

"The soaps. I don't know if you noticed them," she said, pointing at the shelf on the wall. "They're new. And all hand-made. I bet you'd recognize some of the ingredients though." She gave me a big wink.

That was *odd*. I smiled weakly and tried once again to turn away.

"Listen," she said, her voice dropping into a more serious tone, "I just want you to know I don't believe anything they're saying about you around town."

A chill ran through me. I truly had no clue who this girl was or why she had been so excited to meet me, but those were things I could let drop. Rumors around town, though, that was a thread I needed to pull. "I'm afraid that could cover a lot of different topics. Who is *they*?"

"Liz Coleman for one. She was in here yesterday. She's actually one of our best customers," she said. "But once she started talking badly about your aunt, I showed her the door. After I took her money."

I gave her a sideways look. "What exactly was she saying?"

The girl twirled the end of her shiny ponytail. "Well, you know, that the Warrens are a blight on this town. That you make people disappear. That you, I don't know, destroy crops or something?"

"What?" I practically shouted the word. "That's ridiculous. Why would we do any of those things? I mean, how could we do any of those things?"

The clerk suddenly looked uncomfortable. I would have thought all the previous stuff would have made her uncomfortable, but I guess we all have different tolerances. She shrugged. "Well, you know."

I straightened up. Unfortunately, I did know what she was getting at. *Witches gotta blight*, I guess. But how did *she* know? What was going on here?

"I don't believe any of it. I mean, not the part about you guys being . . ." She held up her hands in claws and hissed.

"Cats?"

"No, silly."

She hissed again.

"Vampires?"

"Now you're just messing with me."

To some extent I was. But I didn't mean to be. It was just all so shocking. This was the kind of gossip people spread hundreds of years ago. Anyone who knew us knew that we only ever tried to help the citizens of this town. We did not make people disappear. Or ruin crops. The mere suggestion was absurd.

Suddenly, I remembered all the planters with dead flowers at the end of people's driveways.

"I should be going," I said quickly.

"Sure. But come back. Anytime. I'd love to talk more about things."

Things? I hurried to the door. I almost made it outside,

when the clerk called after me, "And tell your aunt Nixie said hi."

I spun back around in the threshold of the door.

"I just love Nora. She's my hero."

I WAS GLAD TO have a moment to myself on the way back to the library. The sun had come out from behind the clouds and the wind had died again, but my mood had darkened considerably.

I had found of the idea of Uncle Gideon's crow having a secret life amusing, but when it came to my aunt, the prospect was far less entertaining.

Nora's my hero?

Nora did not have friends, let alone fans.

That being said, the shop clerk was the least of my concerns. Now that I had some distance, I found myself replaying my conversation with Mary. Again, she said Nora had always been kind to her. What could that possibly mean? And why hadn't Nora filled us in on her relationship with Mary when the topic had first come up? I was not one to be throwing stones, given the secrets I had kept from my family, but I was starting to suspect Nora had been keeping more than a few of her own. And given the stakes of our current situation, that was, well, it was unacceptable!

Now, if I could only tell her that in such a way that she wouldn't hang me by my fingernails.

I was so distracted by my thoughts I didn't notice the man smiling at me from the picnic table in front of the library until I was almost right beside him.

"Brynn Warren?"

I met the man's smile, taking in his kind eyes and white, bushy mustache. "You must be Christina's father. Thank you for agreeing to talk to me."

"Ben Scott. But please just call me Ben," he said, getting up to offer me his hand. "I hope you don't mind me waiting outside. Christina filled me in, and I thought it might be less awkward chatting about my first love if it wasn't in front of my daughter." He jerked a thumb back at the library.

"Of course." I took the spot across from him at the picnic table as he sat back down. "I'm sorry if I brought up an uncomfortable topic for you and your daughter. I had no idea that Constance was . . ." I struggled to find the right word.

"An old flame?"

I nodded.

"She was certainly that. If you'd asked me then, I would've sworn we'd have gotten married, but life had other plans." A touch of sadness came to Ben's eye. "It was a bit of a shock to hear she was gone."

"I'm so sorry." I let a moment pass before asking, "Did you two meet doing community theatre?"

"Oh no, Connie and I went to school together, but she was a year older." He waggled his eyebrows, just like Christina had. "Older woman."

I laughed.

"She wouldn't give me the time of day back in school though. It took me a while to grow into the handsome specimen you see before you."

I laughed some more. "What was Constance like back then? I only met her recently."

"Connie was full of life. She had the voice of an angel, and she loved to use it." His face shone at the memory. "Do you know Roxie? She runs the dance studio in town?"

"I do."

"Roxie was her idol. She had left for Vegas by then. I think Constance dreamed of doing the same, but she would have gone to New York. I promised to go with her. But it was all just talk." He leaned back, planting his hands on his knees. "If things had been different, I think we both would have been happy with settling down and raising a family in Evenfall."

"If you don't mind me asking, what happened?"

Ben's face darkened.

"I'm sorry if it's too personal."

"No, I'll tell you what happened." Ben looked up at the oak tree towering above us. "It was that family of hers."

"I've heard it was Rippert Sr.'s will that drove the family apart."

"The will was only the beginning. It's what they did to her afterward. That was the real offense. And I'll never forgive them for it."

Chapter 20

"I T ALL STARTED with her father getting sick."

It had taken Ben some time to get his emotions in check, but once he had, the sad look returned to his face, and he launched into the story.

"Stroke actually. He'd had a few little ones in the past, but then the big one hit. There was nothing wrong with his mind, but he wasn't able to walk afterward. He needed someone in the house round the clock. Connie never hesitated. Wouldn't hear of putting him in a home. And not that the others offered, but she wouldn't have accepted help from them either. She was like a mother to those kids. She wanted them to live their lives."

"This is what I don't understand. It sounds like there was a lot of love in the family. I know Rippert Sr. was hard on the kids, but—"

"Hard on them? Ha! That's an understatement. Those kids could never do anything right."

"But wasn't Constance included in that treatment?"

"She was. But to a lesser extent. She looked a lot like her mother. Seeing his wife in Connie I think held him back at times."

"Is that what came between you and Constance? The fact that she was caring for her dad?"

"No. No. We were making it work, as people like to say nowadays. I would come by the house and spend time with Connie while her father slept. He had mellowed quite a bit toward the end. It wasn't easy, but we both knew the situation wouldn't last forever."

"So, when did it all change?"

"When Connie changed," he said, shaking his head. "That damned will of her father's. Why that man cut his other children out of the estate has always been a mystery to me. But the even bigger mystery was why Connie went along with it. That was the fight that ended us."

"What do you mean?"

"When the old man died, and the others found out about the will, they were not happy, to say the least. The way they turned on her? After all she had done for them?"

"How exactly did they turn on her?"

He rapped the table with his knuckles. "They accused her of horrible things. They said she tricked her father into writing that new will. But she had nothing to do with it. I can't prove it, but Beatty knows the truth. Those siblings of hers though—led by Rip—accused her of using the time she spent caring for her father to whisper poison in his ear. But she never said one unkind word about any of them."

"I can't imagine how that made her feel."

"It nearly killed her." Ben frowned, anger creasing his face.

"That's truly awful."

"And, unfortunately, that's not the worst of it. I think Connie could have gotten past those first accusations, but what Rip accused her of next?"

I didn't prod. Ben was clearly building himself up to what was coming.

"He accused Connie of more than just getting their father to change the will." He pinned his lips together. "He implied she helped the old man along."

A chill ran over me. "He accused Constance of killing their father?"

He nodded. "After Connie told me that, I went out looking for Rip. Found him in the town square. Laid him out flat. I'm not proud of it. But boy did it feel good." Ben's fist clenched with the memory. "You know what really burns me?"

I shook my head.

"I doubt Rip ever believed any of it. He was just so angry about being cut out of the will. He lashed out in the worst way possible."

"It sounds like you loved Constance a lot."

He smiled and the anger drained from his face. "Do you believe in soul mates?"

I nodded.

"Connie was mine."

"So, what happened?" My words came out almost sounding like a plea.

Ben sighed. "Connie was so torn up by everything that had happened. I just wanted to make it better, so I went to her with an idea." He shrugged. "Why not just split up the estate? Rip wanted the house. Give him the house. John wanted the land. Let him have it. Mary didn't want anything, but that first husband of hers, he sure wanted cash. So, give it to him. We didn't need it. We could make it on our own."

"What did she think of that?"

"At first, she thought it was sweet. She liked that I didn't care about any of it. She said she wanted to respect her father's wishes though. That never sat well with me. Her father had never been fair with those kids when he was alive, and he wasn't being fair now that he was dead. Connie asked me to drop it, but I couldn't. I didn't understand. I knew as long as she lived in that house, on that property, her siblings would never let it go. I couldn't understand why she'd want to live with that kind of bitterness directed toward her. But the truth was, the bitterness was already spreading to Connie. The way those kids turned on her after she had devoted so much of her life to them? That kind of hurt cuts to the bone. I think it got away from her."

"How so?"

"She wanted to hurt them the way they had hurt her." He looked up at the sky. "Anyway, I guess I brought up the idea one time too many, and that's where it all ended for us. Connie accused me of siding with her siblings. I tried to tell her that wasn't the case, but suddenly she was accusing me of believing she had made her father change his will, and that maybe deep down I believed she had something to do with his death."

"I'm so sorry. For everything." I jolted back from the picnic table. Those had not been my words. They had come from my mouth, but they were not mine.

I shot a look over my shoulder, suddenly convinced Constance would be there, but if she was, I couldn't see her.

Ben patted my hand. "It was all a long time ago. Anyway, I tried to make things right between Connie and me, but it wasn't meant to be. Eventually I had to get on with my life. It took a few years, but then I met my wonderful Patty."

"But she wasn't your soul mate." This time the words were mine, but I couldn't believe they had left my mouth. "I am so sorry. I never should have said that."

"Don't worry. And yes, Patty is my soul mate. You can have more than one. I've been fortunate to find two of them in my lifetime."

It surprised me how certain he was.

"I can see by the look on your face you don't agree."

I looked down at my hands.

"One day life might surprise you."

"Thank you for sharing all this with me. I know it couldn't have been easy, and you certainly didn't have to."

"Bah, I think it's done me some good. I know what people think of Connie, but who she became, it wasn't who she was. Not in her heart. I think I needed to tell someone that."

I smiled.

"Now," he said with a groan as he pushed himself up, "I should probably get going. I promised Patty I'd pick up groceries on the way home. She'll have half the town looking for me soon."

"Before you go," I said, reaching out a hand to stop him, "you said Constance told you she wanted to respect her father's wishes. And that it was a mystery to you why Rip Sr. wanted to cut the others out of the will, but did Constance ever try to explain it? Was he simply being vindictive for some reason?"

"That's the part that was so strange. The last few times I spoke to Rip he expressed a lot of regret for how he lived his life, especially how he treated his children. But in answer to your question, no, Connie never said."

I thanked Ben again and got to my feet. I stood by the table as he took his leave.

At one point he looked back and gave me a wave, and I held my hand up in return.

I knew it wasn't just me saying goodbye.

A gentle wind rushed over the lawn, and with it a feeling I hadn't experienced in a long time.

I had helped Constance say goodbye to Ben. Not like I would have before, but it was something.

I tilted my face up to the sun.

Maybe I could find my way back to that place. Losing my gift along with Adam had driven me to cut myself off from everything. But maybe my aunts were right. Maybe there was a way I could reclaim what I had lost.

"Brynn?"

I snapped my eyes open.

"Brynn Warren?"

All the warmth I had been feeling dissipated when I saw the woman calling to me from the shadow of the oak tree. She didn't look angry. Or even unfriendly. But the way she had her bag clutched close to her chest, she most certainly looked nervous. Almost afraid.

"My name is Maureen. I'm Rip's wife."

Chapter 21

I WALKED OVER TO the woman hidden in the shadow of the tree. I almost lost sight of her when yet another cloud racing across the sky cut off the brilliance of the sun.

"I'm sorry if I startled you. I should have introduced myself when you came by the orchard the other day. I apologize for my rudeness."

"There's no need. The circumstances weren't the best."

The muscles flexed in her jaw. "And I'm afraid my husband is particularly gifted at taking any set of circumstances and making them worse."

I waited, not sure how to respond.

"I've made you uncomfortable. I'm sorry."

"Please don't apologize."

"You must be wondering why I've tracked you down."

I blinked in surprise.

"Don't worry. I haven't been following you. I was just at the gift shop." She looked over to Charmed Treasures. "I was chatting with the clerk. She is quite the fan of the Warren women."

"I'm starting to realize that."

"Anyway, she told me you had just stopped in, and I saw you talking with Ben." She looked down at her purse. "But, in all honesty, I have been hoping I would run into you."

"You must know I live at the B&B. You could have stopped by."

She stiffened and retreated deeper into the shadows. "I couldn't do that. Rip might find out."

"Would you like to go somewhere more private to talk?"

"No, that won't be necessary." She opened the latch on her handbag. "This won't take long." She pulled out a faded envelope. "I was hoping you could give this to Rip's brother. He does the lawn work for the town. It wouldn't be difficult to find him."

"I know John," I said, not yet reaching to take the envelope from her. "Why do you need me to give it to him? Why not give it to him yourself?"

"I'm taking a risk by talking to you. If Rip found out I went to see John." She shook her head. "I need a little more time. When things are settled, I'll talk to John myself. Apologize for not getting this to him sooner."

I took the letter from her. I wasn't surprised to see it addressed to John Graves. I was, however, quite shocked to see who it was from. Constance. My gaze snapped back up to hers.

She held up a hand as though to hold me off. "I know."

"How old is this letter?"

"Several years."

"Why do you have it?"

"Rip stole it. Probably took it right out of her mailbox. She would have thought the mail carrier had delivered it."

I suddenly remembered what John had said about Dog bringing him other people's mail. Maybe the crow had been trying to tell John about this letter. A messenger for the dead indeed.

I brought myself back to the moment. "Your husband told me he didn't see much of Constance."

"My husband is a liar, Ms. Warren. It comes as easily to him as breathing. He doesn't even think his lies through. He visited his sister several times a year trying to convince her to give him Graves House. I'm sure he wasn't nice about it either. My guess is every visit he paid hardened her heart against him a little more."

"But the letter?"

"It wouldn't exactly be in his interests to have John and Constance making amends, would it?"

"Is that what this is? Constance trying to make amends?"

"I shouldn't say. The letter was meant to be a private communication between Constance and her brother. I am ashamed for having looked at it myself." Her cheeks reddened. "Suffice it to say, Rip used what was in that letter to keep John angry at his sister, but it was all out of context. Constance was trying to make things right for once."

"I can't believe this," I said, staring at the envelope.

"You can't begin to understand how devious my husband is. That day when you came to the orchard, he already knew the police thought Constance's death was suspicious."

I couldn't say I was shocked. I already knew he had been lying.

"He set you up. He wanted you to question whether John had something to do with his sister's death. And you're not the only one. He planned to use this letter to convince the police John had a motive to kill his sister."

I frowned. What more could Constance have possibly done to John aside from cutting him out of the will?

"If he could make it seem like John had killed Constance that was one less person he'd have to fight for the estate. Not that he's going to get one brick of that house. Constance would have made sure of that. Of course, Rip's ridiculous plan fell apart when he heard John's alibi."

"What alibi?"

"He was in the military for a while with several members of Evenfall's police force. They were drinking together that night. Not that anyone would have believed John could be capable of such an act. Rip never understood his brother. What it meant to be a good man."

"It's hard to believe Rip would want people to think John was guilty just to further his own aims. Despite his feelings for his brother, that would mean he didn't care if the real killer was found or not." As I said the words, I realized it could mean something much worse. Maybe Rip wasn't concerned with finding the real murderer because he already knew who the killer was.

I locked gazes with Maureen. I needed to ask her something, and I wanted to see her reaction when I did. "Rip said you're his alibi. I need to know the truth. Was he home with you the night of the murder?"

"I'll tell you what I told the police," she said, holding my gaze steady. "He was when I went to bed. At eight o'clock. With a sleeping pill."

A bitter gust of wind swirled around us.

"Ms. Warren, I know your family has a reputation for helping people in unusual circumstances, so I'm trusting you to deliver that letter. John deserves to know what is in it even if it is too late for him to do anything about it. I will never forgive myself for not getting it to him sooner."

"It sounds like you care a lot about John."

She gave me an unpleasant smile. "It didn't take long after my wedding for me to realize I had chosen the wrong Graves man."

She turned to leave, but I couldn't let that happen. Not yet. "Maureen?"

She raised an eyebrow.

"You must know the police are looking at my aunt as a potential suspect. I realize I can't expect you to believe Nora is innocent based on my word, but I'm giving it to you anyway. So, if there's anything you know that could help her, I would be so grateful if you shared it with me. Any detail that's been bothering you? Anything strange about your husband's behavior?"

Maureen sighed, almost as though she had been waiting to be asked. "There is one thing." She stepped in closer. "The past few days Rip has been spending a lot of time on the phone. That's not so unusual, but he's been secretive about it. I was worried he might have picked up on what I've been doing." She shot me a quick look, realizing she had said more than she'd intended. "Never mind all that, it's of no importance to you. The point is, I was suspicious, so I waited until he was distracted, then I looked at his caller list. The same unlisted number kept coming up. Yesterday, Rip was in the shower, and the number called again, so I answered it."

My heartbeat quickened.

"A young woman was on the other end. But it's not what you think," she added quickly. "You see, all Graves family members have a particular lilt to their voice, so even though I've only met her a handful of times, I am almost certain about who it was."

I gripped the letter in my hand.

"It was his niece, Liz Coleman, Mary's daughter."

I paused, then shook my head. "They're family. Maybe they reconnected over Constance's death."

Maureen's eyes narrowed. "Have you not been listening to a word I've said? My husband is not the type of man who reconnects with family over the passing of a loved one. No, Ms. Warren, I don't know what they've been talking about, but it's not a reunion."

I nodded. "Thank you. Thank you for telling me that." I didn't know what it meant, but it somehow felt like an important piece to the puzzle.

"Don't thank me. Just deliver that letter. And again, don't tell John where you got it. I can't have things blowing up just yet. I need more time. Rip needs to believe I'm still on his side."

Maureen turned again, and this time I didn't stop her.

I stared at the letter in my hand. I wanted so badly to read it. I didn't believe John was a killer, but Maureen had said quite clearly this letter contained a motive. A motive beyond being cut out of the estate. I needed to know what that was, even if John did have a rock-solid alibi.

But too many people had already read this letter. It would be wrong to add myself to that list.

Then again, this wasn't just about Constance Graves's family, it was about mine too.

I waved the envelope in the air debating what to do, when I noticed a strange smell coming from it. I brought it carefully to my nose. It was the same scent from the soap in the gift shop, but this time I knew what it was.

I knew what it was!

I had to get home.

I stuffed the letter in my bag. I would give it to John tomorrow. That meant, of course, I would have all night to agonize about whether or not I should read it. But none of that was important right now.

I had to talk to Nora.

She had a whole lot of explaining to do.

Chapter 22

I WALKED AROUND THE B&B, through the iron gate, to the back of the property, hoping to get into the greenhouse unnoticed. I had to check one thing before confronting Nora with the day's events. Given the tension that already existed between us, I didn't want to make things worse unless I was sure about what I thought might be going on.

Thankfully I found the conservatory empty.

Late afternoon sunlight filtered through the glass, casting a lovely glow on the verdant plants, but I wasn't feeling the peaceful vibe.

Now, where was it?

I walked up and down the rows of plants. If memory served, the one I was looking for was quite small and looked a little like an African violet. The flowers were different, though, much more striking.

It took three passes before a small clay pot finally caught my eye. After digging through the dark green fronds of some larger plants, I found my way back to the tiny beauty sitting underneath them by the glass. I pulled it up to my sight line and turned it in the sun. There weren't many plants with jet black flowers, but this was one of them. Actually, it was only the petals that were black. The pistil was canary yellow, trimmed in red.

Time for the moment of truth.

I brought the small pot to my nose and gave it a sniff.

Nothing.

Well, there was a little something, but the scent emanating from the small flowers was too faint for me to be sure it was the fragrance I had recognized in the shop.

I put the pot back where I had found it and planted my hands on my hips.

Now what?

If I went to Nora without proof, there was a good chance she would deny everything, which was really aggravating given all the grief she had been giving me about keeping secrets.

I gazed absentmindedly around the greenhouse until my eyes landed on the cabinets Nora had bought from the library.

Of course! The dried plants often had a more pungent smell.

I hurried over to the tallest stack and drew my finger over the labels of the tiny drawers until I found the B section.

Baboon Flower. Baby's Tears. Baneberry.

I skipped ahead.

Birch. Bird of Paradise.

No. No.

Black Gum. Blackberry. Bloodroot.

No.

There!

I wiggled the little drawer I had landed on open just far enough for me to reach inside and pull out a satchel filled with dried flowers. I loosened the strings holding it shut and brought it up to my nose.

Before I had even truly inhaled, I knew.

It was plain as day. This was the scent I had picked up on in the gift shop, and this was the scent on the letter Maureen had given me.

Black quartz flower.

The same black quartz flower Izzy said could break the warding spell she had put on the house.

It was an incredibly rare plant, one that only witches grew.

Unbelievable.

Nora had really gone too far this time.

I pulled the strings on the satchel closed, but I did not put it back in the drawer. Instead, I took it with me as I strode out of the greenhouse, up the path to the B&B.

I was mad. There was no denying it. Nora had accused both Izzy and I of not doing enough to help her, and yet here she was actively working against us.

I followed the voices coming from the dining room.

Not to mention the fact she felt entitled to knowing all of my most intimate feelings, but she had no problem keeping secrets of her own.

No, this was unacceptable, and I had no problem telling her so.

My steps faltered when I entered the dining room.

The special family dinner Izzy had planned was all laid out. Roast chicken, mashed potatoes, freshly baked rolls, crisp green beans in lemon-butter sauce. There was even a peach pie for dessert. All Nora's favorite comfort foods.

It was the perfect apology dinner.

But suddenly I was having a difficult time remembering what it was *I* was supposed to be apologizing for.

Nora was perched in her chair at the head of the table, looking like a queen, a smug expression on her face.

My uncertainty vanished.

"Brynn," Izzy said, clasping her hands to her chest. "There you are, darling. Look who decided to join us for dinner."

She directed my gaze over to her sister, who was delicately laying her napkin across her lap.

"Izzy tells me you have something you'd like to say?" Nora prodded, arching an eyebrow.

"Yes, I do." I strode around the table and dropped the satchel of black quartz flower on her plate. "Exactly how many other secrets are you keeping from us?"

Chapter 23

WHAT ON EARTH?" Nora said, shooting me a look before lifting the satchel. I saw the moment she recognized the scent. "So?"

I folded my arms over my chest. "Would you care to explain why it is I've been smelling this all over town?"

"No, I would not," Nora said, putting the satchel down delicately at the corner of the table before once again adjusting the napkin on her lap. "And frankly it's none of your business if I've made a friend."

Izzy rushed over, a huge smile on her face. "Norrie! You've made a friend? How wonderful! Does this friend have a name? I want to hear everything."

"Izzy," I snapped. "You're missing the point here."

"What point is that, darling?"

"Well, the friend's name is Nixie. She works at Charmed Treasures and she makes soap. With black quartz flower apparently."

Izzy's face dropped in confusion. "Black quartz flower? Black quartz flower!" Her eyes flashed over to her sister.

"Nora, did you give this Nixie black quartz flower to make *soap*?"

Nora shrugged. "I don't see what the problem is. The girl's been pestering me endlessly about, well, everything, and she has an interest in plants and making natural soaps, so I helped her out a little."

"By giving her one of the rarest flowers on the planet to dabble with?"

"It's wonderful for the skin," Nora said dismissively.

"Yes, wonderful for the skin." Izzy nodded. "And wonderful for dissolving spells. Especially ones used for, say, warding houses?"

"What are you talking about?" Nora asked, then her eyes grew wide with realization, but she caught herself quickly. "You used that spell? Really, Sister, out of all the incantations you could have chosen, we both know that one is rudimentary at best."

Izzy's jaw dropped. "I was upset. And in a hurry. And I didn't see you offering!"

"Aside from the fact you made her feel terrible about it," I said, "do you see what this means? The person who planted the murder weapon in your greenhouse must have used that soap, and I just so happen to know Rip's wife is a likely candidate." I was willing to bet Maureen had purchased the soap from the gift shop before finding me, and she had put it in her purse with the letter. The smell was strong enough for the paper to soak it up. "Which also means Rip himself—"

"Is our murderer," Nora finished, pushing her chair back. "Right. Let's go, then. Evenfall can't have a killer on the loose. I've prepared a number of spells for this occasion. Some may consider them to be in the realm of black magic, as they are quite painful, but given he's a murderer, I don't see an issue."

"No, no, no," I said, feeling my face twist. "We can't say for sure Rip is the murderer. Other people could have used that soap."

Nora narrowed her eyes. "And how exactly do *you* know his wife uses it?"

"I ran into her today. She smelled of it." I didn't want to lie, but I knew if I told her about the letter, she'd take it from me in a heartbeat, and I wasn't sure that was something I wanted to be responsible for.

"Well," Nora said matter-of-factly, "given how things have turned out, I believe it's fortuitous I gave the girl the black quartz flower. It has provided us with a clue."

"And would you like to say something to me?" Izzy asked.

Nora sighed. "I suppose you could make an argument for an apology," she said slowly before quickly adding, "but truly, out of all the warding spells, Izzy."

"You never stop," I said.

"Excuse me," Nora replied, flashing me her haughtiest look. "I came to this dinner under the pretense I would be the one receiving an apology, and here you are throwing accusations at me. And for what? Dabbling in homemade cosmetics?"

"That is not what I'm upset about, and you know it," I said firmly. "While it is concerning this Nixie seems to know more than she should about us, that's not the problem. The issue is you're keeping secrets. Nixie isn't the only person I ran into today. Mary Coleman had some interesting things to say about you."

"Oh, ho, ho, I'm keeping secrets," Nora said, placing her hand on her chest, completely disregarding the part about Mary. "Me? What about you, dear niece? You don't think it might have been a good idea to mention you were no longer practicing magic to your coven? To your family? To me?"

I couldn't ignore the hurt in her voice. "You're right. I do owe you an apology. I'm sorry I didn't tell you the truth about what was going on with me, but—"

"But?" Nora blinked. "It looks like I'm not the only one who's failing at the apologies."

"*But* you don't exactly make it easy. You can be a little *bossy* at times."

"That is true," Izzy said, wrinkling her nose.

"Bossy? Bossy! You two are infuriating! The house could be on fire, but neither one of you would mention it for fear of hurting someone's feelings." Nora rose to her feet. "Do you not see what is at stake? How many times do I have to say it? Brynn, what you are going through is temporary, but the consequences of your actions may well be permanent."

"*Temporary?*" Suddenly the dishes on the table began rattling. "You think the loss of my husband is temporary?"

"Maybe we should all take a breath," Izzy said, putting her hands up.

"I thought you were in control of your powers," Nora said, looking over the dinner table.

"I am," I replied tightly. "Are you?"

"I don't care who's doing it," Izzy said, "but given that the dishes are Mother's, could you both please stop? Now, Brynn, I think what Nora was trying to say is—"

"I can speak for myself, Sister," Nora snapped. "And Brynn knows exactly what I meant. She is purposely misinterpreting what I'm saying so that we'll both feel bad and once again drop the issue."

"And what exactly is the issue, Nora?"

She slapped the table with the palm of her hand. "You did not die with Adam!"

An icy silence filled the room.

"There," Nora said, albeit without much of the fire. "I've said it. Now we can move on."

"Move on?" I spun on my heel.

"Brynn," Izzy said, rushing after me.

I held up a hand. "I need a moment." I took a few steps away, then suddenly whirled back around. "But while I'm gone, Izzy, you may want to ask your sister how she knows Mary Coleman. I could have sworn she said she didn't know anyone from Constance's family, but Mary seems to think otherwise." I said the words to Izzy, but my gaze had been focused solely on Nora.

My aunt said nothing, but I could see in her eyes I had hit on something.

I spun back around and headed out of the room.

"Okay, darling," Izzy called after me. "But come back later if you're hungry." She let out a sigh I could hear from the hallway. "There will be lots of leftovers."

Chapter 24

"BEFORE YOU SAY anything, I know you must have heard what happened in the dining room." I pointed to the exposed vent in the brick wall. "And you probably also know about my decision to stop practicing magic. But, before we go any further, I need to make one thing clear."

My uncle looked slightly alarmed as I dropped myself into the chair across from him.

"I don't want to talk about it."

Dog cawed from his perch in the far corner of the room.

I shot a look over my shoulder. "I don't want to talk about it with you either."

It appeared as though Gideon had been having a pretty cozy evening before I had barged in. He had a book on his lap and a steaming cup of tea at his side. I felt a little bad, but he was part of this family too. It wasn't fair he always got to opt out of everything. Not that I wanted to talk about it.

My uncle cautiously peered at me over the glasses sitting low on his nose.

"I mean it." I folded my arms over my chest. "Nora just doesn't know when to quit sometimes."

He cleared his throat. "Ah, Nora. In my experience, my sister has—"

"Not that Izzy was much help."

"Izzy has always tried to be the peacemak—"

"Gideon. I told you I don't want to talk about it."

My uncle pressed his lips shut.

We sat in silence awhile before he dared ask, "Shall we talk about something else or . . . ?" He cast a hopeful glance down at the novel in his lap.

"Constance Graves."

He closed the book.

I filled Gideon in on everything I had learned so far—from the rose petal, to Rip's many lies, to John and Mary's regrets, to Liz's obvious anger, and the soap that could have broken the warding on the house. I finished with, "I have all of this background on the family, but I can't get it to point in any conclusive direction. Yes, Rip is the obvious candidate. I know he still wants Graves House. But I can't prove anything."

"You still believe the answer lies in Constance's will?"

"I don't know anymore. It doesn't make sense. That family has been in a stalemate for decades, and that new will could have either motivated someone to get their inheritance sooner or made someone angry enough to kill, but the police would have to know all this, and yet they're still focused on Nora."

Gideon nodded. "The crime had to be done quickly, and it would have required a lot of luck on the killer's part to get in and out the house without being spotted, so it makes sense the police would look to us as suspects, but I can't imagine what motive they think we have."

"Exactly, Nora had no reason to kill Constance. And the murder weapon isn't proof. They have to at least consider the possibility the killer left it there before fleeing the property." I rubbed a hand over my face. "But I have a feeling none of that matters. They've found their suspect and now they're making their case."

Gideon nodded. "I have the same feeling."

"You haven't *seen* anything though."

"No."

"You would tell us if you had?"

My uncle held my gaze steady in his own. "I would."

Again, Gideon had fallen into the habit of not telling anyone his premonitions unless they were minor, like the vase falling over in the sunroom. It was too hard for him to know the worst and not be able to prevent it. Now, one of my aunts—I won't say which, but she's the pushy one with the red hair—thought that wasn't entirely true. She believed he did have the power to do something with his premonitions. But without a guarantee, Gideon wanted no part of it. Not after my parents. Not after Lydia.

"I also have a bad feeling about the town hall meeting tomorrow," I said, looking over at Dog. He appeared to be dozing. "I'm starting to think it is some sort of setup."

"How so?"

"I don't know. I mean, I'm sure Liz Coleman will say terrible things. I got that much from when I met her, but I can't shake the feeling she has something up her sleeve."

Gideon and I fell into silence, lost in our own thoughts.

"Going back to Constance though," my uncle finally said.

I raised an eyebrow.

"Maybe it wasn't just one thing that moved her to change her will. Families are funny." He wagged a finger in the air. "Actually, the entire time you were telling me about the Graves siblings, I couldn't help but think of one of the Grimm Brothers' tales."

I pulled the blanket resting on the back of my chair down onto my lap. "Really?"

"Have you ever heard the story 'The Mouse, the Bird, and the Sausage'?"

I frowned. "I can honestly say I have not."

"Well," Gideon said, resting his elbows on the armrests of his chair and pyramiding his fingers, "in it the mouse, the bird, and the sausage all live together, and they all have very specific roles when it comes to household chores."

I straightened up. "Wait, wait, wait. The sausage lives with the bird and mouse?"

"Yes."

"And the sausage has chores?"

"Yes, they all have roles," Gideon said, ignoring the question in my voice. "The bird collects wood for the fire, the mouse collects water, and the sausage feeds the three of them."

I frowned again, maybe a little harder. "Do I want to know how the sausage feeds the family?"

My uncle sighed. "If you are unable to suspend your disbelief surrounding the details of the sausage, I'm afraid we will never get through this story."

"Sorry."

"Now, one day," Gideon said, tilting the peak of his fingers toward me, "the bird decides his job is by far the most difficult of the three, so he declares they should all switch roles. The bird decides it will be his job to collect the water, the sausage will collect the wood, and the mouse will cook the dinner."

"Sounds fair."

"Except it all goes terribly wrong."

I probably should have seen that coming, given it was a Grimms' tale. "What happens?"

"The sausage goes out for wood and gets eaten by a dog."

I blinked. "That is unfortunate."

"The mouse tries to season the supper, falls into a pot of boiling water, and dies."

"And the bird?"

"Falls into the well and drowns."

"I can see why this particular Grimms' tale was one of their lesser works."

Gideon leaned back in his chair. "But it does bring up some interesting points about families."

"Like we should all stay in our lanes or die?"

"That is the most obvious interpretation, but I was thinking more about how we all fall into character during family strife. And how we can get stuck in those roles, and how they cause us pain. Maybe Constance was tired of being the villain in her family? It sounds like John was angry at his brother for painting the three of them as victims. And maybe Mary was tired of trying to make amends, and her daughter was tired of seeing her try."

I didn't answer right away. It was certainly something to consider.

"Whatever the case may be, change in families, even the good kind, can cause pain. Look at you. You are a grown woman, capable of making your own choices, but your aunts will always want to look out for you."

"I'm fairly certain I said I didn't want to talk about this."

Gideon held up his hands in defeat. "I had to try." He paused a moment, then added, "That being said, I do want to apologize."

"For what?"

"For setting a terrible example."

Any residual heat I had been feeling from my argument with Nora drained away as I took in the regret evident on my uncle's face. "Gideon, what do you mean? You're still practicing magic."

"But I hid myself away after what happened to Lydia and your parents. There's no denying that."

"I thought you made the choice to isolate yourself because seeing people's futures was overwhelming?"

"That is certainly true, but given the similarities of our

circumstances, I can't help but wonder if I should have tried harder." He shook his head and looked off.

I felt terrible Gideon blamed himself in any way for the choice I was making now. But I didn't want to argue with him. It would only upset him more.

"Anyway," he said abruptly, "I am quite proud of you for getting into town the way you have been, if you don't mind me saying so."

I smiled. "I don't mind at all."

"And look at what you've accomplished," he said, spreading his hands wide.

"It's good of you to say that, but I haven't discovered much."

"Maybe you've given us more than you think. There are a lot of pieces. It may take some time to figure out how they all fit together."

It was funny, but as soon as my uncle had said the word *pieces*, I couldn't help but think I was forgetting one. An important one. Or maybe not forgetting, but not seeing something right in front of me. Actually, the feeling had been with me since the gift shop, and I didn't think it had anything to do with the soap.

"Thanks, Gideon," I said, pushing myself to my feet. "For everything. Even the fairy tale."

"You are very welcome."

"Maybe next story time, though, we could leave out the sausage?" I suggested, walking toward the spiral stairs.

"It does take away from some of the magic, doesn't it?"

I SNUCK BACK DOWN to the main floor as quietly as I could. While I was really hungry, I didn't want to risk running into either one of my aunts. We all needed some time.

I wasn't angry anymore though. Whether I had wanted it or not, Gideon's story *had* given me insight into my own family.

We were all frustrated.

Izzy had to be tired of being the peacemaker all the time. Just look at all the work she had put into dinner, and for what? And then there was Nora. I couldn't help but think she saw herself as the only one in the family to tackle issues head-on. It didn't matter if I agreed with that assessment or not, Nora believed it, and it had to be frustrating. As for me, well, I was tired of being told how to live my life.

I slipped out the front door, shutting it carefully behind me.

The night air was still and rich with the tangy scent of overripe apples.

I stood in the silence of the porch, feeling the heat leave my face.

I was also tired of having the same fight. I wanted to find a way to be close with Nora again. Izzy too. I didn't want to keep secrets from them. But they didn't understand the pain I still carried from losing Adam. They kept saying they wanted me to share it. Like it was the easiest thing in the world. Sharing the pain, though, meant bringing it to the surface, and I didn't know if I could bear that.

I crossed my arms over my waist.

Besides, I was taking steps forward. I had been to town nearly every day this week. Today alone, I had been to the library and the gift shop. And Gideon was right. I had learned a lot.

Suddenly my arms dropped to my sides.

There it was again. That feeling I was missing something.

What was it?

Something Mary had said? Liz? Ben?

No, that wasn't right. It wasn't something someone had said. It was more concrete. Like the soap. But not.

What was it?

I tilted my face up to the dark sky. Not that it was all that dark. The moon was full and white.

White.

There it was again.

Part of me was trying to remember something. I could feel my subconscious furiously digging to bring it up to the surface. It was so close. Right on the tip of my tongue.

Something white.

That was it!

Why hadn't I seen it before?

I had to go!

I ran down the driveway. I had to be sure.

But it was late. Was it too late? I took a quick look at my watch. Late, but not ridiculously so. It would be fine. He would understand. He'd be surprised to see me of course, but not upset. At least I didn't think he would be upset. Actually, I knew a way to guarantee he wouldn't be upset!

I stopped dead in my tracks, whirled around, and sprinted back to the house. I wasn't worried about being quiet this time. This was too important.

Faustus was standing in the threshold of the kitchen, licking his paw as I barreled toward him.

"You need to move, or I am going to jump over you!"

The cat skittered to the side, giving me a look that spoke to the fact I would pay dearly for this affront later. I could live with that.

"Brynn!" Izzy shouted as I ran into the kitchen. "Are you hungry? I could make you up a plate."

"No. No plate. Pie. I need pie."

"You need pie?" Izzy asked, gesturing weakly to the round tin on the counter.

"Excellent."

My aunt hovered behind me as I slid a piece of pie onto a plate and hastily swaddled it in plastic wrap.

"Darling, I'm sure you don't have to use that much wrap if you're just taking it up to the garage."

"It's not for me."

"Not for you? Then who is it for?"

"Mr. Henderson."

"Mr. Henderson? But why? Why would you bring that man pie?" Izzy laughed. "You have me in such a tizzy, I'm talking like a nursery rhyme."

"Sorry. There's no time to explain. I'll tell you everything when I get back." I raced out of the kitchen, then whipped back around, hurried over to Izzy, and kissed her on the cheek. "I want you to know, I see you." I backed up a step and pointed at her. "I see what you do for this family." I took a couple more hurried steps then added, "And the world is a better place with you in it, Izzy Warren."

My aunt smiled, her fingertips at her cheek where I had kissed her. "Thank you. And good luck!"

Chapter 25

I BANGED ON MR. Henderson's door as loudly as I dared, not wanting to rouse the neighborhood.

I waited a minute or two, but when there was no answer, I knocked again.

This time only seconds passed before the door whipped open. "Brynn, why are you here this time of night?" Mr. Henderson shot his head out and did a quick side to side scan of the street. "Is something after you?"

"No, no, it's nothing like that. And I'm sorry for calling on you so late, but it is important. Could I come in?"

He hesitated.

"I brought pie." I lifted the plate.

"Is that peach?"

I nodded.

"Peach is my favorite." He stepped to the side for me to enter. "Well, hurry up, then. It must be nearly ten. Two hours from midnight."

I gave him a sideways look.

He leaned toward me, then whispered, "The witching hour."

"Right. Of course." I nodded, matching his serious expression.

Once we were inside, he said, "Can I make you a cup of tea?"

"I don't want to be a bother."

"No bother. My mother always used to say nothing soothes like a cup of tea on a cold night. I think I'll have one myself. It will go well with the pie." He hurried toward the kitchen, calling out behind him, "Make yourself at home. I'll just be a minute."

I took a deep breath, trying to calm my nerves. I didn't want to alarm Mr. Henderson any more than I already had, and I also didn't want to get too excited, to prevent being disappointed over what I was hoping to find.

I wandered around the living room. There were lots of shelves loaded down with interesting knickknacks. Mr. Henderson had only moved in two years ago, but he had really made the little Arts & Crafts Bungalow his own. I eyed the brass model planes and the 1940s typewriter — before moving on to a row of books. My face dropped once I caught a few of the titles on the shelf. *Magical Creatures from Around the World*, *Haunted Places*, *Witches Among Us*.

"Are you interested in the paranormal?"

I spun around to face Mr. Henderson, who was carrying a sturdy wood tray with tea and pie.

"I, uh, not particularly," I said, feeling my cheeks burn.

"Well, if the mood ever strikes, you're welcome to borrow any of my books. Living in a town like Evenfall, I think it's in your best interest."

"I'm sure you're right." I sat on the sofa and reached for the teacup Mr. Henderson indicated was mine.

"Now, what brings you over this late?"

I took a long sip as I considered how I was going to handle this. As a general rule I didn't like lying, but given the circumstances, I thought I could forgive myself just this once. "This is a little embarrassing."

Mr. Henderson perked up with interest.

"The other day, you mentioned something about seeing a ghost?"

"Yes?"

"I think I may have seen one too."

My neighbor's teacup rattled in its saucer. He put it down quickly. "I knew I couldn't be the only one." His eyes twinkled with excitement.

"I didn't say anything when you first brought it up because my aunt was with me. She doesn't believe in those sorts of things."

"I understand. Izzy is a very sweet lady, but not everyone is gifted with the ability to see what's right in front of them."

I choked a little on my tea. "Excuse me." I was a bad witch. Very bad. "Anyway, the night Constance Graves passed—"

"Terrible tragedy that. The police told me they were looking into the circumstances of her accident. They made copies of some of my security files. Although I don't see how that will help them figure out how she fell."

He obviously hadn't heard all the talk about Constance's death being suspicious. It would only be a matter of time, but for now, that suited my purposes just fine. "It was that night that I saw . . . what I saw. It's hard to describe exactly."

"That's what I've been trying to tell you. It takes a trained eye, my dear. A trained eye."

"Could you tell me again what you saw that night?" I asked as sweetly as I could. "It might help me be sure I'm not imagining things."

"Certainly." He nodded sagely. "Well, like I said, it was a

woman. Of that I'm sure. She was very beautiful, with long dark hair. She also wore a flowing white robe that trailed to the grass. She glided across my lawn to yours. I bet you saw her right after I did. She would have floated right through the bars of your fence."

"Was any of this caught on your security footage?"

He shot me a look that spoke to how adorable he thought I was in my ignorance. "You should know, my dear, ghosts are far too smart to be caught on any recording devices."

"Oh, of course." It was in fact impossible for ghosts to be caught on camera.

"But," he said, holding up a finger, a sly smile on his face. "One of the cameras did manage to catch the corner of her gown."

"What?" I set down my cup with a bit of clatter. "Can I see it?"

Mr. Henderson hesitated, studying me.

"It's just," I paused, forcing an embarrassed smile, "my aunts think I'm crazy. It would make me feel better to see something concrete."

"I know what that's like." He pushed himself to his feet. "Come with me."

I followed Mr. Henderson into his study. It was a cozy space. There was a fireplace across from his desk, more bookshelves, and a multitude of little lamps that gave the place a soft glow. My neighbor moved to sit in the leather chair in front of the computer on his desk and jiggled the mouse. He then gestured for me to come in behind him. "I tried to show the officers, but they dismissed it as a sheet from the clothesline next door. So foolish."

I couldn't help but agree. Very foolish indeed.

He clicked a few files, and a number of small screens came to life. "I currently only have cameras on the front of the house and the side by the driveway. I've been focusing on the doors for obvious reasons. But I intend to install them in the back, I just haven't got around to it."

I pointed at the screen. "This is the side of your house?"

"That's right."

I studied the live feed. He had the camera positioned on the back edge of the bungalow, facing toward the street, covering his driveway and the side door. None of that mattered though. I was more interested in the tiny sliver of frame that captured the iron fence of our yard where Mr. Henderson had caught sight of his ghost.

"I've tagged the exact moment where the ghost comes into view. Just let me queue it up." He opened another window, then clicked with his mouse to start the recording just before the little mark indicated on the bar at the bottom of the screen.

"What time of night is this exactly?"

He squinted. "It looks like eighteen minutes past nine."

So approximately, fifteen, twenty minutes after the murder.

"Now, keep your eyes peeled. It only lasts a second." He hit play. "Ready. Wait for it. There!"

The flash of white happened so fast I didn't catch anything. "Can you pause it on the exact frame?"

"I can indeed." Mr. Henderson fiddled some more. "I've actually gotten quite good at this," he said, smiling up at me. "Here. I'll put it in slow motion."

He restarted the video. Nothing happened at first, then a frame with a little white flashed on the screen, but it was too blurry to be of use. Another frame clicked into view. Then another. "Pause it!"

I must have startled him because he hit the mouse really hard, and the video stopped precisely where I wanted it to.

I leaned toward the screen.

Chills raced up and down my arms.

It was hard to be one hundred percent sure, but I was willing to bet that was not the corner of a bedsheet I was looking at.

No, I had seen that scalloped edge before. On the nightgown in the gift shop.

It all fit. The woman with the dark hair. The timing. Now this.

And what was it Nixie had said?

I couldn't remember her exact words, but it was something like, *Liz Coleman is one of our best customers.*

Chapter 26

I WOKE UP LATE the following morning with one thing on my mind.

The town hall meeting was today. Liz Coleman's town hall meeting.

I didn't get a lot of sleep after my visit with Mr. Henderson. Once I had gone over everything with Izzy, I realized I was more confused than ever.

Theo had told me Liz had left the bookstore around nine. That didn't give her a lot of time to get changed into a nightgown and over to the B&B, but it wasn't impossible. Especially considering Theo hadn't checked the exact time.

But even if *I* did believe Liz Coleman had been in the area shortly after her aunt had been killed, I would have a tough time convincing the police of that given they already had the recording. And if she had been there, what did it mean? I couldn't just assume she was the murderer.

After talking about it for hours, Izzy and I called it a night. We both needed to get some sleep. I asked her if she was able to get anything out of Nora about her connection to Mary, but apparently my aunt hadn't been in the most communicative of moods after our failed dinner.

Once I was up for the day, I headed directly into town to talk to Nixie. I wanted to ask her if she had receipts for both the soap and the nightgown. I didn't know if she would give them to me or not, but it turned out the point was moot. The shop was closed.

I then spent a good deal of the day trying to track down John Graves. I needed to give him the letter Maureen had entrusted me with, but I didn't have any luck finding him either.

When I got back home, the B&B was uncomfortably quiet. I decided perhaps it was best for us all to have some alone time before going into town. We all needed to be on our best behavior, and if Nora and I got into any more fights beforehand, that wasn't likely to happen.

When it came time to go, I headed down from the loft and over to the B&B. Just as I was reaching for the door, it swung open in front of me.

I blinked a few times to be sure I was seeing what I thought I was seeing.

I had been planning on being extra sweet to Nora given how we had left things, but before I could stop the words from leaving my mouth, I said, "You're kidding me, right?"

My aunt tilted her chin up into the air. "What are you talking about?"

"You don't think," I swirled my finger in front of her, "this all might be a bit much?"

She arched an eyebrow.

Nora was wearing a full-length black velvet jacket that had about a million buttons running down the front and laced, pointy-toed boots.

"Is there a broomstick that goes with this outfit? Maybe a peaked hat?"

"Don't tempt me. I'm not in the business of dressing to make others comfortable." Nora brushed by me, then trotted down the front steps in a manner I never would have attempted in those boots.

Izzy came to my side and linked her arm through mine as we watched Nora stride toward the sidewalk.

I met my aunt's worried eyes with my own. "Tonight's going to be a disaster, isn't it?"

"I would think so. Yes."

Nora suddenly stopped her march and looked back at us. "Well, are you coming? I'm sure there'll be enough room on the pyre for all of us."

Izzy and I let out identical sighs, then followed Nora into the night.

THE SENSE OF dread I was feeling dissipated a little as we approached the retired fire hall. It was a cozy old place, and the warm yellow light spilling out from the windows into the darkness was a welcoming sight.

As we got closer, I spotted the man I had been looking for all day. "You two go on ahead," I said to my aunts. "I'll be right there."

"Where are you going?" Nora called out testily, but I ignored her and hurried over to John Graves.

"Hello, girlie," he said. "Wasn't sure if you and yours would show up for this circus tonight."

"I could say the same about you." I returned the smile he was giving me, but my palms had begun to sweat under my gloves. This wasn't exactly how I wanted to give him the letter. The guilt of keeping it from him, though, had become nearly unbearable. I knew how I would feel if Adam had left a letter and it had been kept from me.

I reached into my bag. "I have something for you."

The younger Graves brother frowned. He took the letter and stared at it a good long time before looking back up at me. "Where did you get this?"

Just then someone caught my attention. A few people

had gathered outside by the front doors of the fire hall, but only one was staring at me. Maureen Graves. There was no mistaking the look of warning on her face. "The person who gave it to me asked that I not tell you where it came from. They want to explain how—"

"It's been opened," John said, holding up the envelope.

"I know. I can promise you I haven't read it. And if the person who passed it along to me doesn't come to you soon, I'll tell you everything I know."

"That's not good enough," he said.

"I know it's not, and I'm so sorry for that. I really am."

I dashed away without looking back. I was certain if I stayed a moment longer, I'd tell him the truth, and I couldn't do that. I didn't know why Maureen wanted to keep it a secret, but I had promised her I wouldn't tell, and for all I knew, she was in danger.

I rushed up the steps of the fire hall, hurried inside, and found my way over to my aunts.

"What was that about?" Izzy asked under her breath.

"I'll tell you later."

The hall, normally empty, except for the antique fire-fighting equipment roped off in the corner, was filled with foldout chairs and a table stocked with homemade cookies, coffee, and tea. Izzy had brought her own special treats to add to the mix. They were made with the intention of heightening feelings of community, so hopefully everyone was hungry.

My eyes trailed over the robust crowd. All the usual people were there. Many of them were smiling when they saw us looking at them, but casting sneaking looks in our direction when they thought we weren't. The tension, how-ever, was clearly getting to some. Poor Birdie Cline, head of the Women's Society, went quite pale when I caught her looking at Nora. Thankfully, our neighbor Minnie Aberna-thy was in the process of handing her a cookie, so there was a good chance she'd recover.

I wasn't at all surprised to see Rip Graves and his wife, Maureen, in the front row. Beside them sat Mary and her daughter. A cold feeling settled in the pit of my stomach when I spotted the thick file Liz had on the seat beside her. She certainly looked prepared.

I had just begun to wonder if John had gone home, when he stepped inside, hat gripped in his hands, face flushed with emotion. He must have tucked the letter away because I couldn't see any sign of it. He took a seat at the back of the room, away from his family.

Also in the back row sat an attendee I hadn't been expecting to see, Nixie from Charmed Treasures. The flash of bright pink hair pulled up in a ponytail made her hard to miss, along with the giant earrings she had on. They were black hats. Black *witches'* hats, to be precise.

Wasn't that just terrific.

When she spotted us, she shot her hand up in greeting. I lifted mine in return, while Nora let out an exasperated sigh.

Just then, I noticed Beatty making his way through the chairs to get over to us.

"Ladies," he said in a tight whisper, "I'm not going to lie. I had been hoping you all would stay home tonight."

"And miss the show?" Nora asked with a smile that didn't quite reach her eyes.

"Look, I realize I'm not your lawyer when it comes to this particular issue, but I'd like to offer you all some advice I sincerely hope you'll take."

"Of course, Beatty," Izzy said. "You know we respect your opinion."

"Then promise me you'll say nothing."

"I can't promise that," Nora said with a dismissive shake of her head.

"Now, I'm being serious. This hall is not a courthouse, but you can rest assured every word that comes out of your mouth will be in the meeting notes, and you do not want anything you say to be misconstrued."

Nora narrowed her eyes. "I'm certainly not going to sit back and say nothing."

"You will if you know what's good for you," Beatty said in the firmest voice I had ever heard him use. "And that goes for all of you. From what I've heard, Liz Coleman is going to try to get a rise out of you, and she's a smart woman with a bit of a mean streak, so don't take the bait. Is that clear?"

Nora took a long breath, then said, "Crystal."

Beatty studied her face, but she was revealing nothing. "Well, good. I hope you mean that. I'm going to go sit back down, but keep in mind what I've said. All of you. Just lay low."

Beatty walked back over to his seat beside Roxie, who gave us a big smile and wave. At least she wasn't worried.

"Okay, everyone, please take your seats. We'd like to begin," a familiar voice called out.

Williams stood at the podium placed at the front of the room. A few other council members sat behind her at a long table. They looked pretty uncomfortable.

My aunts and I hurried to the only three seats left.

Williams clapped her hands to quiet the crowd. "Now, before we get started, I'd like to say a few words on behalf of the council. We know this has been an upsetting time for everyone. Constance Graves was a beloved member of our community, and we will dearly miss her."

There were a few awkward coughs, and a couple of chairs scraped against the floor.

"That being said, and despite what may have brought some of you out here tonight, this is not a trial."

I felt my eyes widen. By saying this was not a trial, this meeting suddenly felt a great deal like a trial. I exchanged looks with Izzy, then looked over to Nora, but she was staring straight ahead.

"Unlike previous town hall meetings, tonight will be an open forum for citizens to express their safety concerns.

The council, however, has requested that comments be solely limited to town safety. Any references to the ongoing criminal investigation will be shut down."

"That's a laugh."

The room fell silent as we all looked over to the man who had spoken.

Rip Graves Jr.

"I don't see how we can talk about town safety," he began, whirling around in his seat to face Nora, "without discussing the fact that my sister has been murdered."

Chapter 27

NORA STIFFENED BESIDE me, but to her credit, she said nothing. I looked down at her hands just to make sure she wasn't working some sort of charm with her fingers, but no, her hands were folded neatly, albeit a little tightly, on her lap.

"Mr. Graves," Williams began, "I am sorry for all that your family has been through. The purpose of the meeting tonight, though, is to discuss concrete security measures that fall within the town's purview."

"Just saying what everyone's thinking." He held up his hands. "But you go ahead. I'll keep quiet."

Williams placed her hands on the podium and took a breath. "Now, is there anyone who would like to begin?"

"I have a concern," a voice called out.

I recognized the woman who had spoken. Jane Robertson. I didn't know her personally, but, if I wasn't mistaken, she taught piano lessons out of her home.

Williams stepped back from the podium and waved out

her hand. She then took her seat with the other council members.

The mousey woman in baggy jeans and a mauve cardigan got up from her seat and walked toward the front of the room. I wasn't too worried about what she might have to say until I caught her exchanging glances with Liz Coleman, who gave her a small nod.

Once Jane Robertson had positioned herself at the podium, she took a moment to smooth her hair and straighten her cardigan. The delay made it all the more shocking when she called out in a startlingly loud voice, "Citizens of Evenfall!"

Thankfully I wasn't the only one who jumped.

"Tonight, I would like to talk to you all about the string of attacks that have ripped through our community. I've heard some of you call it *vandalism*, but that is not what it is. Wanton acts of destruction!" She hit the podium with her fist. "That's what's happening in our town, and we should all be afraid!"

Izzy and I again exchanged looks. *Attacks? Wanton acts of destruction?*

For a small, meek-looking woman, Jane Robertson certainly did have a presence.

"I'm sorry to interrupt," Williams said. "But could you tell us specifically what acts you are referring to?"

"All the dead plants," Jane said in a much quieter voice. "Someone or some*thing* is killing all my fall flowers."

A small murmur ran through the crowd.

"I had three pots of yellow chrysanthemums. Bought them just last week. They're all dead now. I don't know why someone would do such a thing." She looked at Nora. "It's certainly not something a *normal* person would do. That's all I have to say. Thank you."

We all watched Jane Robertson scurry back to her seat. I guess her brand of passion was short-lived. Or she had run out of rehearsed lines. I looked over at Liz Coleman. She was trying to act cool, but there was something in her expression that led me to believe she had hoped that would go better.

Williams stepped back over to the podium. "Thank you, uh, Jane, for sharing your concerns. Although I'm not sure the dead chrysanthemums can be attributed conclusively to vandalism."

"Right you are, Williams. The acts aren't vandalism," a new voice called out. "At least not of the mortal kind."

Another rumble ran through the crowd. At least one person stifled a laugh.

My eyes searched for who had made the comment, but I already knew who was behind it, even before I heard Izzy sigh.

"Did you have something you'd like to add, Mr. Henderson?" The look on Williams's face clearly spoke to the fact she hoped he did not.

"No, no," he said, rocking on his feet. "Other than the fact that blights of the kind Jane is describing are often the handiwork of—"

A loud sneeze cut Mr. Henderson off.

"Sorry!" Nixie called out, holding a hand to her nose. "I have terrible allergies this time of year." She chuckled. "I guess all the plants in town aren't dead."

The crowd joined her in laughter.

I caught the shop girl's eye, and she gave me a wink.

"Right," Williams said, once the crowd had quieted, "I suggest we table this issue until our next formal meeting, and in the meantime, perhaps everyone can monitor their landscaping to see if this is an ongoing problem or not. Now, does anyone else have a topic of concern they would like to raise?"

"I do," a voice boomed from the crowd. I followed it to Frank Booth.

A number of people groaned as he got to his feet and hiked up his pants.

We all knew what was coming.

"Mr. Booth," Williams said before he could begin, "if you are planning to once again complain about the noise of the town's garbage trucks, I would remind you that we have investigated this topic thoroughly."

"And nothing's been done about it!"

"There is nothing to be done. I have, however, been instructed to inform you that if you persist in chasing after the trucks brandishing your broom in a threatening manner, the sanitation workers will contact the authorities. May I recommend a good set of ear plugs?"

"No, you may not."

Williams closed her eyes. "Please take your seat, Mr. Booth."

"I think it's time we get to the issue at hand, don't you?"

The cold dread I had experienced earlier crept back over me as Liz Coleman got to her feet and headed for the podium.

I could tell Williams didn't want to give her the floor, but in the end, there wasn't much she could do but step out of the way. She did, however, whisper something to Liz that looked like a warning.

Liz nodded and rested her file on the podium.

"Good evening, everyone. I am grateful for this opportunity to speak to you all tonight."

The hall went deathly quiet.

"I know many of you won't enjoy hearing what it is I'm about to say, but it's necessary." She paused, allowing some tension to build. "What happened to my aunt was not an accident."

No one breathed.

"The town of Evenfall *is* in danger, and it's all because of one family." Liz Coleman took a long look at me and my aunts. "The Warrens of Ivywood Hollow."

Chapter 28

WILLIAMS JUMPED TO her feet. "Miss Coleman, this is not what we agreed to."

"*We* agreed to nothing," Liz said. "You've been in this town for what? Ten years? My family has been here three hundred."

Williams locked glares with her but then backed away. I think she knew, one way or another, Liz would have her say, and it was probably best to get it over with.

"Now, I know everyone here has heard the stories of the Warren *women*," she began, taking note of the glances being exchanged in the crowd, "but I'm here to tell you they are not just stories. And it's not just about the dying plants or the people who have disappeared."

An alarm sounded in my head. *What people?* I looked to Nora for answers, but she was still staring ahead, completely frozen. I knew my aunt well, though, and something had changed about her. She knew what Liz was talking about.

I had been so focused on Nora, I didn't realize Izzy was

suddenly on her feet. Beatty had half risen to his own to stop her from saying anything, but it was too late.

"What in the stars? Who has disappeared?"

Liz smiled. "You don't know?" she asked sweetly. "Maybe you should ask your sister."

Nora didn't flinch.

"Evanora?" Izzy asked, slowly sitting back down. "What is she talking about?"

"I'm sure I have no idea," Nora answered tightly.

"She knows exactly what I'm talking about. Tell them, Ms. Warren. What happened to my father?"

"Your father?" Izzy asked, still perched on the edge of her seat. "He didn't disappear. He passed not too long ago, I believe."

"Grant was my stepfather," Liz said, gripping the sides of the podium. "Your sister drove my biological father out of town." She slid her gaze away from Izzy to land on Nora. "Isn't that right?"

"Nora," Beatty warned from across the room.

I looked at my aunt. She was hanging in there, but I could feel the disquiet building behind her calm facade. In hindsight coming to this meeting had probably not been a good idea. No, not good at all.

"You couldn't help yourself, could you?"

Nora didn't answer, but I caught her exchanging looks with Mary, who suddenly looked quite *guilty*?

"You saw something you wanted," Liz went on. "And when you couldn't have it, you made sure nobody else could either."

Confusion flickered over Nora's face.

"You sent my father away. I don't know how you did it, but you did. Now we don't know if he's dead or alive," she said with an angry shrug. "All because you couldn't have him. The man you were in love with didn't love you."

Silence filled the room.

I stared at Nora, searching her face for any sign she

knew what Liz was talking about. For a good long time, she remained perfectly still. She could have been a statue. Then, all of the sudden, she chuckled.

It was nothing more than titter at first, but then it grew. I tried to think of a way to quiet her, something that wouldn't make the situation worse, but before I could even blink that chuckle had risen to a howl. Nora was roaring with laughter. Her whole body shook with it. She was completely beside herself. It was like she had never heard anything quite so funny in her entire life.

Unfortunately, everyone else in the hall had gone deathly silent.

But either Nora didn't notice or she didn't care. She just laughed on and on.

After what seemed like hours, my aunt wiped the tears from her face and said, "Oh my. Just the thought of *me* being in love with that man. It's too much." She coughed, blinked a few times, then looked around the room. "Sorry. Where were we?"

Nobody seemed to know anymore.

It was Liz who recovered first. "That was a good performance," she said, a little uncertainty finding its way into her voice, "but I know what I know."

"What is it you know again?" Nora said, still smoothing tears away from the corners of her eyes.

"I know you made my father disappear, and more importantly, I know what everybody else in this room suspects."

Nora rose to her feet. "I would choose your next words carefully." All the previous hilarity had vanished from her voice, and everyone in the room tensed with the sudden feeling of danger.

"Evanora Warren, you are responsible for the murder of my aunt. And I have proof." Liz patted the file in front of her. "Right here."

Chapter 29

"EVERYONE. EVERYONE!" WILLIAMS called out as the crowd erupted in panicked chatter. "We have strayed far from our original path. Liz, I fail to see what connection a love affair that may or may not have happened years ago has to do with your aunt's death. It clearly isn't a motive, and, once again, the purpose of this meeting is not to litigate any crime. We all need to stand down." Williams pointed at Nora. Surprisingly, she sank back down to her chair.

"You're right," Liz said. "It isn't motive for my aunt's death."

Williams took a step toward the podium. "Perhaps we should move on, then."

"The motive for my aunt's death is actually in the town hall meeting notes."

I looked at Nora yet again. She shook her head by way of saying she had no idea what was to come.

Liz raised a sheet of paper into the air. "What I have

here are copies of the notes from a town hall meeting eleven years ago, dated April twenty-first."

"Eleven years ago?" Williams asked. "What possible significance could a meeting from eleven years ago have now?"

"The top agenda item of this particular meeting was Graves House."

Only I could hear Nora mutter under her breath, "Well, fudge."

Fudge? *Fudge!* I stared at my aunt, willing her to look at me, but she had gone still again.

"Here, Evanora Warren is quoted as saying Graves House is a horrific eyesore. That it detracts from the beauty of Evenfall, and someone should . . ." Liz squinted at the paper as though she wanted to be sure she was getting the wording just right. "Someone should burn the house to the ground."

Nora scoffed. "I was hardly the only one in town to grumble about the property. Multiple complaints have been filed over the years."

"My aunt was having the house brought up to code. That's why she was staying with you at Ivywood Hollow?"

"Exactly!" Nora said, snapping her fingers. "There were obviously no hard feelings between us or why else would she stay at the B&B?"

A smug smile spread over Liz's face. "Because that's how my aunt preferred to fight. Up close and personal."

Nora frowned. "What are you talking about?"

"She told you during her stay that while she was bringing the house up to code, she didn't have any plans to improve the esthetics of the family home. Thereby ensuring the house would remain an eyesore for years to come. You were obviously enraged by her plans and decided to do something about it."

"Wait." Nora held up a hand. "Just so I have this straight, you think I killed your aunt because her house wasn't *pretty*?"

Liz turned back to her papers. "This is a quote from you in the *Evenfall Gazette*, dated four years ago." She cleared her throat. "*Constance Graves should be strung up and quartered for what she's done to that beautiful house.*"

Nora turned to me and muttered, "You know, I'm starting to think Beatty's right. I talk far too much." She then said quite loudly, "I'm sure that's a misquote. That doesn't sound at all like something I would say."

The hall went completely quiet again as a number of people in the crowd exchanged awkward looks.

Nora threw her hands up. "Fine, then. It does sound like something I would say. But you all know me. I can, at times, be charmingly dramatic."

"Just so that we can all rest assured you weren't in fact misquoted, let me read from one of your initial complaints to the town council regarding Graves House." She pulled yet another paper from her file. "In the section labeled 'comments from issuer' it reads, *Constance Graves should be strung up and quartered for—*"

"I think we all get your point," Nora snapped. "This is ridiculous. I will have you know, Constance and I quashed that beef years ago. When I realized the town council wasn't going to do anything of use, surprise, surprise," she said, flashing a look at the members, "I went to Constance's house and demanded she fix it up. She said no. I asked her why not. She said revenge. And we left it at that. Beef quashed."

"I'm sorry. You left it at revenge?" Williams asked.

Incredulity came over Nora's face. "Who am I to judge another person's revenge? Constance might have mentioned something about her family, but I didn't pry." She whispered to me, "Actually, I asked her if she needed any help moving her revenge along, but she turned me down." She then directed her attention back to the crowd. "Now that I've become acquainted with more of Constance's family, I can see her desire for revenge was most likely justified."

"You're scrambling," Liz said. "Everyone here knows it. You had the means. You had the motive. And you had the opportunity."

"That's enough!" Williams shouted. "I move to end this meeting."

"And what about you?" a voice called out.

Who said that?

Everyone in the hall turned in their seats to look at me.

Oh. That's who.

I rose shakily to my feet.

So much for laying low.

Chapter 30

I LOOKED AROUND THE room. My gaze landed on a number of concerned faces, but Beatty, he actually looked like he might be sick. This was a bad idea. I knew it was a bad idea. I didn't have any real proof for any of my suspicions. But the way Liz had attacked Nora? I couldn't stand by and do nothing. And now that I was in it, I was really in it.

"Your family has far more motive than ours does."

"What are you talking about?" Liz asked.

I swallowed hard. "I think you know. I think everybody in this room knows."

Rip held up a hand to Liz to let him answer as he swiveled in his seat to face me. "If you're referring to that business with our father's will, that all happened years ago."

"But that's not the only will in question, is it?"

Another rumbling.

Rip narrowed his gaze. "What are you taking about?"

"Everyone knows that you've always wanted Graves House."

"What's your point?"

"Constance was standing in your way."

This time it was Rip who laughed, but it was short-lived and ugly sounding. "What makes you think that's changed?"

My heart banged against my ribs. I was taking a huge risk here, but I couldn't let everyone leave the meeting tonight thinking Nora was the only person with a motive to kill Constance.

I looked over to Roxie, then back to Rip. "Your sister changed her will quite recently. Isn't that right?"

Time suddenly slowed.

Roxie's eyes grew wide as her brother looked at her with horror. The unpleasant smile on Rip's face spread even wider.

I had made a mistake.

"What's this about a new will?" Rip asked.

"She changed her will. And I've been told her intention behind this new one was to finally make someone other than herself happy. Somebody stood to benefit."

Rip let out another laugh. It was even bigger and uglier this time. "You silly little girl."

I tried to keep my expression steady.

"Sure, Connie wanted to make someone happy." He let the sentence hang in the air. "Our father."

"What do you mean?"

"She left everything to the town!" Rip shouted. "On the stipulation the house be made into a museum and the land some sort of park. She insisted on there being a big sign with his name on it. So we could see it every day."

I tried to sort through what this all meant, but I couldn't put anything together. "That changes nothing. You all still had motive."

"What motive?"

"You were angry. Angry she stopped you from getting the house again."

"Yeah, I was angry. Really angry," he said with a nod. "Three years ago."

I felt my mouth drop open, but no words came out.

"That's when Constance changed her will. Three years ago. She made sure we all got copies."

I shot a look at Roxie, who was suddenly looking as ill as her brother.

"No, no. Constance saw Beatty just a couple of weeks ago."

"That may very well be the case, but it wasn't about her will."

This could not be happening. I could feel the eyes of the town on me, waiting, but I already knew it was too late. I had lost them. It didn't matter if Rip still had designs on getting Graves House or not. I had gone after him without having all the facts. No one would believe me now.

A strange noise filtered into my consciousness despite my swirling thoughts.

What was that?

Rattling. Like glasses or dishes knocking together. Just like when Nora and I had been arguing in the dining room.

No. Not now.

I looked over at the treat table. It was very slight, but all of the cups, plates, and silverware were trembling.

"Brynn," Nora hissed under her breath. "Get ahold of yourself."

"Does anyone feel that?" Birdie Cline called out in a panicked voice. "What's happening? Is it an earthquake?"

"Brynn," Izzy whispered. "Stop it."

"I'm trying. I can't."

"You said you were in control."

I thought I was.

Suddenly people were pushing back their chairs and getting to their feet as Liz Coleman shouted out, "Funny how these things always seem to happen when the Warren *women* are around."

Whispers ran through the crowd. Even though I shouldn't have been able to hear them, every one reached my ears.

Strange things always happen in that part of town.

I've always wondered if there wasn't something a little odd about that family.

Back in school, Nora was always a little peculiar.

"Everyone? Everyone!" Williams shouted. "Let's all exit the building in an orderly fashion. I'm sure it's just a tremor."

The rest of what she had to say was drowned out by the crowd.

Izzy grabbed me with one hand and Nora with the other. "You two out first."

Both Nora and I tried to speak but Izzy wasn't having any of it.

"Not one word," she snapped. "From either of you. I've had it. We'll talk about this when we get home."

Chapter 31

I T TOOK A lot for Izzy to get angry. But when she did? It was a little scary.

Nora and I watched her stride through the front doors of Ivywood Hollow and head directly for the fireplace. She shot out her hand and flames swelled up over the logs waiting in the hearth. She then whirled around and pinned us with a ferocious look. "Well, that was a disaster."

I cleared my throat. "Izzy, I'm so sorry."

"No, I don't want to hear from you right now," she said with a point. "There will be time for your apologies later. You promised me everything was fine. How could you lose control of your powers like that? In front of the town?" She shook her head, then turned on her sister. "You. You start talking."

"Don't you think I've done quite enough of that already?" Nora collapsed into the chaise lounge.

"Don't you dare try to be cute with me, Little Sister," Izzy said. "You are going to tell me every detail of your connection to the Graves family. And you're going to do it right now."

"Is everything all right?" a tinny voice came from the iron register by the ceiling.

"Gideon, if you want to say something, then get down here," Izzy snapped. "Otherwise, be quiet."

Silence.

"Sister?"

Nora's shoulders slumped. "It was all such a long time ago. I don't even know where to begin."

"Let's start with Liz Coleman's father, and why she thinks you made him disappear."

Nora rolled her eyes grumpily. "I didn't make him disappear. That would have required far more effort than he was worth."

"Nora," Izzy warned.

A defeated look came over my aunt's face. "Mary came to me. She needed help. Her first husband, Carl, was not a nice man."

Izzy folded her arms over her chest. "Go on."

"She was afraid for her life and her daughter's. She'd spoken to the police, but they were of little help."

"So, you thought you could help her."

Nora nodded.

Izzy tapped her foot on the floor. "Do I even want to ask why you didn't come to me?"

"You know perfectly well why I wouldn't come to you with something like this," Nora said, her voice regaining some of its vigor. "You've always been too afraid of your own magical shadow to do what is necessary. You would have given him a sugar cookie and hoped for the best."

"That's not fair."

Nora met Izzy's eye, then said, "You're right. It's not. The truth is, something needed to be done, and I wanted to spare you from having to perform a spell you clearly wouldn't have been comfortable with when I could take care of the situation myself."

Izzy took a step toward her sister. "And which spell exactly wouldn't I have been comfortable with?"

Nora sank back into the chaise again. "There was only one option as far as I could see."

"Which spell?"

"If I'd had the time, I would have perhaps gone in a different direction."

"Evanora!"

Nora mumbled something into her chest while fiddling with the many buttons of her coat.

"Which. Spell. Did. You. Do?"

"The Night of Terror spell," she finally shouted. "There? Are you happy?"

Izzy blinked a few times, then reached a shaky hand out for the armrest of the sofa behind her. Once she found it, she dropped down into it.

I looked back and forth from one aunt to the other. "What exactly is the Night of Terror spell?"

"It's from the restricted library." Izzy's eyes were wide, but she was staring at nothing I could see. "It's extremely dangerous. Even with a powerful coven, it's extremely dangerous. Highly unpredictable. Nora, you could have died."

My other aunt folded her hands on her lap. "Well, I didn't, and the spell worked."

I had a feeling the name was somewhat self-explanatory, but I still needed to ask. "What exactly does the spell do?"

"It brings a person's worst fears to life," Izzy said, still looking shocked. "It's an illusion if done correctly, but for the person the spell targets, it might as well be real."

I turned back to Nora. "And what were Carl's worst fears?"

"Oh, who remembers." Her face twisted in disgust. "I locked him in a room and put in my ear plugs. As I recall, I managed to get a fair bit of knitting done that night. By morning, Carl was a new man. Quite agreeable. I told him if he ever raised his voice, let alone his hand in anger to anyone again, I'd be back. I don't think he trusted himself around Mary, so he left town. He lives in Nevada now. I paid him a visit a few years back just to be sure he was behaving himself." Her lips curled into something slightly wicked. "He assured me he was. I used a truth spell just to be certain. That being said, I should probably check on him again. Maybe I'll take a trip in February. Get some sun. Buy myself a new hat."

"Enough," Izzy said.

Nora stopped talking and folded her hands once again.

Izzy fixed her sister in her gaze. "Now let's hear the rest of it."

Nora looked back at her in question.

"Well?"

"Everything I told you is the truth." Nora looked over at me. "Didn't Mary say something about my always having been good to her?"

"She did."

"Obviously, she hasn't filled her daughter in on the truth of who her father was," she added. "Not that I could blame her. No one wants a monster in the family."

"I don't doubt any of that," Izzy said. "But you've left something out."

Nora frowned, then pointed a single finger in the air, a moment later she raised another, and then another as though silently counting. "No, I think I've covered all the pertinent details."

"Don't do that."

Nora sighed with what sounded like real exasperation. "I don't know what it is you're referring to."

"Consequences. I am referring to the consequences. They must have been severe given you did the spell without a coven. They would have all gone to you."

Nora looked over to the door, probably subconsciously

wishing for escape. "You know the Warren witches are hardy stock."

Izzy took a steadying breath. "It's a dark spell, Nora. Even if your intentions were pristine, there would have been a price to pay."

"So, I paid it," she said with a shrug.

Izzy pushed herself up off the couch and walked over to her sister. "Where?"

Nora scoffed. "It's fine. It's healed. It was so long ago."

"Where?"

Nora closed her eyes and pointed at the back of her shoulders.

Izzy snapped her fingers and the buttons on Nora's jacket flew open. She then yanked it down and pulled up the black silk turtleneck Nora was wearing underneath. I could only look for a moment at the thin scars crisscrossed over my aunt's back.

"That's right," Nora suddenly said. "Spiders were one of his fears. Hence the, uh, webbing."

Izzy ran her hand over Nora's shoulders. "How did you hide this from me?" she asked in a much gentler voice. "Have you been using a glamor spell?"

She shrugged.

Izzy carefully pulled Nora's shirt back down and then cradled her head. "My dear, dear, sweet, foolish sister."

A strange honking noise came from the register. Was that Gideon blowing his nose? Not that I was judging. My own eyes were stinging.

"Again, it was a long time ago," Nora said, patting Izzy's arm. "I'm fine now. I survived. And Mary and her daughter were free from danger." She looked over at me. "But just so we're clear, it's not something I would recommend." She then pulled away from Izzy's embrace to look up at her. "And if I had to do it again, I would come to you."

"I should hope so."

"It's about time you started pulling your own weight." She shot me a wink.

I smiled. Nora and I had been fighting so much lately. It felt good for us all to be on the same side again.

"Stop that, you two," Izzy snapped.

Or not.

"I'm still mad."

Nora groaned. "But it was forever ago."

"I'm not mad at what you did then. I'm mad about now. Don't you think it would have been a good idea to share all this with us?"

"No, no, let's not go there. I've had a very trying evening. I liked where we were a second ago." She waved her sister in to come cradle her head again, but Izzy folded her arms over her chest. "Besides, I'm not the only one who needs to explain herself. Let's talk about Brynn, shall we?"

Chapter 32

"THANKS A LOT," I grumbled.

Nora smiled at me prettily.

The fire crackled and spit in the hearth as my aunts studied me. Suddenly I felt like I was eight years old again.

"She's right," Izzy said. "Your actions tonight were beyond reckless. And now we have quite the mess to clean up, don't we?"

Nora waved a hand in the air. "I was thinking we could use a memory spell to erase the last part of the evening from people's minds." She dropped the hand to cover her face. "Or why don't we just erase the entire thing. I don't think we accomplished much by way of making me a paragon of citizenry."

"Spell everyone in attendance? Are you mad?" Izzy clutched her forehead. "That's far too complicated. The loose ends would be horrific. No, I was thinking we could send in a news alert to the town paper stating the tremor was real, but there's no danger. The alerts must all be electronic these days, but there has to be a spell for that."

"Oh! Or we could just cause a real earthquake to cover up for Brynn's little shake-up," Nora said. "That could be fun."

"Are you even *trying* to help right now?"

As my aunts continued to discuss all the ways they could go about cleaning up the mess I had made, the reality of what I had done settled in. What had I been thinking challenging Liz like that? Or accusing Rip without evidence? And then there was everything I had been keeping from my aunts. It wasn't as though I hadn't had warning my magic was out of control, but I lied to them about it. Repeatedly. I had lied to myself.

"I am so sorry."

"What's that, darling?" Izzy asked, looking over at me.

I hadn't even realized I'd said the words out loud, but they were worth repeating. "I'm sorry."

She waited for me to go on.

"You're right. I put us all in danger tonight." I felt my cheeks burn as I met her eye and then Nora's. "Actually, you've both been right about a lot of things."

"I love how this is going so far," Nora said with a happy shrug.

"And I know I need to explain, but I can't. Not really. The way I lost control tonight was inexcusable." I picked at my fingers. "There have been a few other instances where my magic has gotten away from me. But I swear to you both, I didn't know. Not for sure. My connection to my magic, it doesn't feel the way it used to."

Izzy stepped toward me, but I put a hand up to stop her.

"I should have told you both everything. But I was afraid." I met Nora's eyes. "I know you don't support my decision to give up magic. And truthfully, I'm questioning whether it's what I want." I took a shaky breath. I wasn't sure if I was explaining any of this properly, but it was too late to stop. "But it hurts. Practicing magic hurts. And I know what it is you want me to do to try to fix things, but I don't think I'm strong enough." I could barely speak past the tightness in my throat. "I don't think I'll ever be strong enough to have Adam's funeral."

"Brynn," Nora began, but I waved her off.

"I thought I could help find out what really happened to Constance without using my powers, but I messed everything up tonight, and now things are even worse than they were before."

I jumped as a loud knock ripped through the parlor.

"Who could that be at this hour?" Izzy asked. She hurried over to the door, then swung it open.

On the other side stood a man in a suit, with two officers in uniform behind him.

"Isabel Warren. Evanora Warren. We'd like you to come with us."

I T HAD ALL happened so fast.

The police hadn't arrested my aunts, but they did take them in for questioning. Beatty apparently had found a lawyer who was already waiting for them at the station. And no, the police did not want me coming along, but they did recommend I keep myself available for questioning at a later date.

In minutes, they were gone.

And it was my fault.

It couldn't have been a coincidence the police had showed up at the B&B after the town hall. People were upset. They would be under pressure to do something. To act.

Well, they weren't the only ones.

If I had time, figuring out what to do wouldn't have been a problem. I would spend days, weeks, months, pondering the perfect spell to help my aunts. I would read every grimoire, weigh all my options, find the perfect bit of magic to use in this situation. But I didn't have the luxury of time.

I needed to do something now.

"Brynn?"

I heard the voice without registering it. My thoughts were swirling.

"Brynn!"

Gideon.

I didn't have time to talk. The time for talking was over. I needed to find out who killed Constance Graves, and I no longer cared how I did it.

I raced into the kitchen, frantically opening and closing cupboards, grabbing everything I thought I might need. Many tools and ingredients were standard. A copper pot. Measuring cups. A long wooden spoon. Wooden spoons were always better for the mixing. The prune juice that was still in the fridge. That would work nicely. And Constance's comb! I couldn't forget that.

"Brynn, I can hear you down there. I need to know what you're planning. We don't want to do anything rash."

I didn't answer. Izzy was right. If Gideon had something to say, he could come down and say it. Now, what else did I need?

Grimoires!

I raced to the library next. I knew just the one I needed. Where was it? Third or fourth shelf, if I wasn't mistaken.

"I shouldn't have to remind you that you haven't practiced magic for quite some time now."

I nodded but said nothing, just ran my finger over the leather backings of the spell books.

"And I know you're upset."

I wasn't that upset. Doing nothing would make me upset. Actually, I felt pretty good. I was finally putting my own selfish needs aside.

"But we should talk about any spells you might be planning."

Aha! There it was. I pulled the heavy book from the

shelf and ran back to the kitchen. This would get me the answers I needed.

The voice from the attic droned on. "Yes, we have all been hoping you would take up magic again."

Exactly, I didn't know what my uncle was complaining about. I laid a tablecloth on the counter and started piling all that I had collected on top of it.

"But we did not mean for you to take it back up like this. Not when you're upset. Not when your *magic* is upset. And especially not alone."

"Do you want to come down and help me?"

As soon as I'd said the words, I regretted them.

Silence followed.

"I'm sorry, Gideon. I shouldn't have said that. But I am doing this."

I wrapped up the tablecloth and slung it over my shoulder.

"Please, let's talk about this. Your magic will not respond the way it used to. It's like calling up a friend after years of not speaking and asking for a loan. Your magic may have feelings about this!"

"Well, if that's the case," I said, heading for the French doors that led to backyard, "you'd better wish me luck."

Because this witch was about to do some serious magic.

Chapter 33

A COOL NIGHT BREEZE carried through the windows above my worktable in the main floor of the carriage house, flickering the candles I had placed around its edges. I wrapped my scarf in another loop around my neck as I eyed my handiwork. As far as I could see, I had just about everything I needed, and it was perfectly arranged.

I'd like to say my aunts would have approved of my craft, but I knew that wasn't the case. Casting a spell on an entire bloodline, by myself, without the help of a coven, was not something they would approve of. Not at all. But I was desperate.

The purpose of the enchantment I had in mind was to make the target, or in this case, targets, believe something that wasn't true, that rumors were being spread about them. And not just any rumors, but rumors of their deepest secrets. It was meant to induce paranoia and panic, and hopefully, in this case, prod the real murderer of Constance Graves to make a mistake. Once I had cast the spell, my plan was to go to the house of the person I suspected most and wait for the magic to do its work. The dilemma, of course, was choosing which family member to watch. Out of the four—Rip, Mary, John, and Liz—I was torn between Rip and Liz. I didn't trust Rip for a second. I knew Maureen wasn't exaggerating when she said lying came as easily as breathing for her husband, and out of all the siblings, he seemed to be the most bitter about being cut from his father's will. But then there was Liz. I believed it was her nightgown I saw in Mr. Henderson's security footage, and she was clearly trying to frame Nora for her aunt's death. I couldn't help but wonder what else she was hiding.

I wasn't sure if I was making the right call, but in the end, I decided I would go to Liz's house. Overall, she was a better candidate for the spell, as Rip's natural arrogance might protect him from some of the paranoia. Only time would tell if I had chosen correctly.

I swept a bit of dust from the counter, sending a spider scuttling to the safety of the wall, and then lit three more candles, placing them in a triangle around the workspace. Time for the spell. I reached for the heavy grimoire I had brought in from the library, but a sudden flurry of wings in the window forced me back.

"Dog!"

I brought a hand to my heart as the crow found his footing. I had not been expecting visitors. Once I had recovered myself, I fixed the bird in my sights. "I suppose Gideon sent you?"

He didn't answer. Not that I had really expected him to.

"Okay, you can stay, but—"

I yelped and clutched my chest again as a furry set of claws impaled the bottom ledge of the window frame.

"Faustus?"

The cat pulled himself up on the sill beside Dog. They gave each other filthy looks, but then settled in, and turned their attention to me.

Wasn't this just terrific. It looked like I was going to

have an audience for my first magical performance in, well, forever.

"Right. Fine. You both can stay, but you have to be quiet."

Silence.

"Glad we're agreed."

I opened the grimoire and flipped the pages.

I knew the spell was in here somewhere. I could almost see it in my mind's eye. It was on the right-hand side of the page, and the edges were bordered with a string of hand-drawn fires. Because grimoires were often personal collections of spells, they didn't usually have a table of contents, but, really, that was something the witching community needed to work on.

Then again, I could just use magic to find it.

There was a time when my skills were so honed, I could have just snapped my fingers, and the book would have opened to the right page. Or I could have called on the night wind to flip through the pages for me until the right one was found. I almost thought about giving it a try, but my neglected skills were not sharp, and I didn't want anything to go wrong before the main event.

I turned page after page by hand until I finally found it.

"There you are."

Wildfyre Magick.

I traced the words written in calligraphy with my fingertips. When it came to spells, everything needed to be done with care, even the way an incantation was written. For those of us not artistically inclined, it was one of the hardest skills to master. It required so much patience. But most witches believed *the powers that be* were pleased when great pains were taken to make the words on the page a thing of beauty, and it never hurt to have the powers in a good mood.

I read over the words in front of me. The spell had both a potion component and an incantation, but neither was overly complicated. It certainly shouldn't test the limits of my abilities. At least my past abilities.

I could do this.

I had to. My family needed me.

I bent down to retrieve Adam's old Bunsen burner from underneath the table. The last thing I needed for the spell. I blew the dust from it and connected it to the line coming from the wall, being careful to avoid the candles. I then clicked on the gas and cracked the flint lighter above the shooting stream. Faustus hissed when the flame came to life.

"Sorry," I murmured, fiddling with the gear at the base of the jet.

The cat merely licked his paw in response.

I slid the burner to the midpoint of the table, then carefully lowered the cooking platform over the top of the flame. Next came the copper pot I had taken from the kitchen. I gingerly placed it on top of the setup, taking time to make sure it was centered. Spilled milk may not be a big deal, but spilled potions were never advisable.

I stood back to admire my handiwork.

Perfect.

Using a Bunsen burner wasn't the most romantic way to cook up a spell, but it would have to do. I wasn't about to use the giant cauldron Nora kept hidden in the greenhouse. The only place big enough to operate it was the firepit in the backyard, and Mr. Henderson might be on the lookout. That would really send him over the edge.

I set to grinding the necessary herbs for the spell together with a mortar and pestle, and it didn't take long for them to react to one another. A strange pungent smell came swirling up to my nose. Charcoal, smoke, and just a hint of sulfur. Again, perfect. Next, I needed something to represent the Graves family. I pulled a hair from the comb Constance had used, then wrapped it around a dried twig I found in one of Nora's many jars. It was from an arborvitae tree, Latin for the tree of life. In this case, though, it would stand in for a family tree. I placed the herbs and twig into the mini cauldron. Now I needed a base. It could be water, but for this particular spell I had something better. The half a bottle of prune juice. The last glass from it had been served to Constance. Symbolism was always good in spellcasting. I dumped the contents into the pot and cranked up the flame.

A new acrid stench rose up from the brew. Burnt prunes. Not the most pleasant aroma, but then this wasn't one of Izzy's spells. Darker magic usually was more pungent.

I wasn't the only one put off by the scent because the instant my spoon touched the potion to mix it together, Faustus sneezed, making Dog jump.

I hid a smile.

The potion would need a couple of minutes to simmer, so I sat down to practice the spell. Apart from the title, the words had been updated to modern English, but it was still best to go over them a few times to avoid any mistakes.

About ten minutes later, I gave the bubbling stew a sniff, then drained it through a sieve into a mason jar.

"There," I said, planting my hands on my hips. "That part wasn't so hard."

Dog let out a noisy caw.

"I know I'm not done." I frowned at the bird. "I'm just working myself up to the next part."

I let the potion cool in the glass for a minute or two before picking it up.

"Okay." I plugged my nose. "Here goes nothing."

I tossed the contents into my mouth and swallowed hard. The liquid burned a path down to my stomach.

"Gah." My body shuddered. "Done."

Faustus and Dog looked at me skeptically.

"Don't worry. This next part will be far more impressive." I rubbed my hands together. Time for the incantation.

"Here we go," I said, giving my audience a wink before closing my eyes.

I had been expecting to feel a tingling of magic running through my veins at this point, but seeing as I could crack concrete without feeling anything, I wasn't too concerned.

I clenched my fists by my sides, then cast out the words of the invocation.

> *Winds of night, winds of night,*
> *Stoke the fire, blind the sight,*
> *Fuel the rumors, real or not,*
> *Grow the fear in every Graves heart.*
> *Blaze the panic, force the fear,*
> *Drive out the culpable, bring them near.*
> *In the mind horrid fascinations churn*
> *In the wildfire the guilty burn.*

I opened my eyes.

A literal cricket sounded in the corner of the garage.

Huh.

Dog, Faustus, and I exchanged looks.

Normally with these types of spells something happened right away. I had assumed a telltale rush of power would automatically surge through my body and out into the world. But that certainly hadn't happened.

I frowned. I had done the spell correctly. I was sure of it.

Granted, I didn't have the help of a coven. But that shouldn't matter for this. I used to be able to handle far more powerful spells.

Of course, once again, the key phrase was *used to*.

No, I needed to give it some time. The spell would work.

Just as I had the thought, out of nowhere, a hot gust of wind hit my shoulders, jolting my body forward, and sending my arms flying back.

I caught myself before I hit the ground, then spun around looking for the source, but there was nothing to see. Everything was still. In fact, the punch of wind had come and gone so quickly it was almost like it had never happened.

The only clue left behind was the fur on Faustus's back. It was standing straight up.

"That was unexpected."

The cat gave me a sideways look.

"I'm sure it's fine. Whatever that was, it's gone."

Suddenly, the wind gusted again, sending me spinning in a complete circle. When it stopped, I stood frozen in front of the worktable, arms out for balance.

Both Dog and Faustus looked quite concerned now.

I dropped my arms. "Okay, that too was strange. But you saw me do the spell. It went off without a hitch." I had barely gotten the words out when a scorching heat enveloped my feet. It felt like I had been dropped barefoot into blistering hot sand. But there was no sand, and I was not barefoot. The heat was purely magical.

I could see the wind this time. It was circling my boots, and along with the dust and dirt it had stirred up from the floor, it was streaked with angry-looking flames.

I blinked. Hmm, a tiny tornado with flaming, mystical winds. The grimoire hadn't mentioned that as a possibility. A footnote might have been nice.

But I could deal with this. What kind of witch was I if I couldn't handle a little heat? I just needed to think this through.

Except thinking became almost impossible when the current of fire spinning around me swirled in on itself, tightening and changing its shape. Now it had a sharp peak at its front directing its course.

A part of me was still clinging to the hope everything was fine, but I knew that wasn't the case.

The blazing stream of air circled round and round me, looking like it would never stop, but then it flipped up from the ground and zipped through the air like a rocket. For a moment I worried it would escape the confines of the garage, but, after making one final pass around the room, the sizzling ribbon dropped into a nosedive, headed directly for my feet.

Oh dear.

I let out a squeak as the wind funneled into my toes, racing up my legs into the rest of my body. I tried to breathe, but couldn't manage anything more than the tiniest gasp of air.

This was wrong. Very wrong.

The whole purpose of a spell was to harmoniously bond a witch with her magic for a joint cause. Nothing about this felt harmonious.

I knew something had to give as my arms and head flung back in a futile attempt to make more room for the power swirling inside me, but I didn't know what that something was until my feet left the floor.

Uh-oh.

Dog and Faustus stared at me with impossibly wide eyes as I rose into the air, higher and higher, until I stopped a few feet off the ground, boots dangling.

The blistering hot wind churned and roiled inside me. Then, just when I thought I couldn't take it anymore, the magic exploded out, hurtling a blast of searing air in all directions. A second later, I dropped to the floor.

Faustus's ears flattened against his head, and Dog skittered about on the window ledge as the wind rushed past, extinguishing the candles.

I jumped up and ran over to the worktable, blinking in the darkness. "You guys okay?"

Dog let out a muted caw while Faustus shot me a horrifically dirty look before settling into what I knew would be a very thorough bath.

"I'm so sorry. I don't know what happened."

Dog tilted his head, looking concerned.

"I'm sure it's fine," I said, fumbling to shut off the gas. My fingers were a little shaky. "Granted, it didn't go exactly as expected, but I think my magic was just trying to make a point. The spell should be back on track now."

Dog cawed.

"No, I mean it. It's all good." I turned quickly and stumbled over an old paint can, triggering the bird to flap his wings in alarm.

"Really. You don't have to worry." I picked my way over to the front of the garage, pushed open the refinished carriage house doors, and then grabbed the handlebars of the bicycle leaning against the wall. "Everything is under control."

Faustus, who had his face deeply buried in his chest, looked up at me, tongue still hanging out of his mouth.

"Yeah, I don't believe me either." I swung a leg over my bicycle. I pressed down on the pedal and hopped up onto the seat.

Hopefully my spell hadn't gotten too much of a head start.

Chapter 34

THE FROSTY NIGHT air cooled my cheeks as I sped over the darkened streets, my scarf trailing behind me. I tried to stave off the sinking feeling in the pit of my stomach, but I didn't have much success.

Gideon had tried to warn me. For months I had pushed away my powers. What did I expect to happen? My behavior went against everything I had been raised to believe. Magic was a gift, not an entitlement.

In my defense, though, everything had happened so fast. The town hall. Nora's confession about Liz's father. The police coming to the door. I had turned to magic because that's what I had always done. But how had Gideon put it? That what I had done was like asking a friend for money after years of not speaking? I hadn't seen it that way. In all honesty, ever since Adam's death, I felt like my magic owed me.

I squeezed the grips of my handlebars. Was that true? Did I really feel like my magic *owed* me? I was still angry *the powers that be* hadn't helped me save my husband's life, but that had never been promised. That wasn't part of the deal.

I pushed the thoughts away. I couldn't think about this now. I had to stay focused. I had set something in motion tonight, and now I had to see it through.

I glided over the pavement, lit up in the glow of the nearly full moon. My heart pounded at the base of my throat, quickening with every turn of my bicycle's wheels. I didn't slow my pace until I reached Liz's street. I had looked up her address online. Fingers crossed this is where my spell had ended up. And, hopefully, it was in a more cooperative mood.

Under other circumstances, I would have enjoyed the sleepy feel of the neighborhood. It wasn't hard to picture the people who owned these homes, inside, tucked snug in their beds. But these were not normal circumstances, and I could only imagine what the dreams of all those sleeping people would be like if they knew there was a witch riding through their neighborhood chasing a rogue spell designed to stir up a killer.

I stayed on the opposite side of the street, tracking the house numbers until I reached 36 Maplewood Lane.

Liz's house.

I got off my bike and guided it over to a small cluster of trees. I wasn't sure what the spell would drive Liz to do, if anything at all, but I knew I'd have a hard time staying hidden with my bike. Once I had it tucked away, I crept back up to the road, being careful to stick to the shadows. I chose a lookout spot beside a tall lilac bush. The shrub had dropped its leaves, leaving nothing but a tangled mess of gnarled branches to cozy up against.

All the lights were out in the small bungalow across the street.

Nothing to do now but wait.

Fifteen agonizing minutes passed.

With every second that ticked by, my fears grew. Maybe

I had chosen the wrong Graves family member to watch. Maybe I should have gone to the orchard. Maybe my spell hadn't worked at all. Or maybe it was wreaking havoc in another part of town while I waited here wringing my hands.

Suddenly a light clicked on in Liz's house.

My breath caught in my throat.

The spell was taking effect! It had to be. My magic had taken pity on me after all.

And yes, it had taken some time, but, really, that's how the spell was supposed to work. Slowly. Insidiously. It's like those times when you're lying snug in bed, and suddenly you think, *Did I turn off the stove?* or *Did I lock the front door?* The thought is easily dismissed at first, but then it niggles at you until you can't fight it any longer. It's easier just to get up and check. I could only imagine how much worse the compulsion would be for someone who had done something truly awful and believed they were on the brink of being caught.

I stared at the house like a cat watching a mouse hole. Seconds later another light came on. This one lighting up the big bay window at the front of the bungalow.

The view was obscured by gauzy curtains, but I could see the silhouette of a person behind it, pacing from one side of the room to the other.

After four or five passes, the figure stopped, then walked up to the window, pulled back the curtain ever so slightly, and peered outside.

Liz.

I couldn't see her face clearly, but the rigidity of her posture and the quickness of her movements had me convinced she was feeling the effects of the spell. But feeling the effects was one thing, acting on them was another entirely. I needed her to show me evidence of her wrongdoing, to lead me to a clue that would unravel this mess. I needed something concrete.

Suddenly, Liz let the curtain drop back in place. A moment later the lights clicked off.

No! She couldn't be going back to bed. The spell should be too powerful for her to resist it that easily. All my earlier doubts came roaring back, but then the lights mounted on either side of the front door flickered to life.

I let go of a shaky breath and steeled my nerves.

Now wasn't the time for doubts. I had to be ready. This next part could be tricky. Liz might take her car, and if she did, I'd have to grab my bike. As long as she stayed in town, I should be able to keep sight of her. But I didn't think that would happen. If Liz was smart, she would choose to walk to wherever it was she was going. It was easier to stay hidden that way.

Minutes later, Liz came out, dressed all in black. She hurried down her driveway to the sidewalk. I didn't move. I wanted to give her a head start. Not so far that I would lose her if she ducked off the road, but just far enough that she wouldn't be able to sense me following behind her. She crossed the street, getting a little closer to my hiding spot than I would have liked, then turned toward town.

I waited, every muscle tense. Once she was far enough ahead, I hurried out to the sidewalk and—

—someone grabbed my arm.

It took everything in me not to scream, but when I turned and saw who was there, the shock was so great, I don't think I could have mustered the breath to yell even if I wanted to. "Gideon?"

"Fire," he gasped.

He was clearly winded. He must have run all the way here.

"What?"

"Fire," he said, shaking my arm as though that would clear up the confusion.

I looked around. "Fire? What fire?"

"You. Spell."

"Where? At the B&B?!"

"No," he gasped, putting all of his weight on the staff he had gripped in his hand. He then pointed a finger in the direction of Liz's house. "There!"

A tiny fire sprung up on the front lawn of the small bungalow. It was only the size of a pear, but it glowed an unnaturally bright shade of orange.

"What? I don't understand. What's happened?"

"You. Spell. Fires."

"Fires?"

"Yes. They're—"

The small fire on the lawn suddenly jumped in size.

"—everywhere."

Chapter 35

"OH NO. OH no. Oh no."

I ran across the street and stamped on the little fire. Thankfully it went out almost immediately.

But then it popped up again a few feet away!

I ran over and stomped it out too.

I waited almost a full minute to see if it would spring back to life, but nothing happened.

"Okay," I shout-whispered back to Gideon. "I think we're good."

Suddenly the tiny fire sprouted up again not far from my feet, and, I swear, something about the way the flames were dancing, that little fire was laughing at me!

"I have to go," Gideon called out. "There's more on the other side of town. You stay on that one. It's the ringleader."

"What's happening? I don't understand."

"Your spell touched everyone," he said, waving his hands out. "Lots of guilt."

My eyes widened as I looked around the darkened streets. "But I did it just on the Graves family."

"Too much power built up inside of you." My uncle took a deep, deep breath. "I'm really out of shape."

"Gideon, I'm so sorry. I was upset after the police came, and—"

He pointed at the little fire growing at my feet with his staff. I stomped it out. Only to have it, once again, pop up a little distance away. "Don't let that one get out of control. I'll put out the rest, and then it will be easier to stop it. We'll meet at the town square."

"Wait, what? The town square? When? What if I'm still following this one?"

Gideon shot me a pointed look.

"Right. You had a vision."

"Actually," my uncle said, "it wasn't quite a vision. I had been writing haikus when I noticed they were all about you and fires and—we don't have time for this! Go!" My uncle rushed away into the darkness, his staff propelling him along.

This was bad. This was very bad.

I raced over to the little fire and once again stomped it out, casting a look up the street.

No sign of Liz.

Everything in me wanted to race after her. The spell *had* worked. Maybe just a little too well. Obviously, my magic and I still had some issues to work out.

The fire popped up again.

I watched the small flames swell to the size of a pumpkin. The fire danced and twirled and then, unbelievably, it somehow grew two little flame hands, which it planted on its two little flame hips, and it waggled at me. Like it was mocking me!

"Why you little . . ." I ran over and jumped on it with two feet, letting out a small shout of frustration.

The fire popped up again a moment later, and this time, instead of dancing, it gave me a cheeky little wink.

THE LITTLE FIRE kept me busy for at least half an hour. Every time I stamped it out, it popped back up. It never seemed to tire. In fact, it seemed to be having a wonderful time hopping from house to house, leading me around town like some sort of blazing Pied Piper.

I was so focused on the fire, afraid I'd lose sight of it, I didn't even realize it when I reached the town square, not until I heard the clack of a wooden staff hitting the pavement behind me.

"Gideon, please tell me you were able to get all the fires out."

He nodded and came to stand beside me. We both looked down at the small fire swirling just before the steps of the town gazebo. "Now it's time to take care of this one."

The fire looked back at us suspiciously.

"I keep stomping on it, but it just pops back up."

"Mm-hmm," Gideon said. "I think we need another approach." My uncle muttered something under his breath, then hit the sidewalk with his staff.

A second later, a raindrop hit my nose. Then another.

I looked back down at the little fire still shining brightly until a small downpour fell directly on its head.

The fire crackled and spit, then let out a noise that sounded an awful lot like a disappointed *aww* before vanishing in a puff of smoke.

"I guess that takes care of that."

I looked at my uncle. "Couldn't we just have started with the rain?"

Gideon's eyes widened. "No, we could not. I had to make sure all the other fires were completely out first, or this one never would have extinguished. Are you really questioning my methods right now?"

"No, no," I said, shaking my head. "Definitely not."

Gideon harrumphed, then looked me over. "Have you experienced any consequences?"

"You mean other than nearly burning Evenfall to the ground?"

He nodded.

"No. I think I'm fine."

"Hopefully the powers that be are satisfied with the chaos you've put us through." My uncle suddenly frowned at me. "What could you possibly be smiling about?"

I let out a bewildered laugh. "I know. I know. I shouldn't be smiling. Things are bad. So bad. Izzy and Nora are at the police station. Constance's murderer is still roaming free. I created a sentient fire." That one was particularly bad. "But, Gideon," I said, blinking at my uncle, "you're outside."

He shot me a sideways look and made a *hmm* sound. "I didn't have much choice, did I?"

"And I am so, so sorry for that."

He frowned again. "Do I even want to know what you were thinking?"

I sighed and let my shoulders drop. "I'd tell you, but I don't quite understand it myself. Actually, I don't understand any decisions I've been making lately. None of it makes sense." I looked away, brushing the raindrops from my cheeks.

My uncle's voice softened as he said, "Brynn, it's okay. It's okay to feel confused. It's okay to feel lost. It's okay to *feel*."

I shook my head.

"You know if anyone can appreciate your pain, it's me."

I knew that was true. Gideon had *seen* the accident that killed my parents and his fiancée. They were on their way to a friend's wedding, and he was supposed to meet them there. The groom had forgotten the rings at his house, and Gideon had gone to pick them up. Once he had retrieved them, he had the vision. My mother's VW Beetle colliding with a truck.

He tried to make it to them in time, to stop any of it from happening, but it was too late.

Izzy once told me Lydia was still alive when he got there, and that he was able to hold her as she passed. She believed that was why he had been granted the vision, but for Gideon, that wasn't enough.

"Giving up magic was never the answer, you know," my uncle said gently. "In fact, I don't think there is just one answer. It's a process, and you're not meant to do it alone."

I raised an eyebrow.

He chuckled. "You look just like your aunt Nora, you know that?" His smile faded a moment later. "You know what got me through losing your parents and Lydia?"

I waited.

"It was your aunts. They stood by me. I was miserable, much worse than I am now, for a very long time, and they were grieving too, and taking care of you, but they still had the strength to support me. They are incredibly strong women. If you don't think they can handle what you're feeling, you're wrong."

"It's not that I don't think they can handle what I'm feeling." I looked up at the sky. The cloud Gideon created blocked the stars. "It's me. I'm the one who can't handle it."

"You can," he said, his voice uncharacteristically firm. "I know you don't believe that, but it's true. And it's time you started wanting more for yourself than mere existence."

I shot him an uncertain look.

He held up his hands. "I know. I know. I'm not one to talk. But you deserve a full life."

"So do you, Gideon." The corners of my mouth twisted into a smile. "And, again, look. You're outside."

His eyes sparkled as the last few drops of rain fell around us. "I am. I am outside."

"It feels good, doesn't it?"

His chest swelled as he took in a long, slow breath. "It feels wonderful."

We smiled at each other for a second before my uncle's face dropped.

"Gideon? What is it? Are you having another vision?"

"No, but I am seeing something." He pointed his staff in the direction of the town buildings.

I couldn't figure out what had him so transfixed at first, but then I spotted movement. It was a person. A person climbing out of one of the windows of the records building.

Wait. Was that Liz?

Chapter 36

I'D HAD THE thought too late.

She was too far away. I couldn't be sure.

I debated making a run for her, but the building was right beside the woods that ran along the Blackstone River. She'd see me coming. I'd never get there before she lost me in the trees. But I had to know! I had to know if it was Liz.

"Gideon," I said, clutching my uncle's arm. "We need to do something. I think that's Liz Coleman, but I can't be sure. We need a spell."

My uncle's brow furrowed. I could tell he wasn't following. "A spell?" He looked back over to the building, piecing it all together. "I don't know," he stammered. "I'd need to think about it."

"We don't have time!"

I searched Gideon's face, but I could see he was at a loss, just like I was.

The person in the distance dropped from the window ledge to the ground. Time was running out.

Think, Brynn. Think.

Nora needs you.

Suddenly a memory of Nora popped into my head. Nora in her floppy hat and sundress. Nora laughing. Nora swirling me in the air, saying, *You, Brynn Warren, are my kind of witch.*

That was it!

"Gideon! The children's rhyme. The one that trips people. You need to do it."

My uncle stared at me, dumbfounded.

"You know the one. You have to say it."

He shook his head.

"I can't do it," I said. "My magic is too unstable."

"You can do this." Gideon grabbed my hand. "You're not alone this time."

I stared at my uncle, willing his certainty into my heart, then closed my eyes.

"Bumps and lumps, stumbles divine." A familiar tingling sensation ran up my arm from Gideon's hand. *"Trip up anyone from the Graves bloodline."*

My eyes flew open and narrowed in on the person about to disappear into the forest.

I could see the magic of my words rippling over the tips of the wet grass.

The figure was almost at the tree line when—

—she tripped!

I let out a little shout of victory.

It was Liz. It had to be. She recovered almost immediately, disappearing into the cover of the forest, but I knew it was her.

I spun around to face my uncle, a huge smile on my face. "You did that, didn't you? I felt that tingle up my arm."

My uncle beamed back at me. "I may have given you a push, but, otherwise, that was all you, my dear. All you."

BRYNN!"

Was that someone calling my name? It was coming from so far away, and I was very tired.

"Brynn!"

I was dreaming it. No one was calling me.

I jolted at the sound of a bunch of little somethings hitting the window behind my chair. Pebbles? I straightened up, blinking in the sunlight filling the loft.

"Don't make me climb these stairs. Rise and shine!"

I knew that voice.

I pulled the blanket from my lap. I must have fallen asleep in my armchair last night. After what happened in town, Gideon and I had headed home. Izzy and Nora had left a message on the B&B's machine saying they were fine. Well, Izzy actually left the message while Nora muttered indecipherable threats in the background. The police hadn't gotten around to questioning them, and while they were technically allowed to leave, their lawyer thought it would show good faith if they stayed. After that, I made myself a cup of tea, intending to puzzle out why Liz would be breaking into the records building, but all the excitement must have been too much for me.

I wrapped the blanket around my shoulders, and I pushed myself to my feet. It felt way too early for this. I stepped into my slippers, stumbled over to the door, and forced myself outside onto the landing. I grabbed the railing and looked down.

"There she is!"

I brought a hand up to shield the glaring sunlight from my eyes, but the brilliant sparkle coming from Roxie's long boho jacket was nearly as blinding. "What are you doing here?"

"I've got news! News that you're going to want to hear."

All the memories of the town hall came flooding back. I sighed. Roxie's *news* had not been all that useful so far. In fact, it had hurt a lot more than it had helped.

"Just hear me out, Brynn. I feel terrible about last night. I've come to make good."

I climbed down the stairs. "I don't blame you, Roxie. You told me you were speculating. I knew it was all," I paused, searching for the right word, "conjecture."

"Listen to you sounding like Beatty. You wouldn't believe the talking to he gave me last night. I think he'd cut me off entirely if we weren't related. Turns out Constance had been by to talk about some permit issues she was having with the house. Those were the affairs she needed to get in order. Although given how she said it, I don't see how I can be blamed."

We might have to agree to disagree on that point.

"But listen, now I have something that really might help you and your aunts."

I rubbed a hand over my face. "Let's hear it."

"Would it kill you to show a little enthusiasm?"

I shot Roxie a warning look.

"Okay. Okay. So last night, someone," she paused dramatically, flashing me a knowing smile, "broke into the town records building."

Apparently, I wasn't awake enough to realize I needed to register some surprise.

"Is this thing on?" Roxie tapped an invisible microphone. "I thought that would have garnered some reaction."

I blinked. I really needed to step up my cover story game. "Sorry. I haven't had my coffee yet. Why would someone break into the town records building?"

Unperturbed by my lack of reaction, Roxie pressed on. "At first, I, along with everyone else, thought it had to be kids. Vandalism maybe. But then I remembered something."

I waited for her to go on. I wasn't in the mood to beg for information we both knew she was dying to give.

"Well, hearing what happened reminded me of a juicy little story I picked up not too long ago. I probably shouldn't say *juicy*, given all that's happened, but it does involve grown women behaving badly, and we all know how entertaining that can be."

"Which women?"

"Liz Coleman and Joanne Simpson."

I frowned. "Joanne Simpson?" She had passed recently from an aneurysm. I suppose it wasn't surprising I had a keen knowledge of everyone who passed away in town. I never missed reading the obituaries. I couldn't help but feel guilty every time I did, but I couldn't seem to stop either.

"That's right. Do you know where Joanne worked before she passed?"

Suddenly, I found my interest piqued despite my initial skepticism. "She worked for the town, didn't she?"

"That's right. In the *records* department. Anyway," Roxie said, leaning in, "the way I heard it, Liz came in one day and gave Joanne a really hard time requesting to view some sort of paperwork. Marilyn over at the hair studio said it was quite the squabble. Liz yelled something about not caring who owned what, and that she was a Graves and had every right to see what it was she was looking for."

"What was it? What was she looking for?"

"I don't know, but apparently she eventually got to see whatever it was, and she went ballistic."

I squinted. "Ballistic?"

"Flipped over a pencil holder. Sent the pencils flying everywhere."

It didn't sound like much, but for Evenfall that was a pretty big deal.

"It has to mean something, don't you think? Granted, after such a public spat, it's hard to believe Liz would go back to the scene of the crime, as it were, but it can't be a coincidence."

"Huh." Actually, I didn't find it all that surprising, given the spell I had cast. "That is interesting."

Roxie gave me an uncertain look. I could tell she was disappointed by my reaction, but after last night's excitement had worn off, I realized that without the will as motive, I didn't have a whole lot to go on. The fight at the records building was interesting, but it wasn't exactly a smoking gun.

"I hate seeing you so worried. I wish there was more I could do." Roxie patted my arm, then looked up at the B&B.

In the brilliant sunshine, Ivywood Hollow looked almost like a dollhouse with its tower, gables, and gingerbread trim.

After a quiet moment passed, Roxie mused, "It's just so crazy to think about, isn't it? Someone getting in like that?"

I nodded. "It all happened so quickly. The killer had to be someone who'd visited the house before." I wrapped my arms around my waist. "Which goes against any theory it was a Graves family member. I don't think any of the siblings or Liz have been inside."

"Oh, well, I can solve that mystery for you."

I looked back at Roxie.

"Graves House has an almost identical layout to Ivywood Hollow."

"What?"

"They did have the same architect," she said, still studying the house. "I've been in both. And while Ivywood has a few extra bells and whistles, in terms of structure, they're mirror images."

That would explain how the killer knew how to find the hidden staircase, if one of Constance's relatives was in fact responsible.

"Anyway, I should get going," she said, patting my arm again. "Let me know if there's anything else I can do."

I knew Roxie was disappointed. She had been so excited to share her news. And I wanted to make her feel better about the situation, but I didn't know how. I couldn't pretend the circumstances were anything but what they were.

I wrapped the blanket more tightly about my shoulders as Roxie ambled down the driveway.

I was just about to go back inside when the strangest feeling came over me.

It was a beautiful day. Nothing appeared out of place. But all of the sudden, I felt vulnerable. Exposed.

Like someone was watching me.

I looked up and down the street. I couldn't see anyone, aside from Roxie.

Huh.

I stifled a yawn. It had been a late night. I was probably imagining it.

Instead of heading back over to the garage, I decided to go into the B&B. Now that I was up, I could at least get some coffee ready for when Nora and Izzy came home.

The silence waiting for me inside wasn't exactly welcoming. The house felt so different without my aunts there. They both had such a life force, it felt empty without them.

Just then I felt something brush against my legs. I smiled. Of course, the place wasn't completely empty.

I bent to scratch Faustus behind the ears. He wasn't normally one to ask for attention. It was especially unusual given how disappointed he had been in me the night before.

"Things aren't right, are they?"

The cat gave me a slow blink.

I straightened back up. "You must be hungry. Why don't we go see what Izzy has for your breakf—"

A loud bang tore through the still house.

I jolted so hard the blanket wrapped around my shoulders fell to the ground. "What was that?" I looked at Faustus, but he wasn't looking at me. His wide eyes were focused on the landing at the top of the stairs.

I let go of the breath I was holding.

Constance. She was banging the closet door again.

I planted my hands on my hips. Izzy had said they had examined the closet, but it seemed to me, it was time I checked it out for myself.

I laid a hand on the bannister and brought one foot up to

rest on the bottom step. I looked back at the cat. "You coming?" He looked at me but didn't move. If I had to guess, he wasn't going anywhere that didn't lead directly to the kitchen. "I'll take that as a no."

I climbed the stairs, my movements swirling dust motes in the rays of morning sun. Once I made it to the top, I walked carefully toward the closet, almost tiptoeing. I felt a little silly creeping along the hallway of my family home, but I couldn't stop myself. I knew I wasn't alone. If I had to put money on it, I was willing to bet the spirit of our deceased guest was hovering right behind me.

"Okay, Constance," I whispered once I reached the closet. "Let's see what you've got for me."

I pulled the door open.

Nothing. Empty shelves from top to bottom.

I shouldn't have been surprised. Again, Izzy told me they had emptied the closet, but knowing that didn't prevent the disappointment from welling up inside of me. And I knew I wasn't the only one feeling that way.

The hair at the back of my neck prickled with a wave of frustration that wasn't my own.

Now what?

I stepped in closer to the little cupboard and ran my hand over the flat, honey-colored wood of the nearest shelf noting its smooth feel. I couldn't help but admire the artisanship. The closet had been handmade. Its planks were seamlessly aligned, and each shelf was perfectly distanced from the next. Unfortunately, the careful design also made it clear there were no clues here waiting to be found, just a faint scent of potpourri.

"I'm sorry, Constance," I said out loud. "I don't get it."

Maybe she was just frustrated her killer hadn't been found, and this was the only way she could express it?

"I know you must be upset. I'm doing everything I can. Could you maybe give me another clue?"

Bang!

The closet door had swung shut again, barely missing my nose.

"Okay," I said, blinking. "I'm not sure how much that helps."

I stared at the closet a little longer before opening it again. I gave it another search, then threw my hands in the air. "I'm sorry, but there's nothing in there."

Bang!

To me that bang almost sounded like she was saying, *Exactly!*

"So you know there's nothing in there. So maybe the closet is a symbol for something else?"

Silence.

"Okay, not a symbol."

A closet with nothing in it. A closet with nothing in it.

Nope. That wasn't helping.

I chewed on the side of my thumbnail. Most closets did have something in them, and Constance wanted me to find something. Maybe that was it? I had been thinking Constance was trying to lead us to a physical clue her killer had left behind, but what if that wasn't the case? What if Constance was trying to lead me to something of hers? But Constance's things weren't here. I mean, of course they weren't here. This wasn't her house.

My breath caught. What had Roxie just said?

"Graves House has an almost identical layout to Ivywood Hollow." I mumbled the words out loud without meaning to.

Bang! Bang! Bang!

"Graves House has the same layout as Ivywood Hollow!"

Bang!Bang!Bang!Bang!

"You want me to look in the closet at Graves House!"

There were too many bangs to count after that.

Of course that's what she wanted! Why hadn't I seen it before?

But I hadn't, and if Roxie hadn't have come by . . .

Oh no.

I raced down the stairs and out the front door.

I sprinted for the sidewalk, as best I could in my slippers.

I hadn't exactly been overjoyed to see my old dance instructor even though she had gone out of her way to bring me information to make up for what had been a fairly honest mistake. And while I already knew most of what she had come to tell me, by pure fluke, she had given me the very thing I needed to solve another piece of the puzzle!

And I hadn't even thanked her.

Most people would be long gone by now, but I knew Roxie was a slow walker, always stopping to smell the roses.

"Roxie!"

She had made it pretty far up the street, but she still heard me. As she turned, I shouted, "I forgot to tell you something!"

"What is it?" she shouted back.

"Thank you! Thank you so much!"

I could just make out the confused looked on her face. "Wait. Did I make good?"

"Did you make good?" I shouted back. "Roxie," I threw my hands wide in the air, "you're a star!"

She laughed and threw a *get out of here* hand at me before wiggling her hips and turning in a sparkling pirouette.

I shot her a wave and ran back up the driveway.

There was so much I needed to do. I needed a plan. I couldn't just walk over to Graves House and break in in broad daylight. I needed to wait until dark. And I needed to choose an appropriate breaking-and-entering outfit. Oh! And I would need a spell to open any locked doors. I'd have to talk to Gideon about that. I also needed to—

Uh-oh.

There was something I needed to do before I did any of those things.

I skidded back into the B&B to find a very annoyed-looking cat waiting for me.

"Sorry! Sorry."

Faustus turned and walked toward the kitchen, his fluffy tail sticking straight up in the air.

I had so many things I needed to do, but feeding the cat breakfast definitely came first.

E VEN THOUGH I was wearing gloves, my hands felt icy as I, once again, rode through the dark streets of Evenfall on my bicycle. But while the night was cold, the sky was clear, and the pavement shone under the streetlamps.

Izzy and Nora still hadn't returned home by the time I had left. I didn't like at all what that might mean. I could only hope whatever I found tonight would put an end to this once and for all.

As I glided onto Constance's street, I immediately picked up on the familiar feel of its layout. It was just like ours. The same wide road. The same tall trees. The same beautiful old homes.

Well, the same beautiful old homes with the exception of Graves House.

Despite all the comparisons to Ivywood Hollow, I could already see the houses had gone in two very different directions.

I had to use all of my strength to get up the hill to reach Constance's home. Where our street ended, hers carried on up a fairly short, but steep, slope. The exertion left me struggling to catch my breath, but when I made it to the top and finally got my first real look at the house, I found it difficult to breathe for entirely different reasons.

From town the house still looked stately, its battle scars softened by distance. But up here, bathed in moonlight, I couldn't help but think Nora had been right. It looked every bit like a haunted house.

The design had so much in common with the B&B—the

side tower and gables, the tall windows on every floor, the wraparound porch that hugged the lower level—all of it was the same. Sadly, the similarities only served to highlight the decay of Graves House. It was in a terrible state. The shingles on the roof were curled and battered, and the paint had peeled in too many places to count. Most disheartening for me, though, was the porch. It had completely caved in on one side, ruining the beautiful lines of the lower level. If the structure had fallen apart due to lack of funds, that would have been one thing, but to let it rot out of pure spite, that was something else entirely.

I found it hard to believe Constance had actually been living here. I eyed the blue tarp flapping against one of the outer walls. It was the only sign the place hadn't been abandoned.

As I sat balancing on my bike, taking in the pitiable sight, a disturbing sensation came over me. All of a sudden, I felt quite certain I wasn't just staring at the house; the house was staring back at me.

The feelings I was picking up on were not welcoming, and they made me wonder if Graves House had somehow taken on some of its mistress's bitterness and made it its own. I'd certainly heard tales of stranger things.

I shook off the sensation.

I had a job to do.

I tucked my bike away in the ditch on the opposite side of the street, grabbed the flashlight from my jacket pocket, and hurried back up to the road.

When I made it halfway across the street, I stopped short.

There it was again. That feeling like I was being watched. And not by the house this time.

My heart pounded in my chest. I looked around but couldn't see anyone.

I frowned. It was probably just the circumstances getting to me. There was definitely something about sneaking around at night, trying to break into someone else's house, that could put a witch on edge.

I crept up to the foot of the porch and climbed the creaky steps, hoping they wouldn't cave beneath my feet. I then reached for the handle on the front door and gave it a turn.

Locked.

No surprise there.

I had spent the later part of the afternoon with Gideon, going over what to do in this particular scenario. While I wanted to believe all my magic issues had been sorted after the events of the previous night, I couldn't be sure. So, Gideon and I had practiced an unlocking finger charm. We practiced it over and over as though I were a witchling again. I had been hoping Gideon might come with me tonight, but I think he was overwhelmed by everything I had already put him through. On the bright side, he hadn't had any more dire visions. At least not any he was willing to share. So that was something.

I put my flashlight between my knees and rubbed my hands together to warm my fingers.

I could do this. Just a few quick movements with my hands and the lock should click open. I took a deep breath and closed my eyes.

Snap with one hand. Snap with the other. Double tap the left fist with the right and flip both palms open to the sky.

I had not heard a click.

I opened my eyes and tried the door handle anyway. Still locked.

It was probably just the pressure of the moment. Another try should do the trick.

Snap. Snap. Double tap. Flip.

Nothing.

Okay, they do say the third time's a charm.

Snap. Snap. Double tap. Flip.

Still nothing.

"Oh, come on," I muttered. Yes, I had neglected my powers, but I had learned my lesson! At least I thought I had. My magic, apparently, was still a little miffed.

I took another breath before trying again. This time I muttered the words as I performed the actions, "Snap. Snap. Double tap. Fl—"

"What are you doing?"

Chapter 37

I SPUN AROUND AND pressed my back against the door. I may have also screamed a little.

Once I was certain I had not in fact had a heart attack, I was able to stammer, "It's you." Oh yes, I knew the girl in front of me. There was no mistaking that bright pink hair. The earrings were different though. Tonight, they were in the shape of cats with their backs arched. I couldn't remember her name though. The fright must have startled it right out of me. "Hi, you."

"Nixie," she said, an amused smile. "And hi."

"I was just . . ." I threw a look back at the door. "What are you doing here?"

"I live down the street. I'm staying with my aunt and uncle while I go to school. I thought I saw you speeding by, so I decided to check it out."

"Right. Right."

She looked me up and down. "And you were just?"

"I was just . . ." I was just a terrible liar is what I was.

"Skulking around Constance Graves's house?" she offered.

"*Skulking* is an ugly word."

"What about breaking in? How do you feel about those words?"

"Those are terrible words. Just terrible."

"Are you looking for something that will help Nora? I heard she'd been arrested."

I frowned. Once again, I couldn't help but think this girl knew far too much about things she probably shouldn't. "Not arrested, no. They're questioning her."

She nodded. "And, again, you think there's something in Constance's house that could help prove Nora's innocence?"

"No," I said, shaking my head. "Definitely not."

"Why do you have a flashlight, then?"

I looked down at the torch in my hand as though it had just appeared there.

"And why do you even need a flashlight? Can't you just cast a spell so an orb of light will follow you around?"

I blinked at her. *An orb of light?*

"Or a cloud of sparks? Or a flame that rests in the palm of your hand?" She smiled. "That would be super cool."

"No, not super cool. Ridiculous. That all is ridiculous." I could actually do the flame in the hand thing, and it was very cool. But no. Just no. This was not happening. Besides, I'd had enough of fires lately. "Nixie, I'm not sure what you've heard, but I think you've been misinformed."

"Oh, I haven't heard anything. Other than from Liz. And she's not exactly an unbiased source. You and your aunts have the town locked down. Whenever I try to get anyone to say anything about the Warren women and the *help* they provide"—she put air quotes around the word *help*—"nobody seems to know what I'm talking about. Or, at least, they act that way."

I frowned. "Right." I didn't want to have to spell the girl, especially given my difficulties as of late, but this was bad. She obviously knew a lot. Again, too much. And I had things to do tonight. But could I really risk that kind of enchantment with my magic behaving so unpredictably?

"You're thinking about wiping my memory, aren't you?"

My eyes widened. "What? Wipe your memory? That's crazy," I stammered. "How would I even do something like that?"

"Don't bother. You'd be wasting your time. Nora's already tried it. Several times. It doesn't work. I'm immune."

Apparently, my aunt still had a few secrets up her sleeve. "You're immune?"

"Yeah, I come from a long line of witch hunters. I'm not proud, if that's what you're thinking. I'm actually, like, super ashamed. But what can you do? You can't pick your family. Anyway, the point is, I don't think your magic works on me."

"I'm sorry, but I have no idea what you're talking about."

"Right." The girl gave me an exaggerated wink. "So how are you planning to get in?" she asked, eyeing the house. "That thing you were doing with your fingers obviously wasn't working."

I stared at the girl a moment longer, then said, "Well, if I was hypothetically breaking in, I guess I'd have to smash a window or something."

"Smash a window?" She blinked. "That glass is original. See the way the light swirls in the panes?"

I didn't look where Nixie was pointing. I was kind of afraid to take my eyes off of her.

"You are not *smashing* a window."

I planted my hands on my hips. "Then I don't know what I'm going to do. Hypothetically speaking. I guess I'll break a door, or—"

Nixie held something up in the air. "You could just use this," she said with a shrug.

"Is that a key?"

"It is. And I'll give it to you." She folded her arms across her chest, burying the key underneath her arm. "On one condition."

"Okay." I gave her a sidelong look. "What condition?"

"You do magic for me. Right here. Right now."

Chapter 38

WHAT?"

I had said the word too sharply. I tried to diffuse the situation with a laugh, but I was convincing no one. "What is this magic you keep going on about?" Again, I was such a terrible liar. "And why? Why do you have a key to Constance Graves's house?"

"I am, or *was*, Constance Graves's neighbor. Why does any neighbor have a key? In case of emergency. I'm assuming this is an emergency?" She held out the key again.

I nodded. This was most definitely an emergency. I reached out to grab the key, but she yanked her hand away. "I said it was going to cost you."

"How much?" I patted my coat. "I don't have any money on me, but I could get some."

"I don't want money. I already told you what I want. It doesn't have to be anything big like turning yourself into a bat."

She had me confused with a vampire again.

"Or making a poison apple."

That was the evil queen.

"Or flying on a broomstick."

I didn't have anything for that one, but I did prefer my bicycle.

"It could just be something small," she pleaded, clutching her hands to her chest, "like levitating off the ground or something."

I rubbed my forehead. That had been last night's trick. "Look, Nixie, there's been some sort of misunderstanding here."

"No! Stop it. Don't do that."

I dropped my hand to look at her.

"Both you and Nora act like I'm crazy. But I'm not. You know I'm not. I know what I know. My grandfather told me stories when I was little, and I saw something once. Something I definitely can't explain." She shook her head. "I just need proof. For my own sake."

I felt for the girl. I really did. We both knew the truth. And she was not crazy.

"*Please.* I promise I won't tell anyone."

There was so much desperate longing in the girl's eyes, it nearly broke my heart. "I hear what you're saying. I really do."

"But you won't do it." She threw her hands in the air. "Great. That's just great."

I frowned. "That's not *exactly* what I was going to say."

Hope lit up in the girl's eyes.

"What I was going to say was, even if I did want to do this absolutely ridiculous and totally deniable thing you want me to do, I'm not sure I could do it right now."

Nixie's face dropped. "What are you talking about?"

I scratched my temple. "You see, I've been going through some personal issues, and you noticed it earlier when I was trying to unlock the door? Not much was happening."

"So, what are you saying? You're broken?"

"Hypothetically speaking, yes. Kind of. It's an on-and-off thing."

"Seriously? You're telling me I finally get this close to seeing some magic." She pinched her fingers in the air. "And my witch is a dud?"

I blinked. *Dud* seemed a little harsh.

She held the key out to me.

I looked at her outstretched hand. "Wait. What are you doing?"

"Just take it," she said, jerking it around.

"Really?"

"Just drop it by the store when you're done. Who knows? Maybe you will find something to prove your aunt's innocence, and she'll show me some magic. Now, Nora, there's a real witch."

I scoffed a little but took the key just the same. "Thank you, Nixie."

"Whatever." She turned and trotted down the front steps of the house.

"Really," I called out after her. "I won't forget this."

"Yeah. Yeah." She kept walking across the dark lawn. "And good luck in there. Watch out for ghosts."

I clutched the key in my hand and smiled. "Always."

MINUTES LATER, I was inside Graves House with the door shut behind me.

I swept the flashlight around the front hall. The interior of the home was clean enough. It wasn't as though there were any cobwebs hanging from the ceiling or dust sheets thrown over furniture, but there was a very sad feel to the place. The furnishings all looked decades old and the walls and floors were dull from lack of maintenance. It was clear, no one had thought of this house as a home in a very long time.

There was something else missing, too. I couldn't put

my finger on it at first, but then it came to me. It wasn't just the house that had a feeling of neglect, there was no indication of care here at all. No family photos. No sign of a pet. There weren't even any plants.

Suddenly, a prickle ran over my neck. I couldn't be sure, but I was willing to bet Constance was with me again.

Time to get to it.

Initially I had been planning to go directly to the staircase, but there was one thing I needed to check first. I crept down the main hallway, passing just by the kitchen, headed for the back of the house, my footfalls echoing much too loudly for my liking. When I reached the doors that led to the backyard, I was surprised to find them closed off with two-by-fours, but the oak board and batten wall beside them was still in perfect condition. I could have been looking at the walls of Ivywood Hollow. And the similarities didn't end there. Even though the paneled interior walls appeared flush with that of the outside, through some architectural wizardry, I knew that wasn't quite the case. Thankfully, though, I didn't have to search for the hidden panel to prove my hunch. There was no need. The light from my torch had found a small brass doorknob. I pulled the camouflaged section of the wall open to reveal a narrow staircase, identical to the one in my family's home.

At least one of my suspicions had been confirmed. It would have been easy for anyone who had lived in this house to find their way quickly through the B&B.

I hurried back to the main staircase. I could have taken the secret steps, but in all honesty, they were a little creepy. The entire house was a little creepy. And while it may seem silly, given I was used to being the *thing* people feared going bump in the night, even witches have their limits.

I grabbed the bannister so like the one in my family's home. This was it. The moment of truth. Stars above, I hoped Constance hadn't led me here on a wild-goose chase, but as the saying goes, there was only one way to find out.

Each step I climbed creaked beneath my feet. When I reached the top, the darkness of the second floor engulfed me, and I found myself wishing I had brought a bigger flashlight.

I swept the small circle of illumination I did have over the wall to the left of me, taking small steps as I did. If Roxie was right, and the house was a mirror image of Ivywood Hollow, the closet should be just ahead. I was finding it difficult to judge how far though. The fear and excitement had me disoriented.

I kept the light of my torch moving along the wall. Step after step, it revealed nothing but an uninterrupted flow of wainscotting and faded wallpaper. Panic fluttered in my chest.

Suddenly the light hit upon the handcrafted wood casing of a closet door.

Without a thought, I raced over, grabbed the handle, and whipped it open.

My heart sank. More empty shelves.

I swooped my flashlight over each one, but the beam revealed nothing.

No, this couldn't be right. I had been so sure. The closet was identical. And Constance had brought me here. There had to be a reason why.

I ran my hand over the dusty shelves feeling for something that might have been left behind, something I couldn't see with the narrow beam of the flashlight, but, again, there was nothing.

I looked up to the ceiling. Maybe there was a crawl space?

The roof was seamless. Not a nook or cranny in sight.

My hand dropped to my side, flooding the floor of the small enclosure with light.

The floor.

I dropped to my knees. There was a grubby bit of old carpet covering the hardwood. I shone my flashlight behind me and to both sides. It certainly didn't match any carpet I could see. I gave the fabric a sharp pull. It came loose in my hand.

My chest tightened as I tossed the little rug aside and pointed the flashlight down at the floor. I choked back a shout. I would never have noticed it had I not admired the woodworking at the B&B earlier, but I had, and now what I saw here was unmistakable. The boards were not flush. There were spaces between a select few, thin lines in the shape of a square.

I ran my gloved palms along the floor back into the closet until I hit the wall. I then reached to either side, tiptoeing my fingers along the edge, searching by touch, until I found what I was looking for. Hinges.

I jerked back on my heels and pressed down on the floor. It sprang up under my touch. Near frantic, I forced my hands underneath the panel of wood and thrust it up.

A small metal box lay tucked in the subfloor.

"Yes." My voice, though quiet, seemed to ripple through the stillness of the house.

I lifted the container, ignoring the cobwebs clinging to its sides. I sat back into a cross-legged position and set it down in front of me. It probably wasn't wise to stay in the house any longer than I had to, but I had to know what was inside. Now. I jiggled the rusty lid until it came up, creaking in protest.

It was filled nearly to the brim with two thick files of paper. I pulled the first out and opened it up.

Constance's will.

I quickly flipped through it. Even though I wasn't a lawyer, I didn't need to be to see that the sole beneficiary of the estate was, in fact, the town. Exactly as Rip had claimed.

I pulled out the next folder.

Rippert Graves Senior's Last Will and Testament.

I read each page carefully this time. By all accounts, this was the document that had torn the Graves family apart, but there were no earth-shattering revelations. It read like a traditional will. Nothing left out. Everything had been left to Constance. No surprises.

This couldn't be it.

I flipped the final page over to gather the document back up. The motion caused a small envelope to drop into my lap. It had been attached to the will with a rusty paper clip. I picked it up, and turned it over, to see Constance's name written in script on the front.

I carefully pulled out the sheets of paper and brought my flashlight up to the faded handwriting, my heart beating painfully in my chest.

I had to read the letter slowly.

Truthfully, I didn't want to believe what was written in those pages. I found myself going over every sentence, questioning every word. I wanted to reject all of it. The implications were too terrible. Too sad. But the more I read, I knew I couldn't deny what it was telling me. All the pieces fit.

When I finally reached the end, I rocked back on the hand I had pressed to the floor and looked into the darkness of the house, searching for the spirit hidden from my sight.

"Constance," I whispered, "how could you?"

Chapter 39

My dearest Constance,

As you well know, I am not long for this earth. My Last Will and Testament has been signed and remains in the hands of our attorney, Bartholomew Barnes. It is at his insistence I write this letter, despite having spoken my intentions to you directly, as your sister and brothers will be shocked by my decision to make you my sole beneficiary. You know it was never my intention to make you a target for their ill will, but, once again, Bartholomew insists that any attempt to legally mandate my wishes would not stand up in court. Therefore, it is up to you to act as my surrogate. I have not been an exemplary father by any stretch of the imagination, and while I realize anything I do now is both too little and too late, I cannot rest peacefully knowing I did not at least try to make a difference in my children's lives. I also know you love your siblings as well as any mother could love her own children. It is this fact alone that gives me solace. I know you will communicate what follows to each of your siblings.

To my eldest son, Rip Jr., the day you were born was the happiest your mother and I had ever experienced. To be gifted with such a healthy fine boy was a wish come true. Giving you my name was one of the proudest moments of my life. Your mother and I had such hopes and dreams for you. Hopes and dreams I lost sight of when she died. I know you must have felt growing up there was little you could do right in my eyes. I am deeply sorry for having fostered that belief in you, Son. What's more, as you were so close in age to Constance, it must have been difficult for you to feel any of the maternal love she tried to share with you. You perhaps suffered the most from the loss of your mother. I'm afraid this lack of love, affection, and approval has turned you into a petty young man, who demands respect and admiration from others when it has not been earned. This is why I am not leaving you the family home. I am afraid you have taken our family's role as founders of Evenfall and turned it into some sort of antiquated birthright. I realize these will be difficult words to take in from me, the failed man who is your father. But know I deliver this harsh condemnation out of a place of love. True esteem and self-respect come from achieving something on your own. I will not limit you further by gifting you unearned respect. I know you can be the man I never was if you take these words to heart. Please consider them carefully. I love you.

To my son John, please know that the moment you came to us, your mother and I knew you were a tender soul with a heart too fine for this world. You had your mother's kindness and gentleness. I only wish she had lived longer so you could have known her better. You were kindred spirits in both your temperaments and, of course, your love of animals. I know how badly you wish to fulfill your mother's desire for a hobby farm that cares for neglected animals, and I want this for you too, Son. And it shall be yours, once you have left home and pursued your dream of a career in veterinary science. I know you can do this. Your teachers always remarked on your strong, adept mind. I also know you are shy and that it is far easier for you to hide from the world than it is to put yourself out in it. But the world deserves to know a little of your great heart, so consider this a gentle nudge out of the nest. The moment you receive your degree, Constance has agreed to gift you the lands associated with Graves House. She has also been instructed, by me, to pay any costs associated with your education. I love you, Son.

To my youngest, Mary, let me first begin by saying what a terrible tragedy life has dealt you to never know the angel you had as a mother and to be left with a grieving father who allowed himself to be turned into a bitter old man. I've heard it said that people who are hurt often hurt others, and that was certainly true in my case. I thank the good Lord every day you were given Constance to show you some of the love and comfort families should naturally provide. At this time, I am also leaving you nothing. I fear the man you have chosen to make your husband. I believe him to be of the cruel and domineering type, the type of man I am ashamed to say I modeled for you, if to a lesser extent. If I were to leave you any money now, I believe he would spend it recklessly, leaving you with nothing. Constance has agreed to keep a sum of money dedicated to you should you ever choose to leave your husband. This money should help you rebuild your life into something I pray will be both safe and loving. I realize this meager gift from your father does not make up for all the neglect and pain you have suffered from the time of your birth, but it is all I have to give. Though I was never able to properly show it, I love you, Mary.

Constance, I know I have placed an enormous burden upon you from the time your mother died until now, but I *am trusting you to enact these wishes. You have been both mother and father to your siblings, trying to provide them with love, care, and support when I could not. For this I will be both eternally grateful and remorseful. I am painfully aware that while you cared for your siblings, there was no one to care for you. I hope, now that I am close to death, you will be able to build your own life, perhaps with that Benjamin of yours, and have the happiness you so richly deserve. I pray your siblings always remember the sacrifices you have made for this family, not only while they were growing up, but in these last few years you have cared for me. I have been a terrible burden—I know this— and you have borne it gracefully. Please allow your siblings to read this letter. I am not convinced they appreciate the full breadth of your sacrifice, and they should. I love you, my daughter.*

Your father,
Rippert Graves Sr.

After reading the letter a second time, I found the sadness was still there, but other emotions were now finding their way to the surface. Sympathy. Disbelief. Anger. Anger that Rip Graves Sr. hadn't spoken to his children while he was still alive, and anger at Constance for not sharing her father's final words. So many lives could have turned out differently if Constance had followed through on her father's wishes. Maybe she had tried, but if I were to guess, I didn't think any of her siblings had read this letter.

Now came the question of what I was supposed to do with it. The letter needed to be shared, but how was I supposed to do that without implicating my family any further? And speaking of my family, there was nothing here that would clear Nora. This letter had been hidden from Constance's siblings, so it couldn't even contribute to a motive.

I restacked the papers, meaning to put them all back,

when I realized there was another file tightly wedged in the bottom of the box. I pried it out and placed it on my lap.

I gasped softly when I read the stamp at the top of the page.

Evenfall Town Records.

It was proof of ownership for six burial spots in the Graves Family plot. Rippert and Catherine Graves had already been buried in two, but there were four more for their children. Given the historic nature of the graveyard, it was still owned and operated by the town.

It all looked pretty straightforward.

Constance must have inherited ownership of the plot along with the rest of the estate.

I flipped the page. There was an addendum attached.

It took a moment to sort through the legalese, but once I had, I jumped to my feet, sending the other files sliding to the floor. The addendum stipulated that, other than Constance, no other person was allowed to be buried in the Graves's family plot. Rippert and Catherine had obviously wanted their children to be buried in the family gravesite, so it was a cruel move on Constance's part, but I knew she could be cruel. She had proved that by not sharing her father's letter. I also knew this addendum would anger all of the Graves siblings, but if I was right, it would have upset one of them much more than the others.

But it wasn't possible.

Not unless . . .

My blood ran cold. I had done it again. Or rather, before. I had missed something right in front of me!

I stuffed all the papers back into the box.

I had to go. Right now.

If I was right, it would change everything.

Chapter 40

I PEDALED THROUGH THE empty streets, cold wind once again rushing over my face.

I twisted the handles of my bike, wanting to wring my own neck.

I had been so sure. I hadn't even questioned it.

As I neared my destination, I guided my bike up off the road onto the sidewalk, bumping over the cracks I had caused just the other day. I skidded to a stop.

The gold lettering of the bookstore shone in the light from the lamppost.

Lovely Leaves.

I dropped my bike to the ground and hurried over to the window, pressing my nose against the glass, my hands cupped on either side of my face.

I tried to see through to the back of the store, but the shop was all shadow and gloom.

I raced over to the door. I didn't want to disturb Theo. I knew this would upset her, but it was too important to leave. I banged on the wood frame with the side of my fist and waited.

Nothing inside stirred.

I banged again.

Still nothing.

I raced around the side of the building. Theo's car was gone. She often spent the night with her sister. Now what was I going to do?

The key!

I dug my hand into my jacket pocket and fumbled for my key chain. It only took a second to sort out the brass one I had kept from the bookstore. I shoved it in the lock and gave it a turn. When I heard the deadbolt slide back, I pressed down on the latch and stepped inside, closing the door quickly behind me.

Theo would forgive me for the intrusion. She would understand. Actually, she would be heartbroken if I was right about this, but it needed to be done.

I blinked in the darkness and took a step toward the back of the store. The edge of my boot clipped a tower of books, spilling them across the floor. I stepped over the fallen stack and headed into the narrow gap between two large shelves. With every step it felt like the walls were closing in, but the shine from the glass front of the grandfather clock standing tall against the back wall drove me forward.

For an instant, I wanted to be wrong. Yes, I wanted to prove Nora innocent. And yes, I wanted justice for Constance despite everything she had done, but as I rose my gaze to the clock's face, my knees feeling like they might give way, I found myself wishing none of it to be true. Knowing who the killer was also meant knowing how and why it had all gone wrong.

I stared at the clock's frozen hands.

I checked my own wristwatch to be sure, but I already knew.

The clock had stopped at nine fifty-seven.

Theo probably looked at the time before she had gone to bed. The clock stood right beside the door that led to her apartment. She would have remarked how late it was. But the clock had stopped. Maybe that morning. Or the day before. Or the day before that. Theo never took notice of those types of things. She wasn't interested in the mundane details of life. I had been the one to wind the clock. She probably only noticed it that night because she had been taken out of her routine.

The stillness of the bookstore fell over me. It suddenly felt too quiet. Too ordinary. It was as though I couldn't quite fathom how the earth kept on spinning when there was such tragedy playing out in the lives of everyday people.

I had been right. But it all felt very wrong.

Chapter 41

OCTOBER NIGHTS IN Evenfall were made for witches, and this one was no exception.

The yellow moon was rising up from behind the trees of the hemlock forest at the edge of town while bats swooped against the darkening sky. The crisp wind with its traces of wood smoke skittered dried leaves across the pavement as a dog barked endlessly in the distance. The stirrings of night magic put most creatures on edge.

I had learned so much over the past several days. Not just about Constance and her family, but about my family and myself.

I had made so many mistakes, but it was time to do better.

Given this was my mindset, it might seem strange I was headed to confront a killer, alone, not sure if my powers would hold out, in a place I had promised myself I would never go. But that was exactly what I was going to do.

I balled my fists at my sides as I stood outside the gates of the graveyard.

"Come on, Brynn," I whispered into the night. "You can do this. You are in control."

I took one step, then another, not breathing until I had crossed the threshold.

I had to stay focused. It was the only way this would work.

A sense of calm fell over me as I walked the winding path through the old graveyard, mist swirling at my feet. I had come here for one reason. Nothing else mattered. Not the small critter rustling in the bush by my side. Not the insects chirping all around me. Not the tree branches softly groaning and creaking overhead.

No, the only thing that mattered was the woman standing in the distance by the stone slab with the yellow rose bush clinging to its side.

It was the last grave in the row, at the furthermost end of the cemetery.

She didn't look over at me when I passed the worn headstones of her parents' graves.

Rippert John Graves.

Catherine Elizabeth Graves.

She still didn't face me when I passed the freshly dug grave beside theirs with the tarp over the top of it. The headstone wasn't up yet, but I knew it would bear Constance's name.

She didn't look at me even when I came to stand by her side.

We stood together looking at that last headstone.

Grant Coleman.

"You've figured everything out, haven't you?" she asked, eyes still on the grave before her.

"Not everything. But enough."

"I'm not surprised. You're a Warren woman. In my experience, there isn't much you can't do."

I didn't answer.

"I always thought I would be laid to rest here," Mary Coleman said, meeting my eye. "But she couldn't even let me have that."

Chapter 42

"WE'RE A LOT alike, you and me."

I held Mary's gaze but said nothing.

"It's hard to be all alone with our kind of pain." She looked back at the headstone. "Others try to understand, but they can't. Not unless they've been through it." She walked over to touch the top of her husband's grave. "I know I keep saying it, but he was a wonderful man. A *good* man. I can tell your Adam was too."

I swallowed hard. I couldn't let my emotions get the better of me.

"That's what other people can't understand. When you have a love like that, it never lets you go. There is no moving on. Others want you to be whole again, but it's not that simple." She shook her head. "Constance never knew that kind of love. If she had, she never would have done what she did."

I stepped toward the Graves family plot and looked down at the area closest to Grant Coleman's grave. "This was where you wanted to be buried, wasn't it?"

"Grant and I thought we were so lucky when we were able to buy this plot. How perfect. I could be both with him and my family. I never imagined *she* would take that away from me."

I didn't answer.

"Constance was the only mother I had ever known. Let me ask you, how do you raise a child and then treat them the way she treated me?"

I shook my head.

She looked away. "It was that damned will. My father hurt us all so much in life and then *that*." She wrapped her arms across her chest. "That's where it all started. I was under so much pressure back then."

"Pressure from your first husband?"

"He was a monster. When he found out I wasn't getting *our* piece of the family pie, I was afraid for my life. My daughter's life." She stepped even closer to her second husband's grave. "I just couldn't understand why Constance would do that to me. My father was one thing, but she had all the power after he died. She could have split the estate. Everything could have been different."

I thought back to the letter Rip Sr. had written. This was all such a mess. "Did she ever try to explain?"

"We didn't give her much chance. Beatty Barnes made sure we all had copies of the will as soon as our father had died. I remember thinking he was behaving strangely when he came to the door. He looked sick with guilt. It didn't take long to figure out why. He knew what was in that will. All he said was that he was sorry for our loss and that I should speak to Constance right away. So that's what the three of us did. We were furious when we headed over to confront her. Even John. Although that didn't last long."

"Rip attacked Constance, didn't he?"

"He was vicious. He accused her of having planned it for years. For taking care of our father just so she could whisper poison in his ear. He said she was the one who had pushed him to change his will. And then he—"

"And then he what?" I knew what she would say, given what Ben had told me, but I wanted to hear it from her.

"He accused Constance of *hurrying* our father's death along."

"You mean he accused her of murder."

She patted the top of the gravestone. "He never said those words. I think even he had some shame deep down. But that was the implication." She curled her fingers into a fist. "I'll never forget the look on her face."

Despite everything Constance had done since, I couldn't help but feel for her. It must have been a terrible moment.

"When Rip was through, she asked John and me if we felt the same way."

"What did you say?"

"John didn't say anything. He walked out. He was never good at expressing himself, especially when he was upset. But me, all I could think about was what Carl was going to do to me when I got home." She looked up at the trees. "So, I said I agreed with Rip."

I forced myself to take a breath. My hands trembled with the effort of staying in control, but I had to hang on until she told me everything.

"I don't know what we were thinking. Maybe that we'd shame her into splitting up the estate? All it did, though, was harden her heart in a way I never thought possible." She met my eye again. "I know you think I'm a monster, but I never gave up on trying to make things right with her." Her face twitched. "Ask me how many apology letters I've written."

I didn't say anything.

"Hundreds," she spat. "Year after year, I wrote her letters. They always came back unopened. And every time I got one of those letters back in the mail, it was like Constance was there, telling me, over and over again, *You're still a bad person, Mary. Bad. Bad. Bad.*"

Suddenly I knew I was seeing the creature who had been capable of ending her sister's life.

"And I've had to live with that voice for years. It was better with Grant, but when he died, that voice got so much louder." Her body shuddered, forcing her to grab the headstone for support. "And then I found out about the family plot. Connie's last revenge." She stared at me with an uncomfortable intensity. "I think you know what happened after that."

I held her gaze though every part of me wanted to look away. "The night Constance died you went to the bookstore. Theo said you were upset. You had tried to cancel, but she convinced you to come by. Liz came too, but she didn't stay long."

Mary nodded. "She was worried about me. I had just found out about the addendum. Liz had known about the plot since Grant died. She had handled the arrangements. She didn't want to upset me with it, but I found a copy of the paperwork at her house. She thought maybe there was some legal recourse, but I knew my sister. She'd have everything in order. I was so upset. I thought going to Theo's might calm me down, but it didn't."

"So you left the bookstore. Theo said you left around ten, giving you an alibi, but her timing had been off by at least an hour. The grandfather clock in the store had stopped. You then headed for the graveyard to clean up the site the way you normally did."

Mary looked at me questioningly.

"There was a yellow rose petal in Constance's room at the B&B. We don't grow them."

She nodded.

"Then you left to go home, but on the way, you spotted Constance in the window of the B&B. It's a small town, you would have likely known she was staying with us while

Graves House was undergoing renovations, and the view of the Rosewater Room is clear from the street."

"I saw her in the window on the second floor and all I could think was *when is enough, enough?* I know I hurt my sister. I know I did. But hadn't she already made me pay?" Her gaze drifted away from me to the memory I couldn't see. "I knew then it was never going to stop. As long as she was alive, she'd find a way for me to keep on paying. But to deny me Grant?" Her eyes flashed back to mine. "Tell me, what would you do? What would you do if someone told you that you couldn't lie beside your husband when the time came?"

The truth was, I didn't know, but I couldn't let her derail me. Not now. I had to hang on. "After that you came around the back of the house. Nora had left her mallet out. You picked it up and snuck inside. You knew to use the hidden staircase. Graves House has one too."

"It was all so easy. It was like I was in a dream. I headed up those stairs and—"

"What are you doing?"

Mary and I both jolted as a voice tore through the night. "Get away from my mother!"

Chapter 43

M ARY'S FACE CRUMPLED as she watched her daughter stride toward us.

"I knew you would do this!" Liz shouted at me. "Whatever she's saying, don't listen to her, Mom. She's tricking you."

Mary sighed. "That's not true, honey. I know you want it to be, but it's not."

"The Warrens aren't right," Liz said, coming toward me, shoulders squared, fists clenched. "You know what they can do."

"No, Liz," Mary said, stepping in to head off her daughter. "I know it's my fault you think that, but there's so much I need to tell you. I asked Nora to help me with your father."

Liz looked to her mother, who had grabbed her arm.

"I should have told you sooner. I just didn't want you to have to live with knowing the type of man your father really was."

"No. No," Liz said, shaking free from her mother's grip and pointing at me. "You made her believe that."

I stilled my breath. My hands trembled even harder. "I would never do that."

"In fact, I bet you and your aunts did something to my mother that night. It makes perfect sense. Nora hated my aunt, but she didn't want to get her hands dirty."

"Sweetheart, please," Mary said, reaching for her daughter again, but Liz moved away before she could touch her. "You need to listen to me. There's so much I haven't told you. Maybe if I had, things wouldn't have gotten away from me the way they did."

"Mom, be quiet."

"I'm so sorry, sweetheart. For so much. I never should have called you that night. I should have turned myself in."

"You still can," I said. "It will help if you do."

"Shut up!" Liz shouted, angry tears flashing in her eyes.

I didn't flinch. "It's over. I already know you came to help your mother at the B&B that night. The edge of your nightgown is on Mr. Henderson's security footage. She was waiting for you behind the house, wasn't she? It wouldn't have been hard. We all thought Constance's death was an accident. No one was looking for her. She called you and you came. I also know you broke into the records building trying to get what you probably thought was the only copy of the addendum to the family burial plot. But it's not." I would have gone on with my explanation, but a new voice shattered the quiet around us. A man's voice.

"I found this in the caretaker's shed." The words were said lightly, but they held an undercurrent of menace I couldn't ignore. "So, let's quit with the confessing and put an end to this once and for all."

I had been wondering when Rip would show up.

He lumbered toward us, shovel in hand.

I knew I should have been intimidated, scared, but I was far more afraid of not getting every last detail out of these three. I knew what could happen when I didn't have all the information. I pressed on. "I also know it was Rip who brought the murder weapon back to the B&B," I said, meeting his eye, "and planted it in the greenhouse."

Rip frowned at me. "You have any proof of that?"

I did. The soap. But that wasn't something I could use. "I know Liz must have called you after the murder looking for help. And you were more than happy to oblige. It would be much easier to contest both your father's and Constance's will with another sibling on board. Plus, nobody hated Constance as much as you did."

"Well, it wasn't just that. I also have a soft spot for Mary," he said, tilting his head toward his sister. "Poor kid was the only one my dad hated more than me."

"You initially hoped you could pin the murder on your brother. You had Constance's letter as motive."

He chuckled. "I wondered who Maureen had given it to."

"Constance confessed to John what she did to him in that letter, didn't she?" The words spilled out of me. I knew time was running out. "He never went to veterinary school. He never got his farm."

He shook his head. "It would have been a great motive, and it would have gotten John out of the way of my upcoming lawsuit. Too bad his alibi was so strong. Who knew my little brother still had friends?"

"So, you went with your niece's preference to pin it on us. I'm guessing it was the herbicides from the orchard that killed everyone's plants."

He shrugged and took a step toward me. "Liz did all the heavy lifting. I just provided the supplies."

I took a step back. "What I don't understand is why didn't you sue before now? Why not contest your father's will?"

"Lack of funds." He adjusted his grip on the shovel. "Maureen's daddy's business has remedied that, though, so it's full steam ahead. Now, Mary, why don't you go wait for us by the gates, dear." He looked back at me. "She hasn't been quite right since everything happened with Connie, and I'd like this to go as smoothly as possible."

"You can't possibly think you'll get away with killing me."

"Killing, no," he said, shaking his head. "But I think I can come up with a plan that will make everybody believe you left town. It's common knowledge you've been despondent since your husband's death. Then add to that all the stress of your aunt being accused of murder. It would be a lot for anyone to take. Too much really." Rip stared at me, waiting, probably for me to begin quaking with fear, but I was too drained for that.

I replayed the last few minutes in my head. Had I covered everything? Did I have all the answers? I was hoping I wouldn't need them. But, again, I wasn't taking chances. Not anymore.

"You're a tough one," he said with an ugly smile. "I'll give you that." Rip took another big step toward me. "But foolish. You never should have come to this graveyard alone."

Just then a cold wind rushed through the headstones, swirling fallen leaves into the air. Following close behind came the sound of unearthly laughter.

Liz took a step toward her mother and clutched her arm. Rip's eyes flashed around, looking for the source of the laughter, but it seemed to be coming from everywhere, all at once, even though the graveyard was empty of all other souls.

Well, empty until my aunts materialized just feet in front of Rip, dressed all in black, hair loose and flowing in the wind.

I couldn't see their faces, but I knew their eyes would be glowing bright green.

Rip dropped the shovel as his mouth gaped open.

Izzy stepped toward him. "I'm afraid *you're* the one who's been foolish," she said in a voice that did not sound like her own. "You just said my niece shouldn't have come to the graveyard alone, but there's something you should know."

Nora came to her sister's side.

"Our niece is never truly alone."

Chapter 44

"HOW DID YOU do that?" Rip stammered. "What are you?"

I'm not sure how my aunts would have answered those questions, but they didn't have to. I distracted everyone by dropping to my knees.

I was exhausted. The magic required to keep a glamor spell like that going since we had entered the graveyard was a little more than I could manage after not practicing for so long. Of course, my aunts had done most of the work, but in order to make people disappear, everyone who knows they're actually there has to participate in the spell to keep them hidden or the illusion disappears.

We had started planning right after I had left the bookstore and gone home. Izzy and Nora were back from the police station by then, and I told them everything. After hours of going through different scenarios, we settled on a plan for the following night. We wanted to get as much information as we could before we *encouraged* Mary to go to the police. If the town hall meeting taught me anything, it was that details were important. My talking to Mary alone in the graveyard seemed like the best approach. I knew she felt a kinship with me because of our losses. She had also told me she visited her husband every night, so all we needed to do was wait, in hiding, for her to show up. As for Liz and Rip, their arrival hadn't been a surprise. I knew someone had been following me, and it didn't take long, after discussing it with my aunts, to figure out the most likely candidate. A small locator spell confirmed it. It was Rip. The wildfire magic had gotten to him after all. I was his loose end. He had been following me since that night. I would have thought the spell would have worn off, but Rip, apparently, had a lot of guilt. I could only assume it had taken him so long to confront me in the graveyard because he had called Liz and was waiting for her to show up. That, and it had probably taken him some time to find a shovel.

Izzy came rushing over to where I was kneeling on the grass. "Are you all right, darling?"

I let her help me back up to my feet. "I'm fine. Just tired."

"I'm so proud of you," she said excitedly, burying me in a hug. "You did so well! I knew you could do it! Your magic is back and better than ever! You never faltered."

"*Ahem,*" a voice called over.

Izzy looked back to her sister, who was waving at all the people still cowering in fear.

"Oh right," Izzy whispered. "Not quite done here, are we?" She hurried back to Nora. "Where were we?"

"We were just about to leave for the police station. Everyone's ready to confess."

Rip shook his head, his eyes darting around the graveyard.

"Are you thinking of running?" Nora asked sweetly. "Because if you are, I think it only fair to warn you." My aunt's eyes flashed an even brighter green. "I love to chase."

Rip stopped moving.

"We're all coming," Mary said, looking at the other two members of her family. "It's time."

The five of them walked back to the path that led out of the graveyard. It was Izzy who noticed first I wasn't following. "Brynn?"

"I'll be along in just a bit. You all go on without me."

Nora shooed the others along, then walked over. Once they were out of earshot, she said, "Well, that was fun. And did you see how I managed to restrain myself? Rippert is lucky I didn't strike him down where he stood for threatening you. Of course, we'll have to dabble with some of their memories. I don't see any way around it. But it was worth it." She stepped in close and touched my arm. "Are you all right?"

"I think so. There's something I need to do."

Nora followed my gaze to the other side of the graveyard. It only took a moment for her to figure out what I had planned. "Oh. Are you sure? Maybe now's not the best time."

I looked back into my aunt's eyes, which had returned to their usual hazel color. "That's the thing. I don't think I'll ever be sure, or that there will ever be a right time, but it's something I need to do. You were right." I turned back to face the gloom. "I haven't been living. And I don't want to be afraid of the memories anymore."

Nora laid a hand on my shoulder. "Would you like some company? This isn't something you should do alone."

I smiled. "As it turns out I don't think I will be alone."

At first my aunt looked confused, but her expression quickly changed to one of surprise. She stared back into the darkness, her eyes searching for what I was seeing. "You don't mean . . . ?"

"I'll meet you at the police station." I squeezed her hand, then stepped toward the path.

"Good luck, Brynn," she called after me. "I'm proud of you."

Now that the wind had died down, peace once again fell over the graveyard. The low-lying mist returned, swirling among the headstones, and the soft moonlight lit up the gravel path.

When I was a few feet away, the person beside my husband's grave turned to face me. "I hope you don't mind my being here."

"Not at all," I said. "I've been wanting to talk to you for quite some time now, Constance."

Chapter 45

Y OU PICKED A lovely spot."
 I couldn't help but agree as my eyes trailed over the burial plot belonging to my husband. I wasn't sure what I had been expecting to feel when I saw the headstone for the first time, but all I felt was calm. It had been done right. My aunts had made sure of that. It was a lovely stone, and it had been beautifully carved. The plot, too, was well cared for. Someone had placed a small chrysanthemum plant at the foot of the stone.

When Constance saw where I was looking, she said, "Mary put those there. I watched her do it."

I nodded.

A long moment passed before Constance finally said, "So, my sister confessed."

I looked back at the spirit before me, her face lovely with its iridescent glow. "She is on her way to the police now."

"It's the right thing to do, I suppose. But, you know, she's not the only one who is responsible."

"Liz and Rip are going too."

"I don't mean either of them," she said, frowning. "I mean me."

Any further words died on my tongue.

"I pushed that girl, *my girl*, into madness, didn't I?" She looked at me, then shook her head. "I was so angry when I was alive, and now all I can think is, *what a waste.*"

"Why didn't you forgive her? I know what they accused you of was terrible. But from what I've heard, Mary tried to make things right."

"She did. But I never saw it that way." Constance gently moved toward a large oak tree. She tried to place her hand on it, but it sunk right through. If I had to guess, she was getting weaker. She wouldn't be slamming any more closet doors. She had stayed too long on the mortal plane. "I heard your uncle tell you that weird fairy tale. But you should know, I never resented my role in our family. I loved taking care of my siblings. That's why I was so hurt when they turned on me. And that's why I couldn't forgive them. For a while, I truly believed all those invitations and letters from Mary were just her way of worming herself back into my life so I'd give her the money. I knew how scared she was of that wretched husband of hers. I figured he put her up to it. But when Carl left, and she fell in love with her new husband," Constance stopped herself short and grimaced, "I believed she was trying to rub her happiness in my face. Her loving husband. Her perfect little family. I couldn't see anything but spite. It just got worse over the years."

She looked off in the distance, her body shining in the moonlight. "After a while I knew she wasn't trying to make me feel bad. It wasn't the money she wanted. No, she wanted my forgiveness. She couldn't live with what she had done. But I was so bitter by that point, the thought gave me pleasure. You see, I could keep the house from Rip. I could keep the farm from John. And I could keep my forgiveness from Mary. It was perfect." She looked back at me. "And it made me a monster."

"But you tried to make things right with John."

A heartbreaking smile came to her face. "Johnny. He was such a sweet boy. He would have been a wonderful veterinarian. I did try to make things right with him. I knew when the three of them came to the house that day his heart wasn't in it. But later on, when he didn't answer my letter, I didn't know what to think."

"You know now he never got it, right?"

"Yes, I do." She squinted. "All things considered, I think Rip needs to go to jail. For a good long time. You won't be able to prove he planted that mallet, but tell that wife of his that the evidence she's looking for is in a shoebox up in the rafters of their garage. Her instincts were right. He is embezzling money from her father's business. She just needs to prove it, so she can get her divorce. And before you say it, I know I should have given my siblings our father's letter. Everything might have been different. Even Rip might have been different. That son of a—"

"I'll make sure Maureen knows."

Constance blinked at me as though she had forgotten momentarily I was there. "And I want you to know, despite what Mary thinks, I did not draw up that addendum to the burial plot to hurt her."

I blinked. "What?"

"I am a monster, but even I'm not that bad."

"Then why did you do it?"

"To get at Rip! It happened this one time after he had come over to bully me into giving him the house yet again. I, of course, turned him away, and as he was leaving, he said something to the effect of, *You know, Connie. No one will remember you when you're dead.* And the idea just came to me. I'd kick them all out of the family plot. Then they'd remember me." She cackled at the memory before regaining her composure. "But it wasn't right."

I couldn't help but smile a little.

"The joke's on me, though, isn't it? I wasn't even think-

ing about Mary. I didn't know she bought the plot beside
ours for Grant. I knew how much she loved him. I've done
terrible things to my family, held terrible grudges, but I
wouldn't have gone that far. At least I'd like to think I
wouldn't have gone that far. If only I could do it all over
again." Constance suddenly looked at me quite intently.
"Don't you go making the same mistakes as me."

I frowned in question.

"You know what I'm talking about. I've been watching
you. You're stuck living in pain. Do you think it's a coincidence you can finally see me the night you decide to visit your
husband's grave?" She wagged a glowing finger in the air.
"Now, this isn't my place, but I know firsthand you can spend
your entire life living in the past, and that is no life at all. And
from what I've heard, your husband wouldn't want that."

The words seemed innocent enough, but there was
something in Constance's expression that made my heart
skip. "What do you mean, from what you've heard?"

"You know as well as I do spirits can't stay here for long,
but we usually stick around long enough to meet up with
another ghost or two. And we talk."

"Constance, what are you saying?"

She held up her hands. "I'll admit, I was eavesdropping
on that fight you had with your aunts. I heard what it was
you wanted, so I asked around a little." She looked over to
the grave. "And, in answer to your question, yes, I do have
a message for you from Adam."

The world tilted beneath my feet. "How is that possible?
He died so long ago."

She gave me a knowing look. "Brynn, you have helped
so many people in this town. Done good for so many families. Do you think the ghosts would let you down? Each
person who has passed in Evenfall since Adam died has
hung on to his message until it could be delivered to you,
and, as it turns out, I get to be the lucky one to do it. Oh
honey, don't cry."

I couldn't stop the tears from running down my face. Ordinarily, the thought of hearing Adam's final words would have been enough to tear down all my defenses, but standing here in the graveyard with Constance, hearing how the passing spirits of Evenfall had banded together to help me, it was more than I could take. I had been so focused on myself, so wrapped up in my own pain, I had forgotten about everything else. I had abandoned all the people who needed me, who needed my gift. But they hadn't forgotten about me.

"I was afraid of this," Constance said. "I can see the guilt on your face, but I want you to know every ghost who passed on the message was happy to do it, and no one begrudges you your time of pain. Besides, it's done us all good. It's true what they say. Giving help is sometimes more healing than receiving it."

I nodded quickly. I didn't know if I'd be able to forgive myself easily or not, but I couldn't focus on that now. I had dreamed of this moment, always believing it was impossible. I could deal with everything else later.

"Right. Where were we?" Constance squinted, then snapped her fingers. "The message. First, though, I need you to promise to do two things for me. Things I can't do now that I'm . . ." She hovered in the air and stuck her tongue out the side of her mouth.

I wiped the tears from my cheeks and smiled. "Constance, nothing would make me happier."

"Ready to get back in the game, huh?"

"So ready." I was surprised by how deeply I meant that.

The first item on Constance's list was not a shock. The second, however, took me aback. "Are you sure that's what you want?"

"Absolutely, I won't be able to rest unless I know it's done. Now back to you. I can feel the light pulling at me, so we'd better get to it."

Suddenly all the insects in the graveyard stopped chirping.

Constance looked around before her eyes settled back on me. "Did you do that?"

I looked around too. "Oh, I guess I did. It will only last a second. I just don't want to miss a word."

She frowned. "You Warren women are a little creepy, you know that?"

I nodded.

"Right. First, I'm sure you won't be surprised to hear your husband wanted you to know that he loves you. Always."

I smiled. The movement sent fresh tears spilling down my cheeks.

"But he also had a request. Now, I'm not quite sure what it means, but hopefully it will make sense to you."

Chapter 46

THE NEXT DAY I set out to fulfill my promises to Constance.

It had been a late night. Not because we were at the police station. Mary, Liz, and Rip had gone in by themselves to make their confessions, but we had waited up to hear from Beatty to make sure it had all been settled. He called around two in the morning. The three had confessed to everything. It was over. For us at least. For Constance's family, the journey was just beginning, and, despite everything, I wanted to help.

Actually, I was grateful to be helping again. It had been too long.

After pedaling around town for nearly an hour, I found John on his lawn mower in front of the library. I didn't have to engage him in a game of chicken to get him to stop this time. I just raised my hand, and he cut the motor.

He sat back in his seat as I walked my bike over to him,

red leaves swirling down around us from the oak tree towering overhead.

He took his cap from his head and rubbed his brow with the back of his hand. "I'm guessing you've heard Mary confessed last night."

I nodded. "How are you doing with everything?"

"Still putting one foot in front of the other." He smiled, somewhat sadly.

"Listen, I want to apologize to you for the other day."

He frowned in confusion.

"About the letter. I made a promise not to tell you where I got it from, but it wasn't fair to you."

He rubbed his chin. "It was Maureen, wasn't it? She called me this morning. Said she wanted to meet up. Have a word about something important."

"I'll let her explain everything." If she was ready to talk to John, the tip I had emailed her last night from Constance must have panned out. "I'm still sorry for my part in it though."

"You're not the one who needs to apologize." John picked at a bit of dirt on his overalls. "What a family, huh? I didn't know Mary was in such a bad way. I should have been there for her. And Connie, if only I had known she was trying to reach out to me."

"It was cruel of Rip to keep that letter from you. I know what he was trying to do. I know he wanted to keep you and Constance at odds, but still, I can't understand it."

"Nah, you wouldn't. You're a good kid." He shook his head and looked up at the sky. "I can't help but think if my mother hadn't died when she did, we all would have turned out different. We could have had happy lives."

"You still can, John."

He looked back at me and smiled. "I didn't mean it that way. I'm happy enough doing my thing. I don't have any complaints."

I adjusted my grip on my bike. "I was actually thinking you might want to expand your *thing*."

He shot me a suspicious look.

"I was talking to a few people from the town council this morning, and as you well know, they're going to try to turn the house into a museum if it can be restored, but when it comes to the land, Constance requested the old hobby farm to be converted into a petting zoo slash animal rehabilitation site. Now, the historical society has a lot of plans for the house, but when it comes to the animal rescue, they're at a loss. A project like that needs someone in charge."

John's chin dropped to his chest. "You don't mean me?"

"It would definitely have to be someone who's passionate about animals," I said, ignoring his comment. "And this person would probably have to make sure the grounds are kept up, so someone with a lawn mower would be ideal."

The wrinkles around John's eyes creased as a genuine smile spread across his face, but it dropped just as quickly. "Given all that's transpired, I'm not sure Connie would want me to be in charge of something like that."

"I have it on pretty good authority that is exactly what Constance would have wanted."

John gave me a sideways look. "Pretty good authority, huh?"

"The best." I nodded sharply.

"You Warren women." The smile returned to his face as he looked down to his lap. "Do you think that means Connie has forgiven me?"

My chest tightened. "John, I know she has."

He peered up at me. "Is she at peace?"

"She is," I said with another nod, "but I think she'd still like to know that you forgive her too."

"I never blamed her for any of it." He pulled a hanky out from his pocket and rubbed his nose. "I hope she knows *that*."

Just then, out of nowhere, Dog flew over the top of both of us and cawed loudly.

My eyes widened. "I think she knows."

John laughed. "I always knew there was something funny about that bird."

B RYNN WARREN, IT'S been an age since I've seen you." Beatrice Saunders beamed at me from behind the wooden counter of the town records building as I came in the door. Beatrice was a fixture in Evenfall. She was the type to always have a smile on her face and a hand outstretched ready to help those in need. I had gone to school with two of Beatrice's kids, so even though I was all grown up, she always looked at me with a warm, motherly gaze. I had missed that look. "How you doing, honey?"

"I can't complain." I walked toward the counter, matching her smile. "How are you? How are the grandkids?"

Beatrice and I chatted a little while. She loved talking about her grandkids, and I found I loved hearing about them. It really had been too long. After a couple of minutes, she asked, "So what can I do for you today?"

I had one last promise I needed to fulfill for Constance. This task had been the one that had given me pause in the graveyard. Yet while I had been taken aback at first, the more I thought about it, the more sense it made to me. I could see why Constance needed me to do this. Although I was a little nervous about it, given it probably wasn't entirely legal.

"Well," I said, opening my messenger bag and pulling out a single piece of paper. "I'm sure you know Constance Graves was staying with us at Ivywood Hollow before her death."

She laughed dryly. "I think the whole town knows that."

"Right, as it turns out, she left behind some important

papers in her room. Now, I've given most of them to Beatty Barnes to look after, but he said this one belongs here." I placed the paper on the counter and gave it a pat for good measure.

"What's this, now?" Beatrice asked, bringing her glasses up to her nose.

"It's the ownership for the Graves family burial plot."

She gave it a thorough look. "This is good to have. We had a break-in recently. A lot of documents were thrown about. In particular the ones having to do with the graveyard."

"I heard. That's why I brought this right over."

She eyed the document closely. "What's this? It looks like there might have been something stapled here at one time." She pointed to the top corner of the page.

"Oh?" I felt my cheeks burn. "There's no other page as far as I know." That was true. There was no other page. There *had* been another page. An addendum. But that had been burned in my fireplace.

Beatrice looked at the page again. For a moment I thought she was going to raise an objection, but all she said was, "Okay, I'll be sure to file this away. Did Beatty make a copy?"

"I don't think so."

"In that case, I'll send him one for the estate. I'm sure, given all that's happened, the more paperwork the better. Just so there are no misunderstandings."

I nodded.

Beatrice's smile dropped into something a touch more sad. "It would be nice to think all the Graves siblings could rest in peace together. Even Mary, if she so chooses."

"It's what Constance wanted." The words came out before I could stop them. I felt my cheeks burn even hotter.

Beatrice gave me a funny look. "You sound pretty certain about that."

"Well," I said, performing a quick finger charm. "I would imagine that would be the case." I patted my cheeks with my magically cold fingertips.

Beatrice gave me a wan smile. "I wouldn't be too sure about that. Constance did have a reputation for being difficult."

"You know," I said, shaking my head, "I think she had a bigger heart than the world ever got to see."

Chapter 47

I 'LL GET IT!"

I trotted toward the front door of Ivywood Hollow. The doorbell had been ringing all day with deliveries. Most were food and supplies. The B&B was reopening in a few days. But some were for the special family event we had planned. One that was long overdue.

"It's probably the roses!" Izzy shouted from the kitchen.

"Did you order them from Nixie?" Nora's voice came from the top of the stairs. "If it's her, I'm not here."

"I thought she was your friend?" I called back to her with a laugh.

"I only said that to make Izzy happy and you know it," Nora grumbled. "That girl has far too many questions. Tell her I'll stop in at the shop tomorrow to settle up. She can pester me then."

I smiled. Nixie was totally Nora's friend.

I opened the door.

At first all I could see was a towering bouquet of yellow roses.

That's right. Yellow roses.

Nora always had plenty of flowers on hand, but she thought it might be nice to have one bouquet as a tribute to Constance, given that she was the one responsible for finally bringing tonight about.

Nixie's face peeked around the bouquet. Her jaw dropped when she saw me.

"Hi," I said. "Why don't you let me take those from you?" I reached for the bouquet but hesitated at the look on Nixie's face.

"I have three questions," she said quite seriously.

"Only three?" I asked, taking the arrangement from her and placing it on the floor.

"First, where did you get that dress?"

I looked down at my black silk gown. "Nora made it for me."

"Will she make one for me? That actually wasn't one of my questions, but I'm adding it to the list."

"She might," I said with a smile. It really was a beautifully tailored dress. "Do you have an occasion in mind?"

"Who needs an occasion? I will wear it every day. I will wear it every night. I will wear it always and call it my precious."

"Okay, then," I said with a chuckle. "Next question?"

"What is going on here tonight?" she asked, trying to peek her head farther in the door. "It's something magical, isn't it?"

I positioned myself to block her view. "I have no idea what you are talking about."

"Brynn! You are killing me! Can I come to whatever this is?"

I smiled. "No. Not tonight. Tonight is for family."

She sighed and her eyebrows formed a peak, resembling that of a sad puppy. I hated to admit it, but the girl was growing on me.

"Was that your third question? I've lost count."

"I probably just need to accept it, don't I?" she said, voice full of resignation.

I raised an eyebrow.

"I'm a witch hunter. You're witches. You're never going to confide in me." Her shoulders slumped. "I'm going to spend my entire life believing in something I'll never have proof of. Truth is, I probably did make the whole thing up. I mean, my family thinks I'm nuts. Maybe they're right."

She was about to go on, but I reached out and grabbed her hand, effectively derailing her.

"What are you doing?" she asked, straightening her dejected posture.

"Nixie, please be quiet. I'm still not back to full strength, so I need to concentrate."

Her eyes grew incredibly wide. "Why? What is happening right now?"

"Close your eyes."

"But—"

"Do it before I change my mind."

Nixie snapped her mouth shut and squeezed her eyes closed.

"Do not tell Nora about any of this. Or Izzy." I stared at Nixie's hand and murmured a few words under my breath. "Okay, open your eyes."

Nixie let out a happy shout. "No! No way! It's the flame!" Pure joy came over her face as she stared at the small pink flame swirling in her hand. "I can't believe this!"

I smiled. It was a nice little fire. And it perfectly matched the color of her hair. I felt quite proud of myself.

"I have to do something!" Nixie went on. "Nobody is going to believe this! I need to take a picture."

Just then the flames went out.

"What happened?" she gasped, looking back and forth from her palm to me. "Where did it go?"

I tilted my head to the side. "Where did what go?"

"Oh," she said, wagging a finger. "I see what you did

there. It's a secret. I won't tell a soul. You can trust me, Brynn."

I laughed.

"But that can't be it. You have to show me more."

"I think that's enough for one day," I said, moving to shut the door. "Thank you for delivering the flowers."

She peeked her face into the closing space. "But you will show me more, right? This isn't the end. Because I'm pretty sure that was the best thing to have ever happened to me."

"Good night, Nixie."

"Good night, Brynn. And thank you for the you-know-what," she said with a big wink. "Talk to you later!"

I clicked the door shut and leaned my back against it.

"What was that all about?"

My aunts, looking quite beautiful in their own silk gowns, were staring at me with their arms crossed over their chests.

"Nothing."

"Mm-hmm," Izzy said. "Well, let's set up. The moon is almost in sight."

I twisted my hands together.

She rushed over and gave my shoulders a squeeze. "Don't worry. It will be all right."

"Nonsense!" Nora shouted.

We both looked at her.

"It won't be all right." A smile spread across her face. "With the three of us together—"

"Four."

We turned to see Gideon coming down the stairs. Both Izzy's and Nora's eyes widened at the sight of him.

My aunts may have been surprised, but I wasn't. Something had changed in Gideon since we had put out all those fires. We had talked about it, and he was warming to the possibility that he could maybe find a way to live outside of the attic. At least for some of the time. He had been experimenting with his poetry, and he was starting to believe that through it, he might be able to get some warning of larger visions before they came to pass and it was too late for him to do anything about what they revealed. Like mini visions before the visions. So far, he said the clues they offered were much more opaque, hints to where things might be headed, but he thought with practice, it could give him more control over his gift. It was hard to say if it would work or not, but he seemed happy with the prospect of things changing, so that was all that mattered to me.

"Gideon," Nora gasped.

"No," he said, holding up a hand. "No fuss from any of you, or I'll go back upstairs."

"Right," Nora said sharply, but her eyes were glistening. "As I was saying, Brynn, with the *four* of us together, tonight will be perfect."

"For Adam," I said.

"For Adam."

I clutched hands with Izzy as Nora strode over to the roses resting on the floor.

She planted her hands on her hips and stared down at the arrangement. "Disgusting." She then scooped them up and marched past us, calling out, "Well, is everyone coming?"

"We're coming," I said. "We're all coming."

Chapter 48

W E'VE GATHERED HERE on this sacred night to honor one of the finest humans the mortal world has ever produced."

The garden had been transformed. Small lanterns glowed softly from every tree, and Nora had made sure all of the fall flowers, from the asters to the zinnias, were blooming, bringing color to every corner of the yard and filling the air with a rich, tranquil scent.

"Adam was more than the husband of our beloved niece. He was a treasured member of our family."

I listened silently, twisting my hands together, as Nora continued telling the story of my husband's life. She spoke of his passion for teaching, his wonder for the world, and his love for us. Really, it wasn't all that different from his human funeral.

The next part, however, would be quite different. And that was the part that had me nervous.

All witch funerals had an enchanted component, a magical tribute given to the one who passed, and I wanted mine to be perfect just in case Adam could see it from wherever he was. I wanted it to be as beautiful as the love he had given me, and I was terrified I would let the both of us down.

When the time came, Nora moved to the side, and I stood in front of my family with my hands still clutched together. A thousand thoughts raced through my head. How was I going to do this? Where would I find the strength? *Why* did I want to do this? I didn't get married to say good-bye. But I pushed them all away to focus on what it was I really wanted to say.

"There are no words that can ever truly express what Adam brought to the world. What he brought to my life." My voice trembled. "My husband was so many things. Intelligent. Funny. Interesting. But more than anything, he was a good, kind man. *Good* and *kind* are simple words, but when you are lucky enough to meet someone rich in both those qualities, the effect is magnificent. Adam was magnificent." Tears welled in my eyes.

"You are doing wonderfully, darling," Izzy called to me.

"No, words alone are not enough to honor the man I had the greatest privilege of calling my husband." I felt a mystical thrum of energy run through the garden in anticipation of my next words. The Warren family had been using them for hundreds of years. "So as is our tradition, I offer my tribute."

I squeezed my fingers into my palms. I could suddenly hear Constance's words to me. Her message from Adam.

He said, tell Brynn that I love her always, and that for my tribute, I want her to show me the stars.

I stilled my thoughts and focused my energy out into the night sky, to the constellations far above me.

Now I just had to bring them down.

I closed my eyes. I didn't need to see the illusion I was creating to know what was happening. Tiny luminous points that were millions of light-years away would suddenly appear to be floating toward us on earth. I could feel the magic running steadily through me, in a way I hadn't in a long time. It felt natural again. As easy as breathing.

I called the specks of light closer to earth.

My uncle sighed. "It's beautiful, Brynn."

"Yes," Nora said. "Adam would be proud."

I knew he would.

Suddenly I could see so clearly the look on his face that night on Carmichael's Bridge. That was the look he would have given me if he were here. The look that was just for me. The one that told me I was pure magic in his eyes.

I would never see it again. Not in this lifetime.

The enormity of the loss gripped me in a way I hadn't allowed it to in a long time, and I could feel the quickening of power that had been building inside me falter. The pain was pushing the magic away, crowding it out.

That was the thing about grief I had come to know so well. It was always too much. The loss always too big. The pain always takes up too much space. It takes all the room you have until there is nothing left, and then it takes even more.

I couldn't hold on to the spell. It had gone from something I could feel and touch inside of me to nothing more than mist running through my fingers.

Suddenly someone gripped my hand.

I opened my eyes. Izzy was at my side.

"I can't hold on," I whispered to her.

"You don't have to, darling," she said, bringing our clasped hands to her chest. "Let it go. You don't have to keep it inside you any longer."

Then someone was holding my other hand. I looked over and met Nora's hazel eyes, sparkling in the light from the lanterns. She held me in her gaze as a single tear slipped down her cheek. She quickly brushed it away, threw back her shoulders, and gave me a brilliant smile. "You can do this, Brynn. You are so strong. A Warren through and through."

I couldn't say if I believed her or not, but the strength of her conviction was enough to get me to try.

I closed my eyes again and took a long, slow breath, breathing through the tightness in my chest. The spell swirled through me once again. Though faint at first, it quickly built on itself, growing in power until it reached a point that I knew it had its own life. The sensation wasn't at all like it had been with the wildfire spell, when my magic had been angry, thrashing at me for release. This was balance and joy, harmony and triumph. It was also love. So much love. All the love I had for my husband but hadn't allowed myself to feel since he passed.

When it was time, I released the magic and let it flow out from me into the world.

A hush fell over the garden, and I opened my eyes.

The illusion of countless stars hovered all around us, infusing the garden with unearthly light.

"It's wonderful," Izzy said, eyes glittering. "Well done, Brynn."

"A magnificent tribute," Gideon added.

"I wish I had been able to do it sooner." The words came out in a rush, surprising me. I hadn't meant to say them, but I didn't regret them either. I could tell my family was about to object, so I added, "That way I could have been sure Adam's spirit would have seen it. Even if I couldn't have seen him."

Just then the stars began to spin, slowly at first, but quickly gaining speed.

"What's happening?" Izzy asked. "Are you doing that, darling?"

I frowned in confusion. "No, I am not doing anything."

We watched as the stars spun faster and faster until the most miraculous thing happened. One after another, each star sparked, then exploded into new life. Suddenly we were surrounded by gleaming, butterflies, dragonflies, and moths. There were others too, but I didn't know their names. In fact, there was only one person, I knew, who would have been able to name them all.

"I have never seen anything like this," Nora said, marveling at the sight of the tiny creatures swirling around us, leaving trails of golden dust in their wake.

Gideon laughed. "I've never even heard of anything like this."

I held out my hand and a tiny firefly landed on my finger.

Adam.

The spectacular show only lasted a moment or two longer before the cloud of winged creatures swirled upward to the sky. The firefly hovered low until it was the last one in sight and then it swirled away too.

I stared into the night sky as my family's arms encircled me.

It was hard to say how long we stayed that way, looking at the stars.

And it would be even harder to speculate how long we would have stayed that way if a bush hadn't rustled behind us.

"What was that?" I whispered to my family still huddled around me.

The four of us turned together to see an extremely wide-eyed Mr. Henderson peering through the hedge, his face in between the rods of the iron fence.

Oh dear.

I pulled myself free from my aunts and uncle and took a step toward him with my hands up in the air. "Mr. Henderson, we can explain everything."

"I don't want your explanations. I know what I saw," he said, quickly straightening his glasses on his nose. "I'd heard rumors, but I never believed—"

"Please, don't be afraid." I took another step toward him. "I know you must have a million questions."

"No. No, I don't." He held up a finger to hold me back.

"There's just one thing I want to know. And I want the truth."

The four of us waited in silence.

"Are you good witches? Or bad witches?"

I let my hands drop to my sides. "Mr. Henderson, we're not good witches *or* bad witches."

I shot a look over my shoulder at Nora. She gave me a wink.

"The truth is," I said, turning back to our neighbor, feeling my eyes glow bright green, "we Warrens are the very *best* witches."

ACKNOWLEDGMENTS

Heartfelt thanks to my editor, Jenn Snyder, who saw the potential in this book when it was little more than an idea. Thank you also to Mary Ann Lasher and Vikki Chu for the beautiful cover, and to all the amazing people at Berkley Prime Crime and Penguin Random House for bringing this book into the hands of readers. As always, many thanks to my agent, Natalie Lakosil, for continuing to believe in me and my work. And special thanks to all the readers, librarians, and bloggers who have supported me in the past. Your kind words have always inspired me to keep writing.

Finally, I am forever indebted to my family and friends who have supported my writing from the beginning. In particular, I am forever grateful to my father, Barry Wallace, for providing me with a plethora of wonderful haikus to use at my will, and to my husband, Hector, who is always kind and patient regardless of the circumstance. I love you both.

PINK-AND-PEACH CLOUDS, FIERY in the sun's dying rays, rolled slowly across the baby blue sky. A riot of birdsong rang out from the trees as a gentle breeze twirled fluffy seedpods in the air. Spring had finally come to Evenfall, Connecticut.

"I just love this time of year," the woman beside me said. "That feeling of warm sunlight on your face. The sight of all the flowers popping up their sleepy heads. The smell of rich, fresh earth bursting with new life." She sighed happily. "Isn't it just magical?"

"I've never cared for it."

I darted a look over to the woman seated on my other side, doing my best to suppress a smile. Some things never changed. While my aunt Izzy tended to see the very best in everyone and everything, my aunt Nora, well, she made an art form out of being perpetually unimpressed.

Then there was me. I was right in the middle. Literally.

I was seated between the two of them on the back porch of our family's Queen Anne tower house, Ivywood Hollow Bed-and-Breakfast. My aunts had suggested we come outside to enjoy the spectacular sunset. It was hard to say if we were succeeding in that particular goal just yet.

"But it's *spring*," Izzy persisted. "What is there not to like about spring?"

"Quite a bit actually," Nora, flashing her long, crimson fingernails in the air. "Where should I begin? The sun is blinding in the early-morning hours. You can't work in the garden without getting completely covered in mud. And then there is all this nonstop *twittering*." She cast a disapproving glance at the trees.

In fairness, she was more of an autumn person.

Izzy sat up in her seat. "Well, all that may be true, but—"

"Then there's the people," Nora went on, not quite through with her rant. She rested an elbow on the armrest of her chair and pointed at us. "Everyone behaves so nonsensically this time of year. They're practically overflowing with hope and excitement. And for what? A mild breeze and a bit of sunshine? Ridiculous." Suddenly a blue bird swooped in out of nowhere and landed on Nora's finger. She blinked at it. "You, my tiny feathered friend, are only proving my point."

The bird twittered prettily then flew away.

"But, Nora," Izzy said with a somewhat nervous-sounding laugh, "wasn't it your idea for us to come out here to enjoy all that spring has to offer?"

"Oh no, Sister. Don't you dare try to pin this on me."

I frowned. *Pin what on who now?*

Izzy huffed a breath. "I knew I shouldn't have included you in this." Her eyes widened when she caught me looking at her. "In this viewing of the sunset," she added, awkwardly, before looking back at Nora. "You haven't liked spring since high school. Wasn't it your junior year when—"

"Absolutely nothing happened." Nora pulled down her oversized black sunglasses to give her sister a ferocious look. "And I do not *hate* spring." She pushed her sunglasses back up and laid her forearms delicately on the armrests of her chair. "I simply think it's overrated."

Izzy held up her hands in defeat.

"Wait, what are we talking about?" I asked, finally getting a word in. There was clearly a great deal being communicated under the surface here. I had a lot of questions, but I opted to start with, "What happened junior year?"

"Absolutely nothing," Nora repeated in a clipped tone.

I twirled my long black braid between my fingers as I looked back and forth between my aunts.

The two of them certainly did paint a contrasting picture. Nora was looking rather elegant this evening—if not a touch severe—in her black silk jumpsuit with a gauze kimono shawl. She had her fiery red hair twisted up into a tight bun on the top of her head, accentuating her long neck and perfect posture. Izzy, in comparison, appeared fresh and sweet in her pink, floral dress with a ruffled hem. Her strawberry blond hair sat loose and curled about her shoulders, wavering charmingly in the breeze.

I had to admit I felt a little undressed in my wrap sweater and jersey leggings. But, in fairness, no one had told me I needed to dress for the occasion. Not that this was an occasion. We were just taking in the sunset. At least I thought that's what we were doing. Suddenly I wasn't so sure.

"Why are we even talking about spring? Or unremarkable junior years?" Nora asked grumpily. "I thought we were supposed to be out here talking about Brynn."

And there it was. I should have known.

I gripped the armrests of my wingback rattan chair to force myself up into a less relaxed posture. "And what is it exactly about me that needs discussion?"

"I have no idea what your aunt is talking about," Izzy said, forcing an overly bright smile to her face. "Have you tried the tea, darling?" She reached for a cut glass mug. "It's a ginger and jasmine mix. I flavored it with honey, cloves, orange slices, blackberries, and just a touch of red pepper for heat."

I eyed the tall pitcher filled with amber liquid sparkling in the slanted rays of the setting sun. Beside it sat a plate covered in freshly baked tarts with a ruby-colored filling.

"They're raspberry," Izzy prodded, following my gaze. "Your favorite."

They looked delicious. I could practically feel the flaky crust breaking apart in my mouth. But we both knew those weren't just any old tarts. I pinned my aunt in my gaze. Her eyes widened again, this time to unparalleled levels of innocence. It was pretty adorable. But I wasn't about to be distracted by her cuteness. "Izzy? What is going on?"

"Oh, just tell her why you've dragged us out here," Nora said with an exasperated sigh. "I'm about to spontaneously combust in all this golden sunlight."

"Are you sure you don't want to try the tea first, darling? Or the tarts?" Izzy asked hopefully.

I raised an eyebrow. "I think I'll wait."

My aunt sighed, then cleared her throat. "This wasn't quite how I wanted to bring the subject up," she said, cutting her sister a look. "But, well, Brynn, your aunt and I have noticed that you seem distracted lately. Like something might be bothering you."

Was that all this was about? I chuckled with relief.

"And Izzy here has a theory on what that *something* might be," Nora said with a sniff. "She also has some ideas about how to fix it."

My chuckle died a swift death. My aunts speculating on my well-being was always disconcerting, but the idea of their fixing any of my theoretical problems was downright terrifying. Time to nip this in the bud. "You don't have to come up with any theories. Or ways to fix anything." I stared off into the endless sky beyond the sorbet-colored clouds. "And you don't have to worry. I know I've been distracted lately, but I promise you it's nothing."

"What's nothing?" Nora asked sharply.

I could feel her studying me, but I kept my gaze on the sky. "It's hard to explain, but I've had this funny feeling lately. I think it's the changing of the seasons. Spring fever maybe."

In fairness, I could see why my aunts might be concerned. A few days ago, I had been kneading dough with Izzy, and she had caught me staring off into space. Apparently, I had been quite still for several minutes without realizing it. Then a day or two after that, I may have snipped the side of my finger with gardening shears helping Nora trim the dead branches off a rose bush. It was a little strange. I wasn't normally so careless. When the feeling came on, it was almost like I had to stop everything I was doing, still all my senses, in order to pick up on *whatever* it was. It was like listening for a soft noise somewhere in the distance. Or trying to catch a faint scent on the breeze. It almost felt like something might be coming. But the funny thing was, as soon as I did focus on the sensation, the feeling would disappear, like it had never existed at all. Again, I had chalked it up to the season. What is spring if not the feeling of anticipation? I was sure it was nothing to worry about.

I knew my aunts might have a bit of trouble with that though. They had raised me since the age of five after my parents died in a car accident. Worrying was a part of their job description, even if I was now over thirty.

I didn't have to look at Nora to feel her gaze narrow in on me. "Spring fever? Since when do you suffer from *spring fever*?" The tone in her voice made it sound like we were talking about malaria or maybe West Nile virus. "Are you sure this strange feeling of yours doesn't have something to do with your work?"

"Or maybe something else?" Izzy asked sweetly, clutching her hands to her chest. Stars above, what was going on with her? She was practically batting her eyelashes at me.

I gave her a look that spoke to the fact that I thought she might be a touch dangerous, then said, "I don't know. Maybe."

"You are not doing a very good job of explaining yourself," Nora said.

I let out an exasperated grunt. "Because there's nothing much to explain. I just keep getting this feeling like something is about to happen, but then nothing ever does. Really, you guys don't need to worry." As if on cue, a warm breeze gusted by, making the trees whisper. I eased back against my chair. Hopefully we could let this conversation go now and just enjoy the evening.

"But what is it exactly you think is about to happen?"

I groaned. Loudly. "I don't know. That's what I'm trying to tell you. Oh! Look! Bunny!" I pointed at a small cottontail hopping across the lawn. I darted glances at both aunts to see if they had spotted it too. But no, they were both still focused on me with matching expressions of concern. "What? Now we don't like bunnies?"

"They eat my vegetables," Nora replied. "Don't change the subject. You do realize that we Warren women are not ones to ignore feelings. Have you spoken to your uncle about this?"

"No, I haven't told Gideon anything. There's no reason to. It's nothing. I'm sure of it." I really was sure. The whole thing was just silly. But at least I was getting some tarts out of it. I reached for the biggest one on the plate, picked it up, and took my long-awaited bite. Chills rushed over my body. It was beyond good. Sweet. Tart. Buttery. It was also, funnily enough, quite relaxing, and encouraging, and dare I say it, *prodding*. Like suddenly I had the urge to give up all my secrets.

I shot Izzy a look.

She smiled and scratched the back of her neck.

"Why didn't you guys just ask me what was going on?" I mumbled, bringing a hand up to cover my mouth. "You didn't have to plan this elaborate ruse." Truth be told, though, I already knew why. Not that long ago I had gone through the darkest period of my life, and I hadn't shared much of anything with my family, but I had come a long way since then. They knew that.

"We didn't know how you would react, darling. You can be quite private."

I swallowed hard and wiped the crumbs from my mouth, and then my lap. "Okay, well, next time just talk to me." I held my palms up. "Really. I have nothing to hide." I turned my palms inward, looking at the crumbs all over my fingers, then quickly grabbed a napkin. "Now, tell me. What was your theory on what was bothering me?"

"It's nothing," Izzy said, shaking her head so quickly it almost looked like a shudder.

I was about to interrogate her further but was distracted by a young couple entering the garden from the side gate. They were newlyweds spending a couple of days at the B&B. Neither one had spotted us yet. They only had eyes for each other.

"They are so sweet together," Izzy mused, a dreamy look coming over her face.

I felt my chest tighten.

They were so sweet together, and so much in love. It was impossible not to see it. It was in every gesture, the way the distance between them closed when they entered a room, the look in their eyes when they said each other's names, even in the way they held hands. It was precious. Truly precious. I had been in love like that once.

"Ridiculous," Nora muttered.

I smiled.

We watched the couple in silence for a little while, before Izzy asked, "Don't *you* think they're sweet together, Brynn?"

I shot up in my seat. Wait a minute.

"What?" Izzy asked nervously. "What is it?"

"Did you know those two would be out here? Is that what you really wanted to talk about? *Love*." I suddenly realized I was using the same tone to speak about love that Nora had used when she was talking about spring.

Izzy's hand flew to her chest. "Brynn, do you really think I would be so conniving as to have that sweet young couple involved in some sort of scheme?"

"Hello!" the young man called out to her with a friendly wave. "Did we come at the right time?"

Nora laughed. Actually, it was more of a cackle.

Izzy smiled weakly and called out, "Yes, just in time for the sunset. Lovely, isn't it?" She sank back into her chair. "Nora is so much better at conniving."

"I'll take that as a compliment," her sister replied, turning her face to the sun.

"Listen," I said in a much gentler tone. "I can see what it is you're trying to do here, and I know you mean well, but you are way off base."

I watched the newlywed husband lower a branch from our magnolia tree for his wife to see up close. Just as it neared her sightline, I heard Nora whisper something under her breath, and one of the pink buds swirled open, much to the couple's delight.

When Nora caught me looking at her, she shrugged and rolled her eyes.

"But, darling," Izzy said, stealing back my attention, "it has been some time now. Isn't there a part of you that misses it?"

"Of course I miss it. I miss *him*. The two can't be separated for me." That was the simple truth of it. I had lost my husband, Adam, to an undiagnosed congenital heart defect almost two years ago. It was a devastating loss. In truth, it had nearly killed me, but I had come a long way since then. I gave my aunt what I hoped was a reassuring smile. "But I can miss those things without feeling like my life is missing something. I am at peace with where I am now. I've had the greatest love anyone could ask for. And even though that part of my life is over, I'm grateful to have had it." I meant the words deeply. It wasn't something I had ever articulated out loud, but I was glad I finally had so that my aunts could understand.

"Now you're just being stubborn," Izzy said with a pout.

I blinked a few times. Normally I would have expected that kind of comment from Nora. "I'm sorry?"

"Is it the family history that's holding you back?" Izzy asked, scooting forward on her seat. "Because you know all that curse nonsense is just that. Nonsense."

I didn't answer. The Warrens did have a history of being unlucky in love. Some might call it a curse, and at times, it had certainly felt that way to me. But no, that was not what was holding me back. I wasn't being held back.

"You are a young woman, Brynn," Izzy went on, undeterred by my silence. She took a quick sip of tea then smiled. I think she surprised herself with how good it was. She recovered quickly though. "You have a long life ahead of you. How can you be so certain that you will never experience love again?"

"I just know." I could have explained further—told them that there was no way another man could ever fill my heart the way Adam had—but a slight prickle had come to my eyes, and I did not want to encourage that prickle to grow into something more. That was something I had come to realize about grief. It never truly goes away. It does lose its all-encompassing grip, but it can come back at any time, as strong as ever. It wasn't necessarily a terrible thing though. It was evidence of having loved deeply. I had to be grateful for that. "Besides, how could I miss love when I have so much of it? I love you. I love Nora. I love Gideon." Just then an enormous cat jumped up onto my lap. "And I definitely love you," I said rubbing the feline's soft ears. "In fact, right now, I think I love you most of all." Faustus, the B&B's resident Maine coon cat, closed his eyes in pleasure as I ran my thumb over the bridge of his nose. He was a lovely large beast with all-black fur, except for the dignified frosting of gray around his face.

"Oh, well, you and the cat should be very happy together," Nora said dryly.

"See?" Izzy said, throwing out a hand in her sister's direction. "Even the *hater of spring* agrees."

"No. No," Nora said. "Leave me out of this. I'm just here as a spectator."

I studied my aunt, but her expression remained hidden behind her sunglasses. She was being uncharacteristically quiet for this conversation.

Clearly Izzy thought so too because she said, "You're not getting off that easily. Tell the truth, is Brynn being stubborn or not?"

Nora regarded me a moment. "Yes, definitely stubborn. But I've always thought stubbornness was more of a virtue than a vice. It shows conviction. Well done, Brynn."

I frowned. "Thank you. I think." I was having trouble following all the twists and turns this evening was taking. I was never going to look at sunsets the same way. "But I have to disagree. I'm not being stubborn. It's just fact. I've had a great love. I'm grateful for that. And right now, I couldn't be happier. I'm completely fulfilled. This is the life I am meant to be living. Even if some areas are going a bit slowly right now."

All of that was true.

I loved running Ivywood Hollow with my aunts. I loved living in the loft above the carriage house. I loved that I was now reconnecting with old friends I had lost touch with over the past few years. And I loved the fact that I had a calling in life that allowed me to help people—the work Nora had referred to earlier. Although it had been a while since I'd truly been able to help anyone. That was the one area of my life that was moving slowly. I guess you could call me a grief counselor of sorts, and living in a small town like Evenfall, there were sometimes dry spells of, well, death.

"Ah. I see what's wrong with you now," Nora said knowingly. "It's not love that you're missing. You want someone to die."

I gasped. "What? I would never! How could you even suggest—"

I saw the corner of my aunt's mouth twitch.

My shoulders dropped from my ears. "You're horrible, you know that?"

"I know," she said happily, reclining further into her seat.

I frowned again.

"All teasing aside," Izzy said, "your well-being is of the utmost importance to us, darling. We just want to know you're happy."

"I am happy. Very, very happy. Couldn't be happier, in fact."

Faustus jumped down from my lap, hitting the porch floor with a loud thump. I guess he didn't like my particular brand of happy.

"You know, I think this conversation has run its course. Why are we wasting time bickering when we are surrounded by all this beauty? I bet everyone in Evenfall is enjoying this sunset."

Suddenly a disembodied voice called out, "Well, I'm not!"

I jumped in my seat. Chills raced up my arms as I spotted a gust of wind swooping over the tall iron gate of the backyard. I realize one can't usually see a breeze, but this was no normal wind. No, this short stream of air was colored with silvery sparkles that danced and gleamed as it cut a path through the sky, bending and twisting like a ribbon caught in a storm. The current rushed up to us; then, in a flash, the twirling sparkles coalesced into the shape of a man, standing right in front of me, his legs going straight through the coffee table.

I could feel my aunts looking at me, wondering what was happening, but I couldn't take my eyes from our newly manifested visitor.

I recognized him instantly. He had quite the distinctive style of dress. The red-and-white-striped collared shirt. The smart-looking suspenders. The fun garters on his sleeves. The bowtie. I had never seen him wear anything else. Probably because I had only ever seen him at work. No, the only difference in his appearance now, from the last time I had seen him, was the shimmering glow and the fact that he was slightly transparent.

"Brynn?" Izzy asked, staring blankly into the space I had focused on.

"It's Mort Sweete. From the candy shop. He's here."

Or at least his spirit was here.

"Oh dear," Izzy said softly.

"Oh dear?" the man shouted. "Oh dear! I think that's an understatement. I'm dead!"

"I am so sorry," I said quickly. "I realize this all must be a shock for you. But I'm here to help. If there's anything I can do, please don't hesitate to ask."

"Okay then," the man said, leaning back and pulling on his suspenders. "I've been murdered. Can you help me with that?"